WARRIORS
TALES
FROM THE
CLANS

WARRIORS

THE NEW PROPHECY

POWER OF THREE

OMEN OF THE STARS

DAWN OF THE CLANS

Book One: The Sun Trail
Book Two: Thunder Rising
Book Three: The First Battle
Book Four: The Blazing Star

EXPLORE THE
WARRIORS
WORLD

Warriors Super Edition: Firestar's Quest
Warriors Super Edition: Bluestar's Prophecy
Warriors Super Edition: SkyClan's Destiny
Warriors Super Edition: Crookedstar's Promise
Warriors Super Edition: Yellowfang's Secret
Warriors Super Edition: Tallstar's Revenge
Warriors Super Edition: Bramblestar's Storm
Warriors Field Guide: Secrets of the Clans
Warriors: Cats of the Clans
Warriors: Code of the Clans
Warriors: Battles of the Clans
Warriors: Enter the Clans
Warriors: The Ultimate Guide
Warriors: The Untold Stories

MANGA

The Lost Warrior
Warrior's Refuge
Warrior's Return
The Rise of Scourge
Tigerstar and Sasha #1: Into the Woods

NOVELLAS

Also by Erin Hunter

SEEKERS

RETURN TO THE WILD

WARRIORS
TALES
FROM THE
CLANS

INCLUDES

Tigerclaw's Fury

Leafpool's Wish

Dovewing's Silence

ERIN
HUNTER

HARPER

An Imprint of HarperCollinsPublishers

Special thanks to Victoria Holmes

Tales from the Clans
Tigerclaw's Fury, Leafpool's Wish, Dovewing's Silence
Copyright © 2014 by Working Partners Limited
Series created by Working Partners Limited

ISBN 978-0-06-229085-4

14 15 16 17 18   CG/OPM   10 9 8 7 6 5 4 3 2 1
❖
First Edition

CONTENTS

WARRIORS

TIGERCLAW'S
FURY

ALLEGIANCES

THUNDERCLAN

LEADER   **BLUESTAR**—blue-gray she-cat, tinged with silver around her muzzle

DEPUTY   **FIREHEART**—handsome ginger tom
APPRENTICE, CLOUDPAW

MEDICINE CAT   **YELLOWFANG**—old dark gray she-cat with a broad, flattened face, formerly of ShadowClan
APPRENTICE, CINDERPELT

WARRIORS   (toms, and she-cats without kits)

WHITESTORM—big white tom
APPRENTICE, BRIGHTPAW

DARKSTRIPE—sleek black-and-gray tabby tom
APPRENTICE, FERNPAW

LONGTAIL—pale tabby tom with dark black stripes
APPRENTICE, SWIFTPAW

RUNNINGWIND—swift tabby tom

MOUSEFUR—small dusky-brown she-cat
APPRENTICE, THORNPAW

BRACKENFUR—golden-brown tabby tom

DUSTPELT—dark brown tabby tom
APPRENTICE, ASHPAW

SANDSTORM—pale ginger she-cat

APPRENTICES   (more than six moons old, in training to become warriors)

SWIFTPAW—black-and-white tom

CLOUDPAW—long-haired white tom

BRIGHTPAW—she-cat, white with ginger splotches

THORNPAW—golden-brown tabby tom

FERNPAW—pale gray with darker flecks, she-cat, pale green eyes

ASHPAW—pale gray with darker flecks, tom, dark blue eyes

QUEENS (she-cats expecting or nursing kits)

FROSTFUR—beautiful white coat and blue eyes

BRINDLEFACE—pretty tabby

GOLDENFLOWER—pale ginger coat

SPECKLETAIL—pale tabby, and the oldest nursery queen

WILLOWPELT—very pale gray she-cat with unusual blue eyes

ELDERS (former warriors and queens, now retired)

HALFTAIL—big dark brown tabby tom with part of his tail missing

SMALLEAR—gray tom with very small ears; the oldest tom in ThunderClan

PATCHPELT—small black-and-white tom

ONE-EYE—pale gray she-cat, the oldest cat in ThunderClan; virtually blind and deaf

DAPPLETAIL—once-pretty tortoiseshell she-cat with a lovely dappled coat

SHADOWCLAN

LEADER   **NIGHTSTAR**—old black tom

DEPUTY   **CINDERFUR**—thin gray tom

MEDICINE CAT   **RUNNINGNOSE**—small gray-and-white tom

WARRIORS

APPLEFUR—mottled brown she-cat

BOULDER—silver tabby tom

FERNSHADE—tortoiseshell she-cat

FLINTFANG—older gray tom

RATSCAR—scarred dark brown tom

ROWANBERRY—brown-and-cream she-cat

RUSSETFUR—dark ginger she-cat

WETFOOT—gray tabby tom
APPRENTICE, OAKPAW

LITTLECLOUD—very small tabby tom

WHITETHROAT—black tom with white chest and paws

QUEENS

DAWNCLOUD—small tabby

DARKFLOWER—black she-cat

TALLPOPPY—long-legged light brown tabby she-cat

WINDCLAN

LEADER

TALLSTAR—black-and-white tom with a very long tail

DEPUTY

DEADFOOT—black tom with a twisted paw

MEDICINE CAT

BARKFACE—short-tailed brown tom

WARRIORS

MUDCLAW—mottled dark brown tom
APPRENTICE, WEBPAW

TORNEAR—tabby tom
APPRENTICE, TAWNYPAW

ONEWHISKER—brown tabby tom
APPRENTICE, WHITEPAW

RUNNINGBROOK—light gray tabby she-cat

RAVENPAW—sleek black cat who lives on the farm with Barley

SMUDGE—plump, friendly black-and-white kitten who lives in a house at the edge of the forest; a kittypet

SNAG—huge tabby tom

STUMPYTAIL—brown tabby tom

TANGLEBURR—gray-and-brown she-cat, formerly of ShadowClan

TIGERCLAW—big dark brown tabby tom with unusually long front claws, formerly of ThunderClan

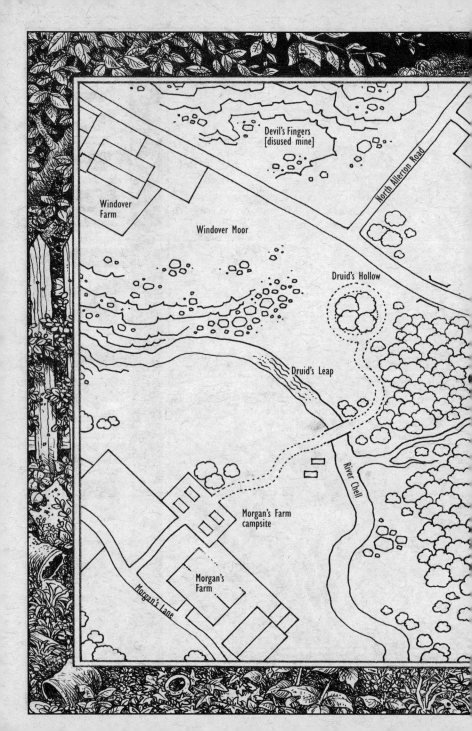

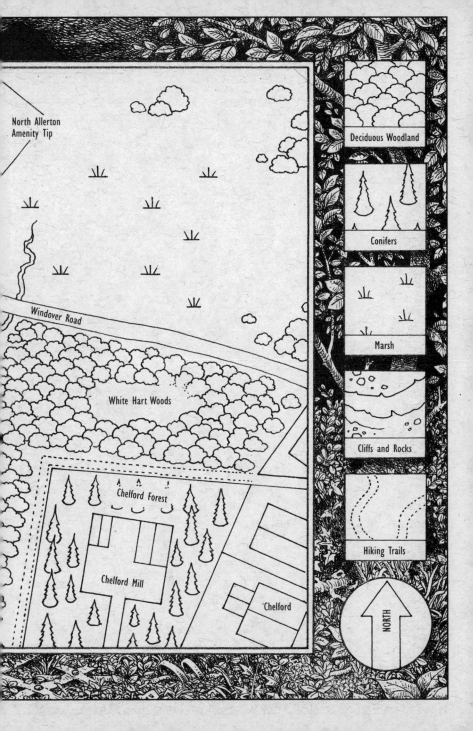

North Allerton
Amenity Tip

Windover Road

White Hart Woods

Chelford Forest

Chelford Mill

Chelford

Deciduous Woodland

Conifers

Marsh

Cliffs and Rocks

Hiking Trails

NORTH

CHAPTER 1

"Kill him!"

"Blind him!"

"Drive him out of the forest!"

The wound in Tigerclaw's belly pulsed with agony, and he felt warm, sticky blood pooling beneath his paws. His Clanmates' furious words seemed to be coming from a long way off, as if he were underwater, cocooned in peaceful cold. *You lost!* screeched a voice inside his head. *Beaten by kittypets and fools!* Tigerclaw felt his lip curl up in a snarl. *I lost this battle,* he conceded silently. *But for as long as there is blood in my veins, I will not give up.*

"Tigerclaw," Bluestar meowed, "have you anything to say in your defense?" The ThunderClan leader's blue-gray fur was streaked with blood—Tigerclaw's as well as her own—and her eyes were dull and unfocused. Tigerclaw felt a thrill of satisfaction that his actions, his careful plans, had left her shattered and flailing inside. He knew a broken cat when he saw one; this was the end of Bluestar's leadership, even if he hadn't managed to take her last lives. The thought numbed the pain in his belly and gave strength to his trembling legs.

"Defend myself to *you*, you gutless excuse for a warrior?" he hissed. "What sort of a leader are you? Keeping the peace with other Clans. *Helping* them! You barely punished Fireheart and Graystripe for feeding RiverClan, and you sent them to fetch WindClan home! I would have never shown such kittypet softness. I would have brought back the days of TigerClan. I would have made ThunderClan great!"

"And how many cats would have died for it?" Bluestar replied softly. She shook herself, then lifted her head. "If you have nothing else to say, then I sentence you to exile," she declared. "You will leave ThunderClan territory now, and if any cat sees you here after sunrise tomorrow, they have my permission to kill you."

"Kill me?" Tigerclaw echoed. "I'd like to see any of them try."

"Fireheart beat you!" Graystripe yowled.

"Fireheart." Tigerclaw slowly turned his head to look at the ginger kittypet. *A warrior name will never make you forestborn, no matter what your Clanmates tell you!* "Cross my path again, you stinking furball, and we'll see who's the stronger."

Fireheart sprang up, tail lashing, even though one of his eyes was swollen shut from a blow from Tigerclaw's paw. "Any time, Tigerclaw," he spat.

"No!" Bluestar interrupted them. "No more fighting. Tigerclaw, leave my sight."

Tigerclaw made himself stand up, in spite of the trembling that shook his paws. A fresh wave of blood oozed from his belly as the edges of the wound shifted. He heard gasps from the cats around him but ignored them. *Pain is nothing! Defeat is nothing!*

"Don't think I'm finished," he warned, staring at the battle-stunned faces around him. "I'll be a leader yet. And any cat who comes with me will be well looked after." He looked for his closest ally in ThunderClan, the cat who'd always told him that he should have been leader by now. "Darkstripe?"

The black-striped tabby stayed where he was, sitting among the warriors. "I trusted you, Tigerclaw," he whimpered. "I thought you were the finest warrior in the forest. But you plotted with that . . . that *tyrant*." Tigerclaw guessed he was speaking of Brokentail, the exiled ShadowClan leader who now lived in ThunderClan's camp. "And you said nothing. And now you expect me to come with you?" He dropped his head, unable to meet Tigerclaw's gaze.

Traitor! You dare to deny me in front of all these cats? You'll pay for this with every hair on your pelt!

Tigerclaw forced his fur to stay flat. "I needed Brokentail's help to make contact with the rogue cats. If you choose to take this personally, that's your problem," he sniffed. He looked at another cat who'd listened to his plans, promised to stand by him when he brought clear, strong leadership to their Clan. "Longtail?"

The pale tabby almost leaped out of his skin. "Come with you, Tigerclaw? Into exile?" He sounded horrified. "I—no, I can't. I'm loyal to ThunderClan!"

You're a pathetic coward, more like! Tigerclaw screeched silently. He scanned the ranks of cats, looking for a hint of understanding, a recognition that this weak and kittypet-favoring Clan was no place for a true warrior. "What about you, Dustpelt?" he growled. "You'll have richer pickings with me than you ever will in ThunderClan."

The young brown tabby got deliberately to his paws and picked his way through the surrounding cats until he stood in front of Tigerclaw. "I looked up to you," he admitted. "I wanted to be like you. But Redtail was my mentor. I owe him more than any cat. And you killed him." His eyes grew huge and he started to shake. "You killed him and betrayed the Clan. I'd rather die than follow you."

Redtail deserved to die! He was too much like Bluestar, always looking for peace and reconciliation. It was only luck that Oakheart hadn't killed him before being caught by that rockfall. Redtail would have never survived that battle.

"Tigerclaw!" Bluestar broke into his memories of dust and falling stones and the bright red slash opening up in Redtail's throat. "No more of this. Go now."

Tigerclaw lifted his head and met her gaze. "I'm going. But I'll be back; you can be sure of that. I'll be revenged on you all!" He turned and walked away, gritting his teeth against the pain in his belly. *I will not show them how badly I have been wounded!* He paused as he drew level with Fireheart. "And as for you . . ." he growled. "Keep your eyes open, Fireheart. Keep your ears pricked. Keep looking behind you. Because one day I'll find you, and then you'll be crow-food."

"You're crow-food now," Fireheart snapped, but the stench of fear rose from him.

Tigerclaw stared into the warrior's wide green eyes. *You know already that I will kill you one day. Your last breath will be gasped beneath my paws. Your last drop of blood will be spilled on my fur. Stones will break and the sky will fall when we meet in our final battle.*

With a flick of his tail that felt as if it was ripping his belly apart, he walked across the clearing without looking back. From inside the nursery he heard the tiny mewls of his son and daughter, Bramblekit and Tawnykit, quickly hushed by their mother, Goldenflower. *I will come back for you,* Tigerclaw vowed. He would not leave his kits to be raised in this Clan of weaklings. They deserved to learn from his example, to model themselves on his courage and skill in battle. *Some skill you showed today!* came the voice in his head again. *Thistleclaw would have clouted you over the ears for letting yourself get beaten by a kittypet and a star-crazed old she-cat.*

Thistleclaw wouldn't have dared to take on the leader of his Clan! Tigerclaw lashed back. *If he hadn't let Bluestar become deputy in the first place, everything would be different. He would have chosen me to succeed him, and ThunderClan would be as strong as we deserve!*

He pushed his way through the gorse tunnel, hardly noticing the thorns that clutched at his blood-matted fur. The barricade had been ripped and scattered by fleeing cats, cats who had sworn to fight alongside Tigerclaw until he had killed Bluestar, on the promise that he would make them his foremost warriors in the new ThunderClan. Tigerclaw spat onto the dusty earth. He should have known better than to rely on those half-trained rogues. Only a forestborn cat had the true instincts of a warrior. The ShadowClan outlaws had disappointed him, too, made soft by moons of surviving alone, too easily cowed by cats fighting to defend their home. Tigerclaw needed more time with them, to remind them of the training they had received under Brokenstar. The former ShadowClan leader may have been criticized for asking too much of his warriors, but he had made his Clan the most feared and powerful in the forest. Who could judge him for that?

And Tigerclaw might still have won if RiverClan hadn't turned up at the tipping point of the battle, Mistyfoot and Leopardfur bounding in to rescue the Clan cats who had been their sworn enemies just a few moons earlier. Why did the Clans show so much mercy to one another? What did it matter to RiverClan if ThunderClan lost its leader? Tigerclaw felt his hackles rise. Of course, it was in RiverClan's interests to keep Bluestar in command, weak and addled and unable to maintain her grip on Sunningrocks. It was probably Crookedstar's greatest fear to have Tigerclaw in charge of his closest neighbors.

The dappled shadows cast by breeze-stirred oak and beech leaves gave way to cool damp gloom beneath the pine trees that bordered Twolegplace. Tigerclaw paused for a moment to check that no cat was following him, but the woods were silent apart from the call of a blackbird and a tree branch resting against another with a soft creak. He let himself sink down on a patch of moss, letting out a grunt of pain. He craned his neck to study the wound on his belly. Fireheart had been lucky to get so close to him. But if he'd really wanted to hurt Tigerclaw, he should have gone for his neck.

Tigerclaw dragged some loose moss against the wound, hissing as he pressed it hard to stem the bleeding. His head swam with pain, and he fought off a wave of blackness that rose behind his eyes. He pictured the Clan he had left behind, battle-bruised and cowering in the dust. Did he really want to command warriors that were so nearly beaten by a half-trained patrol of rogues? Fireheart had taken all the credit for winning, as always, and every cat had been hanging on his words, gazing in doe-eyed admiration. If they were so willing to listen to a kittypet, they didn't deserve a leader such as Tigerclaw. How dare Bluestar cast him out? Had she forgotten how many times he had won battles for ThunderClan, found food for his Clanmates, defended the borders against their enemies? They owed him everything! But in the end they had treated him worse than a lice-riddled fox. He could have been the best leader ThunderClan had ever known!

Better than your father, Pinestar, purred the voice in his ear. *He betrayed his Clan—betrayed you—when he left to become a kittypet. You would never walk away from your Clanmates if you were their leader.*

The moss under his paw started to overflow with blood. With a grunt, Tigerclaw cast it aside and looked around for another clump. There was no more soft green moss, but he spotted some dry leaf-mulch within reach. He clawed it against his belly, packing it into the cut. He felt a burst of triumph against his surroundings: The forest had tried to deny him moss, but he had found something else!

Tigerclaw half sat up, pricking his ears as he stared into

the trees. As clear as stars, his path stretched out before him. There was more than one Clan in the forest. More than one chance to become a leader. His destiny must lie elsewhere. Tigerclaw would return to ThunderClan only to crush his former Clanmates in battle. He would not fail again.

CHAPTER 2

The air beneath the pine trees grew colder and the ground under Tigerclaw started to feel damp. He licked it to get some moisture, then heaved himself to his paws. He couldn't stay here; the evening border patrol would be coming this way soon. He didn't want to see pity in the eyes of his Clanmates if they found him wounded and exhausted, still inside ThunderClan territory. Wincing with every step, Tigerclaw limped deeper into the pine trees. He stayed away from Twolegplace, with its curious kittypets and stray dogs. Instead he headed for the wooden den behind a tall fence of pine trunks, where the Twolegs that cut down trees came in the daytime. He squeezed through the fence, leaving a smear of blood on the stripped wooden post. There was a gap the height of a rabbit below the wooden den. Tigerclaw crawled into the shadows and lay full-length on the earth. There was a faint hint of mouse from farther under the den, but Tigerclaw didn't have the strength to pursue the scent, let alone a scampering piece of prey.

Where is the moss that lines your nest in the warriors' den? Where are the feathers? Is this how your life will be from now on, huddled on bare dirt, starving because you're too weak to feed yourself?

Tigerclaw's belly rumbled, but he pressed his cheek deeper into the soil to block out the sound. Right now, sleep was more important than food. Once he had rested, once he had eaten, then he could begin the destruction of ThunderClan.

He dreamed that he was on fire, scorched by the claw marks that Fireheart had left in his skin. He thrashed with his paws, but sleep held him fast, clutching him in a semi-conscious daze. He was dimly aware of the daylight seeping in from outside, but before he could rouse himself and go out in search of food, it seemed that night was falling again, shrinking Tigerclaw's world to a blur of pain and tortured sleep. He lashed out blindly at screeches from the mist that surrounded him, felt claws rake his fur and teeth snap close to his ears. He whirled, stumbling on legs that felt heavy and sore, but there was nothing except damp gray clouds behind him. *Too slow,* hissed the voice. *Don't let Fireheart and Bluestar catch you! They'll crush you like a bug!*

"Never!" roared Tigerclaw. He woke with a start, breathless and writhing on his back. His belly burned like fire and his claws were unsheathed, clogged with dirt. He crawled out from beneath the wooden den into a cool, pale dawn. How many days had he lain here? One? Two? More? His vision blurred for a moment, and he shook his head to clear it. His mouth was as dry and sore as if he had swallowed feathers, so he limped over to a puddle that lay in a muddy rut close to the fence. The water was black and brackish, but he forced himself to lap until his throat had stopped hurting.

A blackbird pecked at the ground farther along the fence.

Tigerclaw gathered his haunches beneath him and crept toward the bird, testing each of his legs. He felt weak, but a careful check of his belly showed that the wound had stopped bleeding and the edges were starting to crust over with dark red scabs. As long as he didn't stretch too much, he should be able to hunt. *Better to die from hunting than from letting myself starve.*

As he drew closer to the bird, he stepped onto a heap of pine needles that crackled. The blackbird let out a squawk and flapped noisily into the air. Tigerclaw cursed under his breath and sat down. He licked the ruffled, dusty fur on his chest. It tasted of blood and soil. He spat, then turned and stared into the shadows beneath the wooden den. He'd been aware of rustlings during his restless sleep, the muffled squeaks of mice and a mouthwatering scent in the musty air. It would be a cramped and difficult place to hunt, but no worse than some of the bramble thickets he'd scoured before.

Crouching low, feeling the wound in his belly strain, Tigerclaw slipped under the den. The soil rose up on the far side, blocking out the light. Tigerclaw headed for the thickest shadows, feeling his whiskers quiver as he picked up the scents of tiny furred creatures. He paused for a moment to let his eyes adjust to the half-light, then lunged toward the tiny twin glints that gave away a mouse staring back at him, terrified. There was a satisfying fat crunch under his paws, a high-pitched squeak cut short, and Tigerclaw buried his muzzle in the warm blood and fur of his fresh-kill. He saw no need to thank StarClan for his prey; it was his catch, his alone.

The mouse sent strength surging through his legs, and

Tigerclaw emerged, blinking, into the light, shaking loose soil from his pelt. He squeezed between the wooden posts and set off through the pine trees at an uneven trot, gritting his teeth against the pain in his belly. He was outside ThunderClan scent marks here, but there was precious little undergrowth, so a passing patrol would spot him from a long way off. The tall wooden fences and red stone walls that marked the edge of Twolegplace loomed through the trees. The trunks thinned out and brambles and dense clumps of ferns began tangling around Tigerclaw's paws. He lowered his head and began sniffing where fronds had been bent back by a passing creature. *There!* Barely a fox-length from the ThunderClan border, he picked up the acrid, fear-stained scent of the cats who had fought alongside him in the attack.

Fought? More like turned tail like frightened kits! came the voice in Tigerclaw's head. *You were a fool to trust them!* Tigerclaw flattened his ears. *I had no choice! But now that I am free from my bonds to ThunderClan, things will be different.*

Stepping carefully through the thick grass, Tigerclaw followed the scents along the very edge of Twolegplace. Splashes of blood left a visible trail, and he hoped the cats were not too badly wounded. He didn't have time to nurse anyone. These pitiful creatures were weak enough already. He kept one ear pricked toward ThunderClan territory, listening for a patrol. The sun was high overhead, the shadows at the foot of the Twoleg boundary barely wide enough to conceal him. Tigerclaw guessed that his former Clanmates would be resting after morning patrols, sharing fresh-kill before setting out again. His belly growled at the thought of food, but he forced himself to keep going. He wouldn't be caught taking prey that belonged to ThunderClan!

The rumble of the Thunderpath drifted through the trees, and the scent of scared cats was muffled by the stench of monsters and their foul black breath. Tigerclaw forced his way into a solid clump of brambles, guessing that if he were frightened and wounded, he'd seek the thickest cover. He stiffened as he heard tiny whispers ahead of him.

"Keep still! Someone's coming!"

"Has a ThunderClan patrol found us? We can't stay here and be trapped like rabbits!"

"Hush! They'll hear us!"

Tigerclaw burst through the wall of thorns with a yowl. Five pairs of eyes stared at him in horror. Then, one by one, they blinked and lost the sheen of terror.

"Tigerclaw!" meowed a scrawny brown tom. "You survived!"

"No thanks to you, Clawface," Tigerclaw snarled.

"We were going to come back for you once our wounds had healed," protested a broad-shouldered white tom with one black forepaw. His name was Blackfoot, and like Clawface, he had been a ShadowClan warrior loyal to their leader, Brokenstar, before he had been taken prisoner and his followers driven out of the Clan.

Two other former ShadowClan warriors, a brown tabby named Stumpytail and a gray-and-brown she-cat called Tangleburr, stood up and stepped alongside Tigerclaw to brush their tails against him.

"I'm so pleased to see you," purred Tangleburr, but the row of fur pricking along her spine told Tigerclaw that she was lying. All of these cats, including the former stray Snag, a huge ginger tom who lingered at the back of the makeshift den, watching with wary amber eyes, were terrified to see Tigerclaw risen from the dead. They knew they had failed him, had let themselves get beaten by a bunch of queens and elders in an unguarded camp. Tigerclaw breathed in their fear-scent and felt a thrill of satisfaction. These cats would do anything he wanted. He forced his long claws to stay sheathed, pushed down the urge to rip their ears for leaving him to face his former Clanmates alone. These were the only allies he had for now, and while they were scared of him, and in his debt, he could shape them exactly as he wanted.

He looked around. "Where's Mowgli?" He had found the green-eyed, brown tom among the loners in Twolegplace, spotting at once the potential in his sleek muscles and hard, unflinching gaze. Tigerclaw had vowed to make Mowgli a senior warrior if he fought alongside him, and the brown tom had lapped up his promises as hungrily as any forest-born cat.

Stumpytail shrugged. "I don't know. He got his ears clawed pretty harshly by that brown ThunderClan apprentice—Brackenpaw, I think he's called. We haven't seen him since."

Tigerclaw curled his lip. Beaten by an apprentice? He hoped he hadn't been wrong about Mowgli. Clearly he needed more training, more encouragement to fight to the limits of his strength, even if his opponent still had kitten fluff around his ears.

Clawface limped forward with a scrap of fur and meat in his jaws. He dropped it at Tigerclaw's feet. "I caught this mouse earlier," he mewed. "You can have the rest if you want."

Tigerclaw eyed the pathetic piece of fresh-kill. Would he be showing weakness if he admitted to his hunger and ate it? Or should he take advantage of these cats offering to feed and shelter him? What would a Clan leader do?

Bluestar would look for the weakest elder and give them the fresh-kill, purred the voice. *But is that the kind of leader you want to be?*

Tigerclaw bent his head and devoured the mouse loin in a single bite. He looked up, swiping his tongue around his lips. "We'll need more than that to survive. Who is the least wounded among you?"

Tangleburr raised her tail. "I have a bite on my flank, but it's healing fast." She glanced over her shoulder. "And Snag's fur was thick enough to save him from any deep scratches."

The loner padded out of the shadows. "I'll hunt if you want," he rumbled.

Tigerclaw nodded. "Good. You two, bring back at least two pieces each of fresh-kill."

Tangleburr's eyes widened, but she didn't say anything. *Well done, you're learning,* thought Tigerclaw. The two cats threaded their way out of the brambles.

"Tigerclaw, your belly seems to be bleeding," mewed Blackfoot hesitantly. He stretched out his neck and sniffed at the sticky scarlet fur on Tigerclaw's side.

"It's nothing," snapped Tigerclaw. "It'll heal in a couple of days."

Blackfoot stepped back. "Those ThunderClan cats fought more fiercely than I expected," he admitted. Beside him, Clawface nodded. "Especially that so-called kittypet, Fireheart," Blackfoot went on. "He may have been born in Twolegplace, but he's sure learned how to fight like a warrior."

"He *is* a kittypet!" Tigerclaw spat. "Don't ever speak of him as a warrior. He has no right to be in the forest, no right to speak to Bluestar as if the blood of the Clans runs in his veins." He turned away and paced in a tight circle, flicking his tail. "I will find more cats, and teach you how to fight properly, and then we will take on ThunderClan again and Fireheart will *die!*"

CHAPTER 3

❧

Tigerclaw opened his eyes to thin gray light filtering between the brambles. It was not quite dawn, but the air was warm and stuffy from the sleeping cats around him. Moving carefully in order not to disturb Clawface, who was pressed against his spine, Tigerclaw eased himself up and stepped out of the thicket. The Thunderpath was silent and the forest smelled clear and green. He peered through the trees, recognizing even in the half-light which trunks held the border marks for ThunderClan's territory. He felt his fur start to rise as he pictured Fireheart curled in the warriors' den, dreaming of victory. *Sleep peacefully while you can, kittypet.*

There was a crackle of leaves behind him and Snag appeared, shaking dust from his thick pelt. "Have you spotted a patrol?" he asked.

"No, it's too early." Tigerclaw turned and looked toward the Thunderpath, just visible between the tree trunks. "We can't stay here. We don't want to attract attention from Thunder-Clan, and we need more space for hunting. Wake the others. We'll leave now, before the dawn patrols begin."

Snag vanished back into the brambles, leaving Tigerclaw

alone in the woods where he had been born. *I will come back,* he vowed. *But only when I am strong enough to crush Fireheart and ThunderClan along with him.*

Tangleburr was yawning as she pushed her way out of the brambles, but as soon as she saw Tigerclaw her mouth snapped shut and she lifted her head. "Where are we going?"

Tigerclaw flicked his tail toward the Thunderpath. "We'll cross over and skirt the edge of ShadowClan until we reach the wild part of the forest."

Stumpytail looked alarmed. "What if a patrol catches us? We won't be welcome inside ShadowClan's borders!"

"The sun hasn't risen yet. There won't be any patrols around," meowed Blackfoot.

Tigerclaw led the cats through the long grass between the edge of the trees and the smooth black Thunderpath. The river of stone was silent, still reeking of monsters but damp with dew, making it quite cool and pleasant to walk on. The cats trotted across and plunged into the grass on the far side. None of them said a word as they entered the close-growing pine trees. Tigerclaw saw Blackfoot's fur stand on end, and Clawface's eyes stretch wide as he scanned for hostile former Clanmates. But the woods were as silent here as they had been on the other side of the Thunderpath. The cats crept undisturbed along the fences and walls of Twolegplace until they reached a tangled clump of ancient trees with thick glossy leaves and drooping purple-and-scarlet blooms.

"This is the farthest corner of the territory," Clawface whispered. "These bushes came from Twolegplace, and they're so difficult to get through that ShadowClan uses them as a defense against the wild part of the woods."

"They'll protect us just as well," mewed Tigerclaw. "There must be some way through."

Blackfoot walked along the foot of the branches, which dipped close to the ground. "There is a way," he muttered. "I got through once when I was an apprentice."

Tangleburr twitched her ears. "You were lucky you made it back! Who knows what could have happened to you on the other side."

Snag blinked. "It's just more trees," he meowed. "What were you imagining? A Clan of foxes and badgers, waiting to rip your fur off?"

Tangleburr flicked her tail. "I was a loyal ShadowClan warrior," she huffed. "It wasn't my business to know what went on beyond the Clan boundaries."

"Well, that's changed, hasn't it?" growled Tigerclaw. "Come on." Brushing past Blackfoot, he climbed over a gnarled silver branch and wriggled into the center of the tree. He couldn't see through the dense leaves to the other side, but there was a surprising amount of room among the twisted trunks. He heard the others follow him, and continued to scramble forward, ignoring the tearing pains in his belly. Soon he was surrounded by shiny leaves again, but he forced a way through and plunged into clear space on the other side. The wild part of the woods stretched out in front of him, looking more like ThunderClan than ShadowClan territory, with ancient moss-clad oaks and dappled ash trees rather than straight rows of pine.

The other cats lined up beside him, panting. "So, this is our territory now," murmured Clawface.

Blackfoot pricked his ears. "That fallen tree over there looks as if it could be a den," he meowed. He bounded over the mulch-covered ground, leaping twigs and clumps of fungus growing in the damp soil. He vanished behind the fallen oak for a moment, then reappeared on top of the trunk. "It's perfect!" he yowled. "Come and see!"

Tigerclaw followed the others as they ran like excited kits to explore the oak tree. Finding shelter wasn't a challenge. Even hunting would be easy here, with nothing but the occasional bold kittypet for competition. They needed to begin battle training as soon as possible—and Tigerclaw needed to find others to join them, because he wasn't going to trust victory to these few cats again.

When he reached the far side of the fallen tree, Tangleburr and Stumpytail were already dragging ivy out of a scoop in the ground. "This will make a great nest," meowed Tangleburr through a mouthful of trailing vines.

Snag trotted around the dying branches of the tree. "There's a puddle of water here," he announced. "It tastes fresh enough."

Blackfoot looked at Clawface. "Shall we hunt, and get started on a fresh-kill pile?"

Clawface nodded, but Tigerclaw stepped forward and stopped him in his tracks. "This isn't a game of mini-Clans," he warned. "You don't think I've given up on taking over

ThunderClan? Bluestar is weaker than she has ever been, and she weakens the whole Clan by putting so much faith in a kitty-pet. As soon as we are strong enough, we will attack again!"

There was a flash of uncertainty in the other cats' eyes, and Tigerclaw noticed Blackfoot glance at his belly, as if the white tom was concerned that Tigerclaw's wound would never heal enough to let him go into battle. *Are you sure these cats know that you are in charge?* whispered the voice in his head. *If they don't believe that they need you as much as they need food and shelter, you are nothing to them.*

Tigerclaw unsheathed his claws and let them sink into the soft earth. "Hunt, prepare nests, and make sure we cannot be seen by ShadowClan patrols," he ordered. "Tomorrow we start our training."

"Snag, don't be afraid to use your weight against your oppo-nent. If he can't breathe, he'll be easier to hit." Tigerclaw put out his paw and nudged Snag forward so that he was hanging over Clawface, who was starting to look worried.

Stumpytail pricked his ears. "But now Snag is balancing on three paws, so I could knock him over, couldn't I?" he sug-gested.

"Yes, but be careful where he lands. You don't want to crush Clawface." Tigerclaw stepped back and watched as Snag swiped his paw down toward Clawface at the same moment Stumpytail barged into his haunches. The big ginger tom lurched sideways with a hiss, leaving Clawface to scramble free on the other side. While Snag was on the ground, the other two cats leaped on him.

"Much better," meowed Tigerclaw. He scanned the trees. "Where are Blackfoot and Tangleburr? They should have been back from hunting ages ago."

They had been in the wild woods for three sunrises. All the cats were healing well now—even Tigerclaw's wound had stopped oozing whenever he stretched it—and their temporary den had provided good shelter during a couple of heavy rainfalls. The trees were lush and heavy all around them, and hunting was easy as prey came out to eat the seeds and nuts that had been washed down by the rain.

Stumpytail glanced at Clawface. "They'll be back soon," he mewed.

Tigerclaw pounced on the note of uncertainty in his voice. "Where are they?" he growled.

"They haven't crossed the border, I promise," mewed Clawface, his ears flattened in distress. "But . . . but we've been taking turns to patrol on our side, looking for some sign that ShadowClan is all right. We're worried about our Clanmates. We've been here for a while and haven't heard or seen any border patrols. What if something terrible has happened?"

Tigerclaw narrowed his eyes. "Why should that matter to you? They are not your Clanmates now."

Stumpytail lifted his head. "But they were close to us once. We have not stopped thinking about them just because we no longer live among them." There was a note of defiance in his words that Tigerclaw appreciated. *That kind of loyalty could serve you well,* commented the voice inside his head.

"I'll go look for them," he meowed.

Clawface's eyes widened. "You won't punish them, will you?"

Fear is the key. "That depends on what they have done." Tigerclaw padded away from the training area, a clear, smooth space defined by a tree stump, a row of brambles, and a tiny, gritty stream. He plunged into the undergrowth and followed a half-flattened trail to the wall of tangled trees. He guessed the former ShadowClan cats wouldn't spend time patrolling here because it was impossible to see through the dense green leaves, so he trotted along the edge of the barrier until it yielded to more open woodland, where gnarled mossy oaks gave way to tall, whisker-straight pine trees.

It wasn't long before he spotted Blackfoot's white pelt slinking between the trunks. Tangleburr was a few steps behind, better hidden among the foliage. Tigerclaw stayed where he was, just within scenting distance of the Shadow-Clan border marks, and waited. They seemed to be following the line of the border, not crossing over, but close enough to be seen by any passing cats. They were talking to each other in low, anxious voices.

"Did you forget about battle training?" Tigerclaw meowed when they were within earshot.

Both cats stared at him, guilt shining in their eyes. "We . . . we were just on our way," Blackfoot stammered.

"Don't lie," mewed Tigerclaw, padding up to them and sniffing their fur. "You smell of ShadowClan—more than you did already, I mean. Who have you been talking to?"

Tangleburr flattened her ears. "We didn't cross the border, I promise. We just wanted to see how they were."

Tigerclaw flicked his tail. "How who were?" He wanted to force them to admit that their loyalties still lay with their former Clan, that he would never be able to trust them, that all his training had been for nothing. *You should kill them where they stand,* encouraged the voice.

Blackfoot stepped forward, and Tigerclaw almost flinched as he realized the white tom was as tall and broad-chested as he was. "We have done nothing wrong," Blackfoot insisted. "We just wanted to know why there were so few border patrols. We met Dawncloud and Rowanberry hunting on their own. There is a terrible sickness in ShadowClan, and almost every warrior has been affected. Without hunting patrols, the whole Clan is starving."

"The sickness came from the rats at the Carrionplace," Tangleburr put in. "Runningnose is doing everything he can, but there are too many infected cats."

"Why do you think this is your problem?" Tigerclaw asked mildly. "Your Clanmates will want nothing to do with you because of your connection to Brokenstar."

Blackfoot's eyes flashed. "I was loyal to Brokenstar because he was the leader of my Clan, just as every ShadowClan warrior should have been. I am still a ShadowClan cat, whatever happens."

Tangleburr nodded. "These cats that are sick and starving, they are my kin, my friends. I may have left the territory, but I can't forget them."

For a moment, Tigerclaw felt a stab of envy. He didn't miss a single one of his Clanmates, not treacherous Darkstripe or Longtail, nor the weak and fawning kittypet-lovers among the other warriors. Was he going to lose control of Blackfoot and Tangleburr because of their sentimental attachment to cats who no longer cared about them?

You can't challenge their loyalty, warned the voice. *So use it for your own ends. If ShadowClan is as weak as they say, it poses no threat to your destiny. Remember, mercy is a sign of great power.*

Tigerclaw blinked. "For your own safety, I forbid you to enter ShadowClan's territory," he meowed. "But I want to hear for myself what is happening in their camp. We will wait for the next patrol, and I will speak to them."

They didn't have to wait long. A slow, stumbling crunch of twigs and dried leaves announced the approach of a patrol. Regular pauses told Tigerclaw they were renewing border marks—as if scent alone would keep the ravaged Clan safe. Three cats stumbled into view between the tree trunks. Tiger-claw narrowed his eyes, recognizing Fernshade, Deerfoot, and Boulder. The big gray tom who had been born in Twolegplace spotted the waiting cats first and bounded forward.

"Tangleburr! Blackfoot! Rowanberry told me she had seen you! What are you doing here?" Boulder's eyes were bright, but his ribs showed beneath his pelt and his flanks were tucked up with hunger.

"We live here now," Tangleburr meowed, gesturing with her tail in the direction of the fallen oak. "Stumpytail and Clawface are with us . . . and Tigerclaw."

Boulder's eyes narrowed. "We've heard rumors of an attack on ThunderClan," he meowed. "Was that you?"

Blackfoot flicked his tail. "That's not what we want to talk to you about. What is happening in ShadowClan? Are you really dying from this sickness?"

Fernshade padded forward. She looked older than Tigerclaw remembered, her tortoiseshell fur patched and clumpy, and one eye stuck shut with weeping yellow ooze. "We have been sick from the rats before, but never this bad," she rasped. "Runningnose hasn't slept for a quarter moon, trying to find enough herbs for us all."

"Why are you telling them this?" snarled Deerfoot, shouldering his way between his Clanmates. "These cats are no longer our Clanmates. They turned their back on the warrior code when they chose to follow Brokenstar." He glared at Blackfoot and Tangleburr, then let his gaze rest on Tigerclaw. "And this cat is not to be trusted," he growled softly. "What are you planning, Tigerclaw? I thought your Clanmates would have clawed your fur off by now."

Tigerclaw forced his pelt to lie flat. "I chose to leave," he meowed. "ThunderClan is ruled by a kittypet now that Bluestar listens to Fireheart before anyone else."

Deerfoot's nostrils flared. "I can't imagine you giving up that easily, Tigerclaw."

Tangleburr rested her nose against Fernshade's flank. "You look so tired," she mewed sadly. "Would you like us to hunt for you?"

"No!" snapped Tigerclaw and Deerfoot at the same time.

"We can hunt for ourselves," insisted the ShadowClan cat.

"You owe these cats nothing," hissed Tigerclaw. "I've heard enough. Come, follow me." He turned, and for a moment his heart beat faster as he wondered if Tangleburr and Blackfoot would obey. There was a brief silence, then he heard paw steps padding after him.

"May StarClan light your path!" Fernshade called.

"And yours," Tangleburr whispered in reply.

"We meet again, Tigerclaw!" snarled the ginger cat. "And this time, I won't let you live!"

"Really, Fireheart?" Tigerclaw sneered. "Have you forgotten that you're nothing but a soft-bellied *kittypet*?" He launched himself forward, claws raking the air in search of the orange pelt. All around him, he could hear ThunderClan cats yowling in fury, and the thud and scrape of paws as blows were landed. In his dream, Tigerclaw looked desperately around, trying to see who was fighting alongside him. Was he supposed to take on the whole of his former Clan alone?

But instead of well-trained ranks of warriors matching his strikes, there were nothing but shadows—shadows filled with shrieks and the crash of paw steps, but thin black air nonetheless. Tigerclaw felt Fireheart's claws find the half-healed wound on his belly and he leaped sideways, snapping his teeth where the tom's neck should be.

His jaws closed on a mouthful of dusty leaves, and Tigerclaw woke coughing and churning the leaf-mold with his paws.

"Are you all right?" Clawface asked sleepily from beside him.

"Fine," growled Tigerclaw. He stood up and left the nest, shaking the bad dream from his pelt. If he had to fight every battle alone, he would not give up! Even with an army of shadows, he would still win!

He paused. He had dreamed of shadows fighting alongside him, screeching and matching him blow for blow. He tipped back his head and looked up at the milky sky between the branches. *Was it an omen from StarClan?*

Would it be ShadowClan *that helped him destroy Fireheart?*

CHAPTER 4

❦

Tigerclaw waited until the patrol was nearly on top of him before stepping out from behind the clump of brittle ferns. Rowanberry stopped dead, her brown-and-cream pelt already spiking along her back. Behind her, the patrol scrambled to a halt, staring at Tigerclaw in alarm.

Tigerclaw flicked his tail. "I come in peace," he rumbled. "I know about the sickness in ShadowClan. My friends and I will hunt for you, asking nothing in return except that your former Clanmates are forgiven for their misguided loyalty to Brokenstar. They know they were wrong, and they want to make amends."

Rowanberry peered past him. "I don't see them here, though."

Tigerclaw bent his head. "They don't know I'm talking to you. They would be too proud to beg for your forgiveness, so I am appealing on their behalf. Please, let us stock your fresh-kill pile, find herbs for Runningnose, at least until you have beaten this sickness."

Dawncloud stepped forward, her pale ginger coat glowing in the dawn sunlight. "Do they want to come back to the camp?" she asked.

Tigerclaw shook his head. "No, we will stay out here, in the den we have made for ourselves. I promise, we want nothing else but to help you."

"I can understand why our former Clanmates might want to hunt for us," meowed Flintfang, a gray tom who looked ready to join the elders, if his legs held up long enough to get back to the camp. "But why you, Tigerclaw? You have never been a friend to ShadowClan."

Tigerclaw shrugged. "I am rival to no Clan now that I live outside any borders. Your Clanmates helped me not so long ago, and I am in their debt."

The old tom narrowed his eyes. "I don't know what Night-star would say about this."

"He'd say, 'Pride won't stock the fresh-kill pile!'" retorted Dawncloud spiritedly. "Tigerclaw, it's a generous offer, and we accept."

"But you don't need to bring the fresh-kill to the camp," meowed Flintfang. "We'll meet you here at dawn tomorrow, and take it from you."

Tigerclaw nodded. "Of course, if that's what you wish. Have a safe journey back to your camp. We will be here tomorrow." He turned before the cats could speak again and pushed deeper into the ferns. *Mercy is a sign of great power.* By the time the sun rose again, ShadowClan would be in his debt.

Blackfoot and Tangleburr were delighted to hear that ShadowClan would let them hunt on its behalf, but Clawface was less trusting.

"What if it's a trap?" he muttered. "They may be sick, but they still outnumber us. Once we're inside the camp, anything could happen."

"They're taking the fresh-kill from us on the border," Tigerclaw mewed. "I'm not putting any of us in danger for the sake of filling their bellies."

The ancient oak trees offered good hunting, though the ground was damper than Tigerclaw was used to. Snag managed to knock a squirrel clean out of a tree with a single blow from his paw, and Tangleburr returned with a brace of frogs dangling from her mouth.

"ShadowClan cats *like* them," she mewed defensively when Tigerclaw curled his lip.

By the time they returned to the clump of ferns at the border, Tigerclaw was satisfied with their offering. Enough to make a significant contribution to a Clan's fresh-kill pile, but not so much that it looked like hunting for ShadowClan was the only concern these cats had in their lives. Even after two long hunts the day before, Tigerclaw had insisted on battle practice as the sun sank behind the trees. Tangleburr's strong neck muscles gave her a ferocious bite, and Tigerclaw had been encouraging her to sharpen her teeth on the stump of an old apple tree, which had the strongest wood. Snag was becoming less cautious about using his weight to his advantage, and it had taken Stumpytail several moments to catch his breath after a particularly heavy blow.

"You came."

Tigerclaw ignored the faint note of surprise in Flintfang's

voice. "I always keep my promises," he meowed.

Boulder lowered his head and sniffed the heap of prey. "This will fill our fresh-kill pile better than it has been for days," he commented.

Dawncloud blinked warmly at her former Clanmates. "Thank you. I'll make sure Nightstar knows what you have done. There will be no grudges against you after this."

"Good," Tigerclaw mewed. "And to make sure that Nightstar knows precisely who has helped him, we'll help you take this to the camp."

Boulder tensed. "You said you'd stay out of ShadowClan territory for now. We can't guarantee how our Clanmates will react."

Tigerclaw stepped confidently across the scent line. "As Dawncloud said, your Clanmates will only be grateful for our help." He looked over his shoulder at the cats waiting by the ferns. "Come on, all of you." The former Shadow-Clan cats padded warily to join him. Snag brought up the rear, his nostrils flaring as the scent of the Clan washed over him.

Tigerclaw picked up the squirrel—the largest piece of prey—and gestured with his tail to prompt the others to help. Flintfang narrowed his eyes but said nothing. Dawncloud led the way back through the pines, reaching out with her tail to brush against Stumpytail. Tigerclaw knew they had been close friends as apprentices, and he decided to watch the brown tom closely to make sure his loyalties didn't return too wholeheartedly to his former Clan.

As they approached the thicket of brambles where Shadow-Clan made its camp, a wave of stench filled Tigerclaw's mouth and nose. Behind his mouthful of squirrel, he tried not to retch, and he could tell by the looks of alarm on his companions' faces that they were equally repulsed.

Boulder put down the sparrow he was carrying and halted just outside the entrance to the camp. "No cat has escaped the sickness," he meowed quietly. "If you don't want to risk get-ting infected, you should turn back now."

Tigerclaw lifted his head. "We are not afraid to deliver help," he insisted around his mouthful of squirrel fur. Beside him, Blackfoot nodded, although Snag looked increasingly reluctant to keep going.

They followed Boulder through the gap in the brambles, into the clearing at the center of the camp. Tigerclaw spot-ted the remains of a fresh-kill pile in a corner—now a pitiful scraping of bones and feathers—and strode over to it. He deposited the squirrel and turned to look around. Dozens of eyes gleamed from the shadows under the thorns, and the air was filled with shocked whispers.

Rowanberry emerged from a den. "Dawncloud told us you were going to hunt for us. We didn't expect you to deliver it yourselves."

Tangleburr dropped her frogs on the pile and trotted over to her old Clanmate. "We had to know how you are," she mewed. "Please don't send us away."

There was a faint rustle of branches behind Tigerclaw, and he spun around to see Runningnose, the sickly ShadowClan medicine cat, stumble out beside a black tom who was so thin, his fur looked as if it was sliding from his bones.

"You did a brave thing, coming here," Nightstar rasped.

Tigerclaw dipped his head. "Your former Clanmates would not stand by and let you starve, and my loyalty is to them now. This is not courage, it is merely following the warrior code."

Dawncloud went over to Nightstar. "Look, do you see the fresh-kill pile?" she prompted gently. "We will all fill our bellies tonight!"

"We can still hunt for ourselves," growled a voice from the side of the clearing. Deerfoot walked forward, his eyes glistening with what Tigerclaw thought might be the beginnings of the infection. "These cats left our Clan for a reason. Maybe we should think twice before welcoming them back."

Runningnose flattened his ears. "*These cats*, as you call them, may have saved us all from starving to death," he meowed. "Show them some gratitude, Deerfoot."

Clawface was looking around. "Where's Cinderfur?" he asked. "I heard he'd been made deputy."

Rowanberry padded over to him. Tigerclaw recalled that she and Clawface had been mates a long time ago, and Cinderfur was one of their kits. "He died, Clawface," she whispered, leaning into the fur on his shoulder. "He was the one who brought the sickness into the camp, when he caught an infected rat."

Clawface swayed and took a step back. "He died?" he echoed. "I should have been here, Rowanberry. If I had caught that rat instead . . ."

The she-cat tapped his mouth with her tail. "Hush. Our son walks with StarClan now. He will know what you have done for us today."

Tigerclaw put his head on one side. "Who replaced Cinderfur as deputy?" he asked Nightstar.

The old leader started, as if he had dozed off while still on his feet.

"Nightstar has been too sick to choose a new deputy," Runningnose put in. He stepped a little closer to the black tom so that he was supporting some of his weight. Tigerclaw thought he had never seen a weaker, more pitiful-looking pair of cats. "I fulfill the duties of a deputy for now," the medicine cat went on.

Tigerclaw couldn't imagine that took up much time. There weren't enough healthy cats to organize regular hunting or border patrols, as he and the others had noticed from the other side of the boundary. He felt a stir of curiosity in his belly. A sick, elderly leader, no deputy, a medicine cat run ragged trying to treat the illness that ravaged his Clanmates . . . ShadowClan was sinking faster than a stone in a river.

Nightstar twitched and stood more upright. "Tigerclaw, you are most welcome to stay and share the fresh-kill with us," he meowed formally. He gestured with his tail. "Please help yourself first."

Tigerclaw bowed his head low. "We wouldn't dream of it, Nightstar," he mewed. "We caught this prey for you. Shadow-Clan's need is far greater than ours. But, if you will allow it, we will continue to hunt on your behalf, until your Clanmates are strong and well again."

Nightstar let out a faint purr. "You are so kind," he rasped. "May StarClan light your path, always."

"Oh, they will," Tigerclaw murmured as he turned and summoned his cats with a flick of his tail. Clawface drew reluctantly away from Rowanberry, and Stumpytail cast a yearning glance toward Dawncloud, but they all followed him as he padded out of the camp and into the pine trees.

"I'll show you to the border," Flintfang offered, but Tigerclaw shook his head.

"Stay and eat with your Clanmates," he urged. "We know the way back."

Behind him, the other cats whispered their shock to one another, at finding their former Clan so ill and weak. Snag was sympathetic, vowing to catch every squirrel in the woods if that's what it took to make the cats well again. Tigerclaw listened with half an ear. He didn't care if every ShadowClan cat got sick and died. For now, he had an entire Clan in his debt, and that could only work in his favor.

If mercy is power, then I have never been more powerful.

The following day, Tigerclaw let the others go off and hunt for ShadowClan again, on the understanding that after sunhigh they would have a session of battle training. When the cats had crashed noisily through the bracken, deeper into the woods, Tigerclaw headed in the other direction, toward Twolegplace. The memory of Mowgli nagged at him; the loner may have turned tail and fled during the clash with

ThunderClan warriors, but there had been something about the young brown cat—his eagerness to learn about Clan life, his appetite for battle—that suggested he might still be useful. Tigerclaw pictured the last time he had seen Mowgli, grappling with Fireheart, aiming his claws at the kittypet's throat, before Brackenpaw had caught him off balance and dragged him away. Tigerclaw knew he couldn't judge Mowgli too harshly, not after Fireheart had overpowered him in Bluestar's den. This Twolegplace rogue had skills that could be very helpful indeed. Tigerclaw decided that he was willing to give him one more chance. But if the brown cat failed again, he would regret it more than anything else in his life.

He reached a tall wooden fence and squeezed through a gap between the panels. His head spun as the cloying scents of Twolegplace crashed around him: flowers in colors that were rarely found in the woods, the sickly-sweet smell of too-short grass, and underlying everything, the stench of monsters, spewing their foul breath on the maze of Thunderpaths. Tigerclaw pushed through a bush with pale green leaves and jumped over a low stone wall. On each side, a narrow black path led between red stone Twoleg nests. He had a vague memory of being here before. If he went this way—he turned and trotted over the harsh stone, keeping to the shadow at one side—he could come to a dusty open space where strays came to bask in the sun. Ahead of him, the light grew brighter until he had to screw up his eyes. The sheltered path came to an abrupt end, and Tigerclaw peered into the bright white expanse. Several furry shapes lay on their sides, tails flicking lazily.

A head lifted up close to him. "We've got company," the silver-furred she-cat mewed to her companion.

A fat brown tabby looked over at Tigerclaw. "He stinks."

"That's what forest cats smell like," meowed the first cat. "What are you doing here, stranger? Did you forget how to catch squirrels?"

Tigerclaw ignored them. A flash of movement on the far side of the space had caught his attention. He narrowed his eyes and just made out a lean black shape with a distinctive pointed muzzle before it vanished behind a pile of stones. Pelt pricking, he padded around the edge of the space. Most of the strays paid no attention to him, though one growled at him to stop casting a shadow. Tigerclaw reached the place where he had seen the brown cat disappear and sniffed the broken rocks. He knew that scent . . .

"Mowgli?" he called softly.

He heard a rustle in the long grass behind the stones. "Tigerclaw?" came a cautious whisper. There was a pause, then a thin brown tom slid out. His eyes were huge and wary, and the fur pricked along his spine. "Did . . . did you come looking for me?"

Tigerclaw blinked. "I don't make a habit of coming into Twolegplace," he snarled.

Mowgli slunk closer, his head so low that his muzzle almost touched the ground. "I'm sorry, Tigerclaw," he mewed. "I know I shouldn't have let that cat chase me off. I know how much you wanted that ginger tom killed."

"Mistakes belong to the past," Tigerclaw growled. He

wasn't going to let Mowgli think he wasn't disappointed with him. "I want to know if you'd let it happen again."

The brown cat looked up at him, his green eyes hungry for approval. "Never!" he vowed. "I'd spill the last drop of my blood to fight alongside you again!"

"I won't ask that of you yet," mewed Tigerclaw. "Things have changed. The other cats and I are living near Shadow-Clan now, but I still intend to destroy ThunderClan one day. And kill that ginger cat," he finished with a hiss.

Mowgli stood up straight, almost as tall at the shoulder as Tigerclaw. "Let me finish what I started," he declared. "You won't regret it, Tigerclaw."

"I'll make sure I won't," Tigerclaw meowed. "Come, we have a lot to do." He turned and trotted straight across the open space, deliberately scuffing a small cloud of dust toward the dozing strays. He heard them cough and curse behind him, but he and Mowgli had vanished into the gap between the Twoleg nests before the cats could haul their lazy bodies up.

CHAPTER 5

❧

When Tigerclaw returned to the fallen tree with Mowgli at his heels, Snag looked surprised but greeted his old friend warmly and showed him where he could make a nest. Blackfoot was more cautious.

"Are you sure you can trust him?" he mewed to Tigerclaw.

"If you think he might be a spy for ThunderClan, that's highly unlikely," Tigerclaw pointed out. "Last time Thunder-Clan saw him, he was trying to claw Fireheart's throat."

"I didn't mean that he might favor ThunderClan now," Blackfoot argued. "I just wondered how much we can rely on a cat who turned tail at the first sign of battle. What if he leaves us again?"

"Then he won't come back," Tigerclaw answered. "He knows this is his last chance."

Tangleburr padded over to join them. "We're ready for battle training when you are, Tigerclaw," she mewed. "Oh, and Clawface and I saw some ShadowClan cats by the border while we were hunting. They wanted to know if they could hunt with us tomorrow."

Tigerclaw frowned. "What, in these woods?"

"No," meowed Tangleburr. "Inside ShadowClan territory. That's where they know the best places to find prey. But they thought they might be more successful if we helped."

Tigerclaw felt a ripple of satisfaction run through his fur. Had ShadowClan warriors already realized how much they needed him and his companions? He waited a few moments before replying. "Very well, but we will still hunt separately for ourselves. ShadowClan must understand that we can survive without them."

Tangleburr nodded. "Of course. Thanks, Tigerclaw. I . . . er . . . told Wetfoot that we'd meet them at the border just before sunhigh." She blinked nervously. "If you said it was okay."

Tigerclaw flicked the tip of his tail, just enough to warn Tangleburr that he knew she had promised help too easily. The she-cat looked down at her paws.

Mowgli was looking confused. "I thought you hated the Clans," he meowed.

"Only ThunderClan," Tigerclaw growled. "ShadowClan is suffering from sickness and hunger. If we are strong enough to help them, we will."

Clawface padded past them, heading into the shade of the oak tree. "I might take a nap," he muttered. "Before we practice battle moves."

Tigerclaw blocked him with one paw. "Will you always be able to take a nap before an enemy attacks? No. You'll train now, with the energy that you have. Understand?"

There was a flash of anger in Clawface's eyes, then he

nodded. "I understand, Tigerclaw."

Good, whispered the voice in Tigerclaw's mind. *These cats must make no decisions on their own, not unless you want them to feel more powerful than you.*

Tigerclaw felt his muscles tense across his shoulders. *Never*, he vowed silently.

The following day, as the sun reached the tops of the trees, Tigerclaw was gratified to see the relief in the eyes of the gray tabby tom waiting for them at the border.

"I thought you might change your mind," Wetfoot gabbled as they drew near.

Tangleburr glanced sideways at Tigerclaw. "We will help you if we can," she mewed carefully.

Tigerclaw stepped over the border. "Right, which way are we going first?"

A small, light brown cat pricked his ears. "Wetfoot's leading this patrol," he chirped.

Wetfoot quickly shook his head. "It's fine, Oakpaw. Tigerclaw can lead us."

A bony, black she-cat scraped the mulch on the ground. "My belly thinks my throat's been slashed," she muttered. "Are we hunting or talking?"

"Okay, Darkflower, keep your fur on," teased Blackfoot, and Tigerclaw was reminded with a jolt that his companions—apart from Snag and Mowgli—knew these cats far better than he did, were friends and even kin with them. He couldn't let that become a weakness for him.

"We'll keep to the border with the wild woods," he announced. "Follow me, and wait for my command to begin stalking."

"We usually scent our own prey," Oakpaw began, but Tangleburr cut in.

"Whatever you think best, Tigerclaw," she meowed.

Tigerclaw plunged forward, relishing the feel of the ground beneath his paws, breathing in the green scents of the forest that swallowed him up. Behind him, the other cats matched him stride for stride; ahead of them stretched a swath of silent trees, swollen with prey just waiting to be caught.

"Why exactly did you leave ThunderClan?" meowed Applefur. The mottled brown she-cat was lying in a patch of sunlight, lazily flicking her tail.

Tigerclaw studied her, noticing the gleam of curiosity in her pale green gaze. He had just returned to the ShadowClan camp with another successful hunting patrol. The young warrior Russetfur had impressed him in particular—she had been raised in Twolegplace with Boulder, but she was as sharp and lethal as a forestborn cat when it came to chasing prey. Around him, ShadowClan cats ate peacefully, enjoying the feel of sun on their patchy coats. All except Nightstar, who was too sick to come out of his den; Tigerclaw could hear him coughing behind the screen of brambles.

He traced a line in the dust with one long claw. "You'll hear enough rumors about me to make up your own stories," he meowed.

Applefur blinked and let her cheek rest on the ground. "That's why I'm asking you for the truth."

Tigerclaw stood up and surveyed the clearing. "I cannot be loyal to a Clan that listens to a kittypet over its deputy. I still believe in the warrior code, even if my former Clanmates don't."

"Are you talking about Fireheart?" asked Ratscar, a young warrior with the claw mark that had given him his warrior name standing out against his dark brown fur.

Tigerclaw curled his lip. "If you don't want another stripe in your pelt, you won't mention his name around here," he growled. He nodded to Blackfoot, who was talking to Fernshade. "Come, it's time we left."

A dark gray tom lifted his head from a pigeon he was sharing with the other elders. "Do you have to leave already?" he called. "The sun won't set for a while. I was going to tell you about the time I found a badger stuck in the marshes."

Tigerclaw made himself look disappointed. "Next time, Cedarheart, I'd love to hear that tale. My friends and I have imposed ourselves on your Clan for long enough today." With a flick of his tail, he gathered his companions around him.

"You'll come back tomorrow, won't you?" mewed Runningnose, poking his head out of Nightstar's den. "I . . . I thought you might arrange the hunting patrols for me. I need to look for more herbs across the border."

Tigerclaw tipped his head on one side. "If you wish, Runningnose. We'll be here soon after dawn." He padded out of the camp, letting his companions call their farewells over their shoulders.

They are beginning to need you like the forest needs rain, whispered the voice in his head. *Good work, Tigerclaw.*

The four cats looked excited and proud to have been chosen for Tigerclaw's hunting patrol. Russetfur's lean muscles strained beneath her fox-colored fur as if she was already picturing her first pounce, while Ratscar was flexing his claws, checking them for sharpness. Clawface looked as composed as ever, but his ears were pricked and the tip of his tail twitched. Beside him stood Whitethroat, a black-and-white tom who was small for his age but seemed quick and keen. Tigerclaw wanted to see just how fast he could move.

"I thought we'd hunt something other than ShadowClan prey today," Tigerclaw announced.

Russetfur tipped her head to one side. "What else is there?"

"Perhaps prey from somewhere else?" mewed Clawface, his eyes beginning to gleam.

Tigerclaw nodded. "Let's try ThunderClan," he suggested, watching each warrior closely.

Russetfur and Ratscar braced their shoulders and narrowed their eyes, but Whitethroat took a step back.

"Th . . . ThunderClan?" he stammered. "Really? But that would be stealing!"

Tigerclaw blinked. "Do you have a problem, Whitethroat?"

The little cat looked down at his paws. "I would rather not take prey from ThunderClan, that's all," he meowed.

Clawface crossed to stand beside Tigerclaw. "There are rumors," he began quietly, "that Whitethroat and Littlecloud sought shelter in ThunderClan during the worst of the sickness."

"Do you think that's true?" Tigerclaw hissed.

Clawface studied the black-and-white warrior, who seemed to be trying to shrink inside his own pelt. "I can imagine two frightened cats trying to escape from a Clan that was dying around them," he mewed.

"Then we need to make sure their loyalty to their own Clan hasn't faltered," Tigerclaw stated grimly. Raising his voice, he meowed, "Whitethroat, this is not a hunt-if-you-want-to patrol. You will follow where I lead, is that clear?" He padded over to the warrior and let his claws slide out. "All other Clans are enemies to ShadowClan. If we want to take prey from them, there should be nothing to stop us. Do you understand?"

Looking terrified, the small cat nodded. Tigerclaw let his gaze drift around the clearing until it settled on Littlecloud. The gray tabby was shuffling through some herbs for Running-nose. Tigerclaw curled his lip. Now that Littlecloud was an apprentice medicine cat, it would be hard to test his loyalty in the form of hunting or battle. Tigerclaw would have to keep an eye on him.

"Let's go," he meowed, curling his tail over his back and leading the way out of the camp at a brisk trot. He swiveled his ears to check that four sets of paws were following, then ducked into the tangled, brittle grass where tiny paths would lead them to the tunnel that ran beneath the Thunderpath. Before he ducked into the narrow hole, Tigerclaw paused to take one last breath of ShadowClan scent. Was this where he belonged now? He hadn't been into ThunderClan territory since . . . He pushed aside the memory of Bluestar ordering him to leave and ran into the tunnel. His paw steps echoed hollowly around him for a moment, then he burst into the thick green forest on the other side. *Home!* screeched his traitorous senses as countless smells of leaves and ferns and lush green growing things filled his nose. Woven among them were traces of tiny furred creatures, rustling through the undergrowth, scrambling over mossy tree trunks, leaving their invisible trails for hungry cats to follow.

"Wow!" breathed Ratscar. "This smells like good hunting!"

Tigerclaw nodded. "Stay close to the Thunderpath for now. There's no point drawing attention to ourselves before we've had a chance to catch a decent haul."

He plunged into the bracken, relishing the feel of dew-damp leaves brushing against his spine. Almost at once he heard the crunch of a mouse nibbling on a seed. Dropping into the hunter's crouch, he crept forward, one paw step at a time, until his muzzle pushed aside a frond of bracken and revealed the small brown creature. Tigerclaw bunched his hindquarters beneath him, then sprang silently past the frond to land right on top of the mouse. It let out a faint squeak, soft and warm and delicious-smelling in Tigerclaw's paws. He swallowed the water that had surged into his mouth and buried his prey quickly.

Behind him, the ShadowClan cats were staring open-mouthed.

"That was fast!" Russetfur commented.

Tigerclaw felt a surge of pride. This was his territory now; he knew every hunting trick his ancestors had ever thought up. He shrugged as if it was no big deal and shouldered his way past an elder bush, drooping with heavy white flowers. The scent tickled his nose and almost made him sneeze, but he stopped when he heard a soft crackle on the other side of the bush. Peering through, Tigerclaw spotted three light brown shapes slipping between a pair of tall ash trees, along a trail that led to the border. A ThunderClan patrol! He squinted, identifying Mousefur, Runningwind, and Thornclaw. A memory flashed into Tigerclaw's mind of those three cats sneering at him as he padded from the ThunderClan camp for the last time. Each one had treated him no better than a captured prisoner, battered and defeated by their precious kittypet. Tigerclaw felt a slow flame of rage burn in his belly.

This was too good an opportunity to miss. "ShadowClan cats!" he yowled over his shoulder. *"Attack!"*

CHAPTER 6

❧

Tigerclaw exploded through the bush and launched himself onto Runningwind's narrow brown back. The warrior dropped beneath him like a stone. Tigerclaw let his talons sink into Runningwind's throat and fought back a yowl of delight as blood welled up around his paws. Behind him he heard Mousefur and Thornclaw racing away, their paw steps rapidly fading in the direction of the camp. "Cowards!" Tigerclaw spat.

"Great StarClan!" gasped Russetfur. "You've killed him!"

Tigerclaw stepped off Runningwind's unmoving body. "He should have reacted more quickly," he mewed.

Whitethroat padded forward on trembling legs and lowered his nose to sniff Runningwind's pelt. "But . . . he wasn't expecting to be attacked! He was just on a patrol."

"A good warrior is always ready," growled Tigerclaw. "Now, who is going to help me find the others?"

Clawface scraped his paw along the ground. "For what reason? We have trespassed on their territory. You've *killed* a warrior! We don't want to drag our Clanmates into a battle with ThunderClan. We are not yet strong enough for that!"

Tigerclaw let his hackles rise. "There is always a reason to attack another Clan! More territory, better prey, the chance to prove how strong you are!"

"But we're *not* strong," Ratscar protested. "And we don't want to take over ThunderClan's territory or hunt their prey."

In the distance, they heard cats approaching fast, crashing through undergrowth, not caring how much prey they scared away. Clawface stepped forward. "Tigerclaw, we came here to hunt, not to fight. This is not a battle we can win. Not yet."

Russetfur shifted her paws. "We need to get out of here!"

Tigerclaw forced the fur along his spine to lie flat. *Make them think it's your decision to retreat, not theirs,* warned the voice in his head. *Otherwise this could be the dumbest thing you've ever done.* "Fine. This warrior"—he kicked Runningwind's body and it shuddered like a leaf in the wind—"will be a clear enough message that ShadowClan is growing powerful again." He flicked his tail in the moment before Clawface, Russetfur, and Ratscar plunged into the elder bush and raced back to the Thunderpath. *I gave you the signal to retreat! Remember that!*

Whitethroat stayed where he was, his muzzle buried in the dead warrior's still-warm fur. "Are you coming?" Tigerclaw snarled. Whitethroat didn't move. "Waiting for your ThunderClan friends to arrive, are you?" Tigerclaw spat. "I knew I couldn't trust you. Know this, Whitethroat. You won't be welcome in ShadowClan again, I promise."

"It's this way!" Mousefur screeched from the other side of a clump of bracken. "Hurry!"

Tigerclaw lifted his head and sniffed. Beneath the acrid tang of the Thunderpath, he detected Fireheart and Whitestorm, closing in on him fast. Much as he longed to stay and watch them grieve for Runningwind, he knew he couldn't take them all on. He turned and slipped into the elder bush just as Fireheart pounded into the clearing beneath the ash trees.

"He's dead!" Whitethroat wailed.

Tigerclaw burst out from the bush and tore along the trail through the bracken. Brittle fronds whipped his pelt and stung his eyes. He stopped, flanks heaving, on the edge of the Thunderpath. Suddenly, to Tigerclaw's astonishment, Whitethroat appeared a little way off, struggling through the brambles. He was wide-eyed and panting, and blood smeared his cheek.

Is he leading an attack on ShadowClan? Tigerclaw wondered, bracing himself to run and warn the others. *Traitor!*

Fireheart scrambled out behind Whitethroat, and the black-and-white warrior whipped his head around to stare at the ginger cat.

Bring whoever you want! I will kill them all! Tigerclaw vowed.

Without stopping to speak to Fireheart, Whitethroat flung himself onto the Thunderpath. Tigerclaw took a step back as a monster blasted past, flinging grit and foul smoke into his face. When the air stopped whirling, he saw Fireheart staring in horror at a black-and-white shape that lay in the middle of the Thunderpath. *The monster hit Whitethroat!* Tigerclaw narrowed his eyes. *Will ThunderClan still attack?*

On the unforgiving black stone, Whitethroat stirred. Fireheart ran over to him. He crouched down and seemed to be speaking to Whitethroat, but his words were drowned by another monster roaring past. By the time Tigerclaw could see Fireheart again, he was standing up. Whitethroat was sprawled at his paws, eyes glazed and open, a trickle of blood coming from his mouth. Tigerclaw felt his fur prick. Fireheart was staring straight at him.

"Is chasing puny cats to their deaths the best you can do to defend your territory?" Tigerclaw yowled.

In answer, Fireheart hurtled toward him, narrowly missing two monsters, and launched himself at Tigerclaw. Taken by surprise, Tigerclaw staggered backward, feeling the scents of ThunderClan rise up around him from the thick grass. Fireheart's paws pummeled his ribs, but Tigerclaw wrenched himself free and reared up, flinging the ginger cat onto the ground. Tigerclaw let his full weight crash down on him, sinking his claws into the fur around Fireheart's throat. Fury burned inside him.

"Are you listening, kittypet?" he hissed. "I will kill you, and all your warriors, one by one."

Suddenly there was a roar of thundering paws, and a voice meowed in Tigerclaw's ear, "Did you think we would let you fight alone?"

He turned and looked into Blackfoot's hungry gaze. "No, my friend," mewed Tigerclaw. "I knew you would come."

Blackfoot had brought nearly every cat that wasn't sick with him—including Russetfur and Ratscar, Tigerclaw noticed. As the ShadowClan cats hurtled across the Thunderpath, Mousefur and Whitestorm burst out of the undergrowth. They fought bravely, but the ThunderClan warriors were sorely outnumbered. Even though Fireheart had managed to wriggle free from Tigerclaw, this wasn't a battle that Shadow-Clan would lose.

Mowgli rushed forward and sliced at Fireheart's hind legs with his claws. Fireheart stumbled and Tigerclaw reared over him, bracing himself to deliver the deathblow. Mowgli's eyes glittered in triumph. There was a searing pain in Tigerclaw's belly and he looked down, baffled. A broad gray tabby warrior had lunged into Tigerclaw's exposed stomach, tearing at the newly healed wound. *Graystripe! What is he doing here? He lives in RiverClan!*

Tigerclaw fell onto his paws and looked around. His cats were fighting more than the three ThunderClan warriors now. It looked like a whole RiverClan patrol had come to Fire-heart's rescue. *Always relying on others for help!* Tigerclaw spat. He braced himself as Fireheart and Graystripe tackled him side by side. Tigerclaw was forced back toward the Thunderpath, then his paw got tangled up in a bramble and he fell heavily onto the ground. He looked around for Mowgli or Blackfoot, but they were wrestling with fish-scented cats. Clawface and Russetfur had retreated to the edge of the Thunderpath, flanks heaving and covered in scratches.

Fireheart glanced up to look at the ShadowClan warriors who were leaving, and Tigerclaw felt the ginger cat's weight shift on his shoulders. He wrenched himself free and raced for the Thunderpath. He heard the other ShadowClan cats fall in behind him, but he didn't slow down until they were all deep inside the pine trees. He limped to a halt beside a patch of brambles, his belly burning with pain and his muzzle stinging from scratches. Around him, the other cats slumped onto the ground and began licking their wounds.

A thin voice whined in Tigerclaw's ear: *You ran! You should have stayed and fought! Never start a battle that you cannot finish, you fool.*

Tigerclaw lifted his head. "We must let the rest of ShadowClan know that we were attacked without provocation," he ordered. He caught Clawface's eye and waited for the brown tom to nod. "Tragically, Whitethroat gave his life trying to save his Clanmates from ThunderClan's savagery. He died at Fireheart's paws, trying to reach the safety of his own territory."

Flintfang snarled, "No warrior kills one of my Clanmates without answering to me. Let me go back to ThunderClan now and avenge Whitethroat's death!"

Tigerclaw let his tail rest on Flintfang's shoulder. "Have patience, my friend. Those RiverClan cats might be waiting for us still. Wait until the ThunderClan warriors have to defend themselves alone, and then we will destroy them without losing a single drop of our own blood."

"Whitethroat will not die in vain!" cried Russetfur, and her Clanmates joined in with a wail of grief.

"ThunderClan got lucky today, that's all," Tigerclaw meowed when they fell silent. "This is not a battle that has been lost. Merely one that has been put off for a while." He met Blackfoot's gaze. The white tom seemed to understand what Tigerclaw was saying. What happened today would be reported to the rest of ShadowClan as a moment of tragedy for Whitethroat and a cause for revenge on ThunderClan when they had their chance. Fireheart's days of leading his band of kittypet-lovers would soon be over.

CHAPTER 7

Gray, damp ferns brushed against Tigerclaw's pelt as he walked through the forest. Above him, the sky was pitch-black, without the faintest glimmer of moon or stars. Yet somehow there was just enough light for him to make out the trunks of trees looming toward him and the trace of a path over the slimy ground. The air smelled rotten, like fungus or forgotten fresh-kill. The leaves above Tigerclaw whispered even though there was no wind, and a greasy mist seemed to ooze up from the soil and cling to the fur on his belly. *Where am I?* Tigerclaw wondered. *Is this StarClan?*

"No, this is the Dark Forest," came a meow from behind him.

Tigerclaw froze. He knew that voice! It was the one that talked to him inside his head. Pelt standing on end, he slowly turned around.

A broad-faced she-cat stood among the ferns, her tortoiseshell-and-white fur patched and scarred from long-past battles. Her amber eyes gleamed like tiny gold moons; they seemed much brighter than the rest of the she-cat, and Tigerclaw was uncomfortably aware that he could see the leaves and ground on the other side of her.

"Welcome to the Place of No Stars, Tigerclaw," the she-cat meowed.

"This isn't StarClan, then?"

"*Tchah!*" The old cat spat. "Why would you want to go to StarClan? That place is full of weak-willed cowards who clung to the warrior code like ants to a leaf in a puddle. You will find much better company in the cats here, Tigerclaw."

Tigerclaw shifted his paws. "Who are you? How do you know my name?"

The she-cat purred; it sounded like two dead branches sliding together. "I have been watching you for a long time." She padded forward and stretched out her head to sniff his flank. Tigerclaw tried not to flinch at the stench that came from her breath. "ShadowClan needs a fearless and powerful leader," the old cat murmured. "You know you can give them everything they want, Tigerclaw. And after that . . . we will be waiting."

She turned and started to walk away. "Stop!" cried Tigerclaw. "What do you mean, you'll be waiting? I don't even know who you are!"

The she-cat paused and looked back at him. "My name is Mapleshade," she meowed. "I have walked beside you from the day you were born, guiding your paw steps, laying out your destiny before you. For now, you don't need to know anything else. Much, much more lies ahead of us, Tigerclaw. Be patient, and you will find out everything."

"Wait!" Tigerclaw tried to run after her, but the ferns

tangled around his legs, and Mapleshade vanished into the undergrowth. With a start, he woke up, his fur still damp and carrying the scent of fungus and dying things.

"Ewww!" coughed Stumpytail, scrambling to the other side of the nest. "Did you roll in something bad yesterday?"

Tigerclaw stalked out of the den, ducking under the fallen trunk. "Don't be ridiculous!" he hissed. "Come on, we need to get to the camp."

Blackfoot bounded up beside him. "Has something happened? Did you have a dream from StarClan?"

Tigerclaw shook his head impatiently. "We just need to be there."

He raced through the trees with Mapleshade's words echoing in his ears: *ShadowClan needs a fearless and powerful leader. You can give them everything they want.* He heard the other cats panting and stumbling behind him, but he didn't slow down until he reached the entrance to the camp. At once he heard a low, keening sound, many voices sharing one terrible note of grief.

Runningnose was standing in the middle of the clearing surrounded by cats huddled in misery. His tail dragged in the dirt, and he looked even older than he had the day before. He came to meet Tigerclaw and ushered him to the edge of the camp. "Nightstar died last night," he murmured.

Tigerclaw lowered his head. "I am so sorry for your loss," he mewed. "I hope he walks with StarClan now."

Runningnose's tail twitched. "Wherever Nightstar is, I hope he is at peace. The most important thing to do now is to keep the rest of my Clan safe." He stared at Tigerclaw, his eyes huge and haunted. "My Clanmates are terrified of being leaderless. There is no deputy to take over from Nightstar, and StarClan has sent us no sign of what should happen next. How can I blame these cats if they feel that their ancestors have abandoned them?" His voice rose in a wail of horror. "What if we never recover from what Brokenstar did to us? The wounds run so deep, and nothing I can do will heal them."

Tigerclaw let his tail rest on the old cat's shoulder. "You must be strong," he urged. "Without a leader, your Clanmates will look to you. StarClan hasn't given up on ShadowClan; you mustn't let yourself think that." He hoped Runningnose took his quivering muscles as a sign of grief rather than of the excitement that was building inside him. *This is your moment!* Mapleshade hissed. *Tread carefully. You are stepping onto the thinnest ice, and you must not fall through.*

Tigerclaw squared his shoulders, as if he had reached a decision. "Runningnose, you must lead your Clan until StarClan makes its wishes known. And until that time, my cats and I will do everything we can to help you. I know your Clanmates have been doubly wounded, by Brokenstar and by the sickness from the rats. If you let me, I will help you heal them."

Runningnose sniffed. "Thank you, Tigerclaw," he mewed. "I knew I could rely on you." He limped across the clearing to the lichen-covered rock and hauled himself onto it. "Let all cats old enough to catch their own prey join here beneath the rock!"

The earthen space began to fill with somber-eyed cats,

swirling together like leaves in a stream. Tigerclaw saw
Stumpytail go to sit beside Dawncloud, while Clawface laid
the tip of his tail on Rowanberry's back to guide her to an
empty place.

"What did you say to Runningnose?" whispered Snag in
Tigerclaw's ear.

"That he and his Clanmates will have our utmost support
until StarClan reveals their new leader."

There was a flicker of surprise in Snag's eyes. "That old cat,
and this weak Clan, could need a great deal of support," he
commented.

Tigerclaw nodded. "Indeed. And we will be repaid for it,
don't worry."

"Good," mewed Snag.

"Clanmates!" Runningnose began from on top of the
rock. "Shortly the elders will bring Nightstar's body out from
his den and we can begin our vigil. As we have no deputy to
take his place, I will lead you until StarClan makes its wishes
known. Even as we mourn Nightstar, life must continue.
The worst of the sickness has passed, and we must make
ourselves strong once more. Hunting and border patrols
will be sent out as normal, and battle training will begin
again."

He was interrupted by a tumult of voices.

"We have only just gotten over the sickness! We need more
time to recover!"

"How can we hunt, patrol the borders, and train our
apprentices?"

"We want to serve our Clan, Runningnose, but you're asking too much!"

Runningnose's eyes clouded with confusion, and he took a pace back from the edge of the rock.

Tigerclaw raised his head. "With your permission, cats of ShadowClan, I can help you. My cats and I have kept your fresh-kill pile well stocked for the past moon. Now you are strong enough to hunt for yourselves, so why not let us help with your border patrols, and take over your battle training?" He lowered his eyes and scraped at the ground with one forepaw. "If you wish, that is." *Don't overdo the humility, Tigerclaw,* warned Mapleshade. *It's not terribly convincing.*

Runningnose stepped forward again, blinking in gratitude. "Tigerclaw, we will take all the help we can get," he meowed.

"Wait," called Deerfoot. "ShadowClan has always survived on its own. Why should we let outsiders do everything for us now?"

Tigerclaw met Deerfoot's gaze. "That is not what I am proposing," he mewed. "We merely want to work alongside you, give you time to recover your full strength now that the danger of the sickness has gone." He looked around. "Cats of ShadowClan, never forget that you are surrounded by enemies who will attack the moment they think you have any trace of weakness. You were lucky to be left alone while the sickness was here. Can you keep it a secret forever? It only takes one sharp-eyed cat at a Gathering, one rumor across the border, for other Clans to put your strength to the test. ShadowClan has always been the most feared Clan in the forest. I promise I will not let that change!"

The pine trees shivered as the clearing erupted in yowls of triumph.

"He's right! We can't show weakness to the other Clans!"

"I'll train with you, Tigerclaw! Teach me everything you know!"

"ShadowClan will be feared once more!"

Tigerclaw closed his eyes and basked in the warmth of the cheers. *Remember this moment*, Mapleshade urged. *This is what power feels like.*

CHAPTER 8

❧

Runningnose appeared at his side. "*Please* organize the battle training as you see fit." He gave a slightly embarrassed purr. "Not my area of expertise at all!"

"No problem," Tigerclaw meowed. He flicked his tail. "Blackfoot, Snag, Mowgli? I want each of you to take a warrior and an apprentice. Go through the basic attack and defense moves, then we'll join up for a mock battle later on. Okay?"

His companions nodded. Stumpytail pricked his ears. "What about me?"

"You, Clawface, and Tangleburr can lead hunting patrols," Tigerclaw ordered.

There was a faint cough behind him. "We can arrange our own hunting patrols, Tigerclaw," Deerfoot meowed. His voice was mild but his eyes gleamed with an unspoken challenge.

Tigerclaw bowed his head. "Of course, Deerfoot. I only meant that my cats can help you with restocking the fresh-kill pile."

Deerfoot blinked. Tigerclaw sensed that the warrior was going to question him at every turn, and he felt his claws slide out to grip the soil. *Be patient*, whispered Mapleshade. *There will*

75

be time to deal with him later. Turning away, Tigerclaw nodded to Flintfang and Tallpoppy. "You two come with me."

Tallpoppy twitched her ears. "We don't need battle training," she pointed out. "We have been warriors longer than you, Tigerclaw!" She sounded amused, as if she was speaking to an impudent kit.

Tigerclaw let the fur rise along his spine. "Runningnose said that I was in charge of battle training," he meowed quietly. "I can't do that unless I know the abilities of every warrior in the Clan."

Tallpoppy blinked. "I don't think Runningnose meant it quite like that."

Tigerclaw took one step closer to her. "Really? Would you like to discuss it with him—or do you think he has enough to do already?" He flicked his tail toward the center of the clearing, where Runningnose was helping the elders to drag Nightstar's crumpled body out of the leader's den.

Tallpoppy looked down at her paws. "I won't disturb him now," she meowed. "Flintfang and I will show you how ShadowClan warriors are trained to fight."

Tigerclaw led them to a sandy space among the pines not far from the lake. The forest echoed with the sound of cats striking, pouncing, and retreating as Blackfoot, Snag, and Mowgli tested the rest of the Clan. Tigerclaw stood back and waited for Flintfang and Tallpoppy to demonstrate the established ShadowClan battle moves. He recognized several of them: the stealthy approach, the leap with raised forepaws, the hind leg slice that unbalanced opponents as well as left their back paws bleeding and lame.

"Wait!" Tigerclaw called as Tallpoppy folded gracefully onto the ground after a swift strike from Flintfang. Tigerclaw went over and narrowed his eyes at the brown she-cat. "Why did you roll over so fast? Even if you get knocked over, you still have a chance to grab your opponent with your teeth or claws. If you do this to a smaller cat, or can catch a bigger one off balance, you'll bring them down too."

"I'm sure Tallpoppy would do that in the heat of battle," Flintfang puffed, licking the ruffled fur on his chest. "But we have our claws sheathed now!"

Tigerclaw glared at him. "And how will that help when it comes to a real fight? Unsheathe your claws, both of you, and start taking this seriously. If there's a danger you might get hurt, you'll both sharpen up your moves."

Tallpoppy's eyes widened. "That's how Brokenstar made us train," she mewed. "This is a practice, Tigerclaw, not the real thing. Why risk getting injured when we are at peace?"

"If you're as good at fighting as you say you are, you won't get hurt," Tigerclaw growled. "Now, try that hind leg slice again, Flintfang, and give Tallpoppy something real to avoid."

Flintfang launched himself at Tallpoppy again, and this time Tigerclaw could see his claws glinting amid the thick gray fur on his paws. But Flintfang retracted them a heartbeat before he lashed out at Tallpoppy's hind legs, and once again she dropped to the ground without being touched. Tigerclaw shouldered Flintfang out of the way. "Let me try," he ordered.

He waited until Tallpoppy was standing, then rushed her,

unsheathing his claws and aiming for the soft part of her hind leg just above her paw. Tallpoppy screeched and flung herself away from him. Tigerclaw stopped and looked down at her as she twisted her head around to lick her bleeding leg. "You'll react quicker next time, won't you?" he challenged. Tallpoppy didn't look at him; she just nodded and kept swiping at her torn fur.

"I don't think that was necessary," Flintfang began, but Tigerclaw silenced him with a flick of his tail.

"Let's get back to the camp," he meowed. "The hunting patrols should have returned by now."

Stumpytail and Clawface had done an impressive job of stocking the fresh-kill pile. The cats swarmed around it, keeping their voices low out of respect for Nightstar but unable to hide their delight at such a good haul. Tigerclaw stepped forward just as Oakpaw was about to drag a shrew from the pile.

"I want to say something," Tigerclaw announced. All around him, the cats fell silent. Tigerclaw gestured to the fresh-kill pile. "Every bite we take tonight is dedicated to the memory of Nightstar. ShadowClan has lost a noble leader, and my companions and I are honored to share your grief." He bowed his head in a show of respect. In his mind, Mapleshade let out a rasp of laughter. *Nightstar was weaker than a newborn kit. Don't think these warriors didn't know that.*

"Thank you, Tigerclaw," mewed Runningnose. His voice cracked. "We are honored to have you here—you and all your companions." He stood a little straighter. "On behalf of my

Clanmates, I would like to invite you to move into the camp. You have proven your loyalty to ShadowClan many times over, and it's what Nightstar would have wanted. You belong here now, not outside our borders."

Tigerclaw blinked. He had not expected this so soon, and he could tell by the startled whispers that Runningnose didn't speak on behalf of *all* his Clanmates. Should he make Runningnose wait a little longer, until the whole Clan was desperate for Tigerclaw to join them permanently? *You can win them over more quickly if you're among them all the time,* Mapleshade pointed out. Tigerclaw waited for one more heartbeat, then bowed his head. "You are very generous, Runningnose. If you are sure that this is what Nightstar would want, then we accept." He lifted his head, daring the ShadowClan warriors to challenge something their leader seemed to approve through the words of his medicine cat.

Rowanberry stepped forward. "Welcome to ShadowClan, Tigerclaw." She glanced fondly at Clawface. "And to those of you who have lived among us before, welcome home."

There was a murmur of approval from some of the warriors, and Stumpytail and Dawncloud touched noses. Snag and Mowgli stood at the edge of the crowd, looking wary.

Tigerclaw raised his tail. "Runningnose, I have a great favor to ask. Please may I give my friends Snag and Mowgli warrior names? Only then will they feel as if this is truly their home. I am sure Nightstar would want the same."

Runningnose nodded. "Of course, Tigerclaw. Please, go ahead and choose their names."

Tigerclaw glanced around at the watching cats. "Only if your Clanmates agree," he meowed. "After all, a naming ceremony should be performed by a leader. I don't want to offend anyone."

"I'm sure we'll cope, Tigerclaw," meowed Fernshade drily.

"We don't want the other Clans asking questions at the Gathering about where these cats came from," Wetfoot agreed.

Tigerclaw jumped onto the rock, ignoring the ripple of surprise from the ShadowClan warriors. "Snag, Mowgli, come here, please." The massive ginger tom and the sleek brown cat padded forward until they were standing below him. Tigerclaw took a deep breath. "Snag, Mowgli, do you promise to uphold the warrior code and to protect and defend this Clan, even at the cost of your lives?"

The two cats bowed their heads.

"I do, Tigerclaw."

"I do."

"Then by the powers of StarClan I give you your warrior names. Snag, from this moment on you will be known as Jaggedtooth. StarClan honors your strength and your fighting skills, and we welcome you as a full warrior of ShadowClan." Tigerclaw reached down and rested his muzzle briefly on the broad orange head. Then he turned to the brown tom. "Mowgli, from this moment on you will be known as Nightwhisper. StarClan honors your stealth and your courage, and we welcome you as a full warrior of ShadowClan." Tigerclaw touched his head, and stepped back. "Clanmates, I give you

Jaggedtooth and Nightwhisper!"

"Jaggedtooth! Nightwhisper!" cheered Stumpytail and Blackfoot. Other ShadowClan cats joined in, and the newly named warriors lifted their heads proudly.

"That's not fair! They didn't have to do any training!" grumbled a small voice from the back. Tigerclaw sought out Oakpaw and fixed him with a cold glare; the apprentice ducked his head and said nothing more.

Tigerclaw jumped down from the rock. "And now, Clanmates, we will honor our fallen leader Nightstar with the vigil that he deserves. Come, join me as we pay tribute to him." He padded across to the small black shape that had tried so hard to give strength and leadership to ShadowClan after the defeat of Brokenstar. *How did you ever think you would succeed in following him?* Tigerclaw thought scornfully as he crouched by Nightstar's head. He closed his eyes, listening as the rest of ShadowClan settled around him, pressing their muzzles against the cold, dusk-damp fur.

This Clan belongs to me now, Nightstar. Watch how I make it strong again, feared and respected throughout all the forest.

CHAPTER 9

"Tigerclaw, wake up!"

Tigerclaw stretched and opened his eyes, briefly confused by the tangle of brambles overhead instead of a smooth gray trunk. Then he remembered: He was in the ShadowClan camp now, not hiding in the wild woods like some kind of rogue. He rolled over, feeling the familiar glow of satisfaction. He and his companions had been in the camp for a quarter moon, leading their Clanmates in battle training, joining hunting and border patrols, constantly reassuring Running-nose that StarClan would choose a new leader soon. . . .

"Tigerclaw, you have to come see this!"

Tigerclaw sat up and looked at Clawface. "What is it?" he grumbled. "I'm not on the dawn patrol today."

"I know, I've just returned with it. But something is happening on the other side of the Thunderpath. The forest is on fire!"

Tigerclaw leaped out of his nest and thrust past Clawface. Behind him, the scrawny brown warrior called, "It looked like the flames were right above the ThunderClan camp!"

Tigerclaw pounded through the thorns and raced through

the pine trees, ignoring the brambles that snagged at his pelt. Nightwhisper was standing beside the Thunderpath, straining to see through the trees on the other side. A terrible roaring, crackling sound echoed from ThunderClan territory, and the air was acrid with pale gray smoke. Glimpses of bright orange flames flickered among the trunks, and every so often the distant rumble was splintered by the sound of a tree crashing to the ground. Tigerclaw crouched at the edge of the Thunderpath and scanned for monsters.

"Are you going over there?" Nightwhisper yowled over the noise of the burning trees. "Do you want me to come with you? There might be cats who need our help."

Tigerclaw shook his head. "I'm not going on a rescue mission," he growled. "I just need to see what's going on. Stay here; I want to do this alone."

Nightwhisper shifted his weight onto his front paws as Tigerclaw began to cross, as if he was about to follow. Tigerclaw glared over his shoulder at him. "I said, stay here!" He bounded across the rest of the hard black stone and plunged into the long, cool grass.

At once the scents of ThunderClan bathed his nose, cutting through the smell of cinders. Tigerclaw breathed in deeply, then burst out coughing as sharp smoke pricked the back of his throat. He ducked his head and pushed through the grass into the trees. The leaf-mulch beneath his paws was instantly familiar, and he quickly found his way to an almost invisible trail that led deeper into the woods, toward the ravine. The crackling of the flames grew louder, and Tigerclaw felt his fur grow hot as he neared the camp. As far as he could tell, the trees between the ravine and Twolegplace were burning, and the deafening roar suggested that the fire was heading straight toward the ThunderClan camp. *No!*

This is the Clan that drove you out! Forced you to live as a rogue, turned you away in favor of a kittypet! Mapleshade's voice snarled in his ear.

Tigerclaw curled his lip. *Don't mistake this for caring about my former Clanmates. I want the satisfaction of destroying them myself, not watching them burn like trapped rabbits, that's all.* He wondered if Mapleshade could sense the horror that squirmed in his belly. No cat deserved to die in flames, surely?

He winced as Twoleg shouts rang out close to his ear, and giant figures, muffled by thick dark pelts, crashed through the undergrowth. A two-tone howl sounded from the Thunderpath, and something long and heavy was dragged past him, hissing over the crumpled bracken. Tigerclaw bounded in the other direction, weaving through the oaks and beech trees until the ground fell away steeply into the crevice that had been his home for so many moons. Smoke billowed over the ravine, and flames already licked at the brambles on the far side. Shrieks and yowls of terrified cats cut through the noise of the fire. Tigerclaw crept to the edge of the cliff and peered over.

Frostfur's white pelt gleamed through the smoke as he nudged Bluestar up the path that led out of the camp. The leader stumbled along at a half run, caught up among her fleeing Clanmates.

"Head for the river!" called a voice from below. Tigerclaw felt his muscles tense. Fireheart was in charge, of course. Surely that mouse-brained ThunderClan leader hadn't made him *deputy*? "Keep an eye on your denmates," Fireheart ordered. "Don't lose sight of one another."

That should be me down there, Tigerclaw thought furiously. *I should be saving my Clanmates, not some kittypet!*

Now Fireheart was handing Willowpelt's kits to Longtail and Mousefur, telling them to stay close to the queen, who was carrying the third kit. Tigerclaw scanned the cats for a pale ginger pelt and let out a growl of relief. Goldenflower was at the top of the ravine, racing toward the river. A tiny pale brown shape ran at her heels: Tawnykit had made it out.

Fireheart followed the cats to the top of the slope and paused. "Wait! Is any cat missing?"

Cloudpaw's fluffy white head popped up. He looked as much like a kittypet as ever. "Where are Halftail and Patch-pelt?" he squeaked.

"They're not with me," Smallear called from farther along the path.

"They must still be in camp!" meowed Whitestorm. Tigerclaw shrugged. If elders couldn't manage to save themselves, they were a waste of fresh-kill.

"Where's Bramblekit?" Goldenflower shrieked, and Tigerclaw felt the blood chill in his veins. *Bramblekit!* "He was behind me when I was climbing the ravine!" the queen wailed.

"I'll find them," Fireheart meowed. "It's too dangerous for you to stay here any longer. Whitestorm and Darkstripe, make sure the rest of the Clan make it to the river."

"You can't go back down there!" Sandstorm yowled.

"I have to," Fireheart insisted. *Yes, play the hero, run into fire to show just what a loyal little warrior you are.* Tigerclaw sank his claws into the dusty soil. *Where is Bramblekit?*

"I'm coming too," Sandstorm mewed.

"No!" Whitestorm told her. "We are short of warriors already. We need you to help get the Clan to the river."

"Then I'll come!" Tigerclaw blinked as Cinderpelt staggered back to the edge of the ravine. The pale gray medicine cat looked exhausted, her eyes streaming from the smoke. "I'm no warrior," Cinderpelt mewed. "I'd be no use anyway if we met an enemy patrol."

"No way!" Fireheart hissed.

Then Yellowfang lurched over to them. "I may be old, but I'm steadier on my paws than you," mewed the old medicine cat to Cinderpelt. "The Clan will need your healing skills. I'll go with Fireheart. You stay with the Clan."

Tigerclaw stared in disbelief. Was the life of his son dependent on an ancient medicine cat and an arrogant kittypet?

Cinderpelt looked as if she was going to say something, but Fireheart cut her off. "There's no time to argue. Yellowfang, come with me. The rest of you, head for the river." He turned and ran back down the path with Yellowfang lumbering behind him.

Tigerclaw peered through the smoke, searching desperately for a small dark brown shape. Flames were devouring the ferns around the camp and twining around the slender tree trunks. Two filthy, blurred shapes were just visible at the foot of a birch. Yellowfang rushed forward and grabbed the closest body—Tigerclaw was pretty sure it was Halftail—and started to drag it across the clearing. Fireheart hauled Patchpelt through the gorse tunnel first and managed to get the old tom to the top of the cliff. Yellowfang and Halftail were much slower, and the trees around them exploded in fire before they were halfway up the slope.

"Help! Help!"

Tigerclaw whipped his head around and stared in horror at the tiny cat clinging to the branch of a tree that sprouted from the side of the ravine. "Bramblekit!" he roared. The bark just below his son was smoldering, and in the next heartbeat the whole trunk was ablaze. Tigerclaw was about to launch himself off the top of the cliff when there was a blur of movement and a soot-stained shape raced up the tree.

"Fireheart, help me!" As Bramblekit screamed, he let go of the branch and dropped toward the ground. Tigerclaw watched, unable to breathe, as Fireheart managed to catch the kit in his mouth. There was no way they would make it down the trunk now. Fireheart began to creep along the branch, still carrying Bramblekit. Every hair on Tigerclaw's pelt stood on end, urging him to fly through the air and somehow rescue his son. But his weight would only bring the branch crashing down into the flames. He had to let Fireheart do this alone.

The flames leaped up to reach the branch and there was a terrible crack. The branch started to fall, but Fireheart somehow managed to jump clear at the last moment and grasp the side of the ravine. Bramblekit lurched, and Tigerclaw braced himself to plunge down into the river of fire, but Fireheart kept hold of the tiny cat and began to claw his way to the top of the cliff. Below him, the burning tree filled the ravine with flames, blocking any sight of Yellowfang and Halftail.

Tigerclaw realized he was trembling. *Thank you, StarClan, for sparing my son.* He drew back into the ferns and glowered at Fireheart, who had made it to the rest of his Clanmates and was being fawned over like he had saved the entire forest on his own. *You may have saved my son, but this changes nothing.* Tigerclaw growled under his breath. *I will still kill you when I have the chance.*

CHAPTER 10

❧

"Don't lie there like a dead pigeon! Go for his hind legs!" Tigerclaw hissed. Oakpaw was sprawled on his back, felled by a blow from an apprentice named Rowanpaw. The lithe ginger tom danced out of the way, purring.

"Too slow, Oakpaw!" he taunted.

Tigerclaw lashed his tail. "Are you going to let your enemy speak to you like that?" he challenged Oakpaw.

The pale brown cat scrambled to his feet. "No way!" He launched himself at Rowanpaw, paws flailing. Rowanpaw fell back with a grunt, and Tigerclaw noted with satisfaction that Oakpaw had unsheathed his claws and drawn blood. Slowly, slowly, these ShadowClan cats were learning.

"Is Rowanpaw hurt?" mewed a worried voice behind him. Tigerclaw turned to see Runningnose emerging from a clump of bracken, his nose moist as usual, and his eyes cloudy with concern.

"He's fine," Tigerclaw meowed. "He'll move quicker next time, that's all."

Runningnose nodded. "I trust you to train these apprentices to fight in any battle, Tigerclaw," he murmured. "No cat could doubt your loyalty to our Clan."

Not for a moment, Tigerclaw thought. When he had returned from watching ThunderClan burn, he had let the Shadow-Clan cats believe that his shocked look was due to his fear that the flames would cross the Thunderpath. Tigerclaw had insisted on patrolling that border alone all day, watching long hollow snakes spurt water onto the burning trees while Two-legs scurried about, yelping. Even after three sunrises, the woods still smelled of smoke, and blackened, charred trunks could be seen deep in ThunderClan territory. Tigerclaw wondered if Bluestar had brought her cats back to the ravine yet. All of the dens would need rebuilding, and prey would be scarce, driven off or killed by the flames.

"I wondered if I could have a word?" Runningnose mewed beside him, jerking him out of his thoughts.

"Of course." Tigerclaw checked that Oakpaw and Rowan-paw weren't actually killing each other, then led the medicine cat away from the training area into a circle of hawthorns. "Is something wrong?"

Runningnose blinked. "The full moon is coming. How can ShadowClan go to the Gathering when we have no leader, no deputy?" He scraped at the ground. "But if we don't go, every other Clan will know that something is wrong. Perhaps I should just ask StarClan to send clouds to cover the moon!" He strained to sound lighthearted, but Tigerclaw could smell fear coming from the old cat's ruffled pelt.

"Has StarClan sent you any omens about who should lead ShadowClan?" he asked, trying to keep his voice mild. Inside, something stirred, a feeling of hunger, the certainty that everything he wanted was drawing closer.

Runningnose shook his head. "Nothing," he mewed. "But perhaps I've been too busy, or too tired, to see the signs. My Clan is on the brink of destruction, and it could be my fault!"

Tigerclaw rested his tail on the old cat's shoulder. "Look around you," he urged. "ShadowClan is not on the brink of destruction! Your Clan is full of strong, able warriors. You know in your heart which one will make the best leader." He stepped away from Runningnose, studied him carefully. "You alone know the signs that StarClan might send. Your ancestors trust you enough to be their voice in ShadowClan. You can help them choose the next leader."

Runningnose's head jerked up. "Are you saying that I should fake a sign? I couldn't do that!"

"Of course not," Tigerclaw soothed. "But surely any choice that the medicine cat makes is guided by StarClan, whether he knows it or not?"

Runningnose looked troubled. "You mean, StarClan would ensure that I made the same decision as it would?"

Tigerclaw nodded. "Think about it, Runningnose. There are still several days before the Gathering. Keep watch for signs from your ancestors—but also listen to the voice inside your own mind."

Ha! purred Mapleshade.

Runningnose pushed his way out of the hawthorns, his eyes still troubled. Almost at once the branches on the other side of the little clearing rustled and Jaggedtooth emerged.

"He should choose you, if he has any sense," the ginger tom meowed. "Why didn't you tell him that, and help him make the decision?"

Tigerclaw blinked. "I cannot determine the will of StarClan."

Jaggedtooth's eyes glittered. "I don't share your faith in dead cats," he mewed. "Perhaps that makes things easier?"

Tigerclaw held his gaze and gave him a tiny nod. "You've been a good friend to me, Jaggedtooth. I won't ever forget that."

Jaggedtooth nodded back. "I know," he mewed.

The sky above the pines was as dark as the water in the marshes, but the trees glowed silver in the light of a swollen moon.

"Tomorrow is the night of the Gathering," Tigerclaw heard Fernshade whisper to Rowanberry. "Has Runningnose told you what he's going to tell the other Clans?"

"I don't think he'll need to tell them anything," Russetfur put in. "It's going to be pretty obvious that Nightstar has died and we don't have a leader."

"Or a deputy," added Applefur. "The other Clans will laugh us out of Fourtrees."

"Be patient," urged a quiet voice. Tangleburr had joined them. "There is still time for StarClan to answer our prayers."

There was a stir of movement outside the medicine den, and Runningnose appeared, his gray-and-white pelt lit up by the moonlight. He crossed to the rock and hauled himself onto it. "Let all cats old enough to catch their own prey gather for a meeting!" he called, his thin voice echoing through the trees.

Tigerclaw unfolded himself from the shadows and joined the others as they sat at the foot of the rock. Runningnose looked no bigger or stronger than a kit, and Tigerclaw marveled at the way his Clanmates gazed at him with such respect, such trust that he would restore their Clan to how it should be.

"Clanmates, I know you are troubled about the Gathering," Runningnose began. "I share your fears, but be strong! Have faith in our warrior ancestors to send us a new leader soon!"

There was a murmur from the watching cats, and Deerfoot stood up. "Soon isn't now!" he hissed. "The Gathering is tomorrow! Does StarClan want us to look weak and leaderless in front of the other Clans?"

"Has StarClan given up on us?" wailed Rowanpaw. He was hushed by Stumpytail, who clouted him gently with one paw.

"Of course they haven't given up on us," Runningnose mewed, but his words were drowned by his Clanmates' increasingly noisy protests.

"We'll be pounced on like rats as soon as the Clans hear about Nightstar's death!" yowled Ratscar.

"How can we survive without a leader?" snarled Tallpoppy. "No other Clan has ever turned up at a Gathering without one!"

Runningnose hung his head and said nothing. Tigerclaw could smell the misery coming from him. *Don't give up now,* he urged. *There is still something you can do.*

Suddenly the medicine cat tensed. His ears pricked, and his gaze fixed on something at the foot of the rock. There was a tiny, pale glint among the grass, dappled in the moonlight. Runningnose jumped down and put his muzzle close to it. Then his head shot up in astonishment.

"It's a claw!" he gasped. "Here, at the bottom of the rock. Has any cat lost a claw today?"

Warriors and apprentices shook their heads, and puzzled murmurs spread through the Clan.

Runningnose was studying the claw again. He reached out carefully and touched it with his paw, shifting it so that the other cats could see it. "Look," he whispered. "The moon has cast shadows on it. Not shadows, *stripes.*" He looked up and stared at Tigerclaw. "Stripes like a tiger's pelt."

"It's a sign!" gasped Dawncloud. "It must be!"

"StarClan has chosen our new leader!" called Blackfoot.

"Tigerclaw!" breathed Runningnose, and as one the cats of ShadowClan turned to gaze at Tigerclaw. "StarClan has spoken," the medicine cat mewed. "And we must listen."

Tigerclaw felt the breath catch in his chest. After all this time, the ancestors had chosen him! He had served them for so long, tried to challenge the weak leadership in Thunder-Clan, been driven out and forced to prove his loyalty to a new Clan. And now at last StarClan was rewarding him with a leadership of his own. "Thank you," he whispered.

Tigerclaw closed his eyes and sensed the ranks of shadowed cats swell around him. Like a dark wave they surged through the forest, carrying him along on legs that seemed weightless. He felt a yowl of joy rise inside him as he raced into battle with his Clanmates. "Follow my lead!" he called, and countless warriors fell in behind him, matching their stride to his. Ahead, their enemy quivered with fear. . . .

"Tigerclaw?" Blackfoot mewed quietly. "Runningnose wants to speak with you."

Tigerclaw blinked open his eyes. The medicine cat was standing in front of him, close enough for Tigerclaw to smell his rancid breath.

Runningnose bowed low. "Will you do us the honor of leading us, Tigerclaw? StarClan has spoken, and it has chosen you."

We did it! screeched Mapleshade inside his head. *Didn't I promise you this would happen?*

"And we choose you, too!" yowled Boulder over the heads of his Clanmates. "You have led us out of the darkness after Nightstar's death, and shown us how to be strong again!"

Tigerclaw dipped his head. "I am stunned by the decision of our ancestors," he meowed. "I came late to ShadowClan, though I hope no cat would question my loyalty to each one of you. I never looked for this. If you're sure, and if StarClan has spoken, then I can only say *yes*."

"Hail the new ShadowClan leader!" called Runningnose, and the night air was split with screeches of joy and relief.

There was a faint rustle in the brambles behind Tigerclaw. He turned and saw a pair of amber eyes gleaming. Jagged-tooth limped forward, bleeding from one toe where the claw had been ripped out. Tigerclaw glanced down at the injury. "You took a big risk that it would work," he murmured.

Jaggedtooth lashed his tail. "It paid off," he growled. "You can thank me later."

Tigerclaw turned and padded to the center of the clearing. The other cats fell silent as he sprang onto the rock. Tigerclaw settled his paws on the cold, smooth stone and looked down at his Clanmates: Nightwhisper and Jaggedtooth, former strays who would be loyal to him until their last breath; Running-nose and Littlecloud, *his* medicine cats, watching for signs that StarClan sent to their leader; strong warriors, healthy queens, and apprentices desperate to learn how to fight as bravely as he did. He caught Blackfoot's eye; he would make him deputy before the moon rose above the treetops. Not Jaggedtooth, who needed to understand that Tigerclaw owed him nothing.

Tigerclaw braced his shoulders. He should prepare for the Gathering, when Bluestar would be forced to face him as her equal, at the head of a Clan that could match hers any day.

But that was tomorrow. For now, Tigerclaw was content to listen to his Clanmates calling his new name.

Tigerstar! Tigerstar!

WARRIORS

LEAFPOOL'S
WISH

THUNDERCLAN

LEADER

FIRESTAR—ginger tom with a flame-colored pelt

DEPUTY

GRAYSTRIPE—long-haired gray tom

MEDICINE CAT

LEAFPOOL—light brown tabby she-cat with amber eyes

WARRIORS

(toms, and she-cats without kits)

DUSTPELT—dark brown tabby tom

SANDSTORM—pale ginger she-cat

CLOUDTAIL—long-haired white tom

BRACKENFUR—golden brown tabby tom
APPRENTICE, WHITEPAW

THORNCLAW—golden brown tabby tom

BRIGHTHEART—white she-cat with ginger patches

BRAMBLECLAW—dark brown tabby tom with amber eyes

ASHFUR—pale gray (with darker flecks) tom, dark blue eyes
APPRENTICE, BIRCHPAW

RAINWHISKER—dark gray tom with blue eyes

SQUIRRELFLIGHT—dark ginger she-cat with green eyes

SPIDERLEG—long-limbed black tom with brown underbelly and amber eyes

QUEENS (she-cats expecting or nursing kits)

FERNCLOUD—pale gray (with darker flecks) she-cat, green eyes, mother of Dustpelt's kits

SORRELTAIL—tortoiseshell-and-white she-cat with amber eyes

DAISY—cream-colored, long-furred cat from the horseplace

ELDERS (former warriors and queens, now retired)

GOLDENFLOWER—pale ginger coat, the oldest nursery queen

LONGTAIL—pale tabby tom with dark black stripes, retired early due to failing sight

MOUSEFUR—small dusky brown she-cat

SHADOWCLAN

LEADER **BLACKSTAR**—large white tom with huge jet-black paws

DEPUTY **RUSSETFUR**—dark ginger she-cat

MEDICINE CAT **LITTLECLOUD**—very small tabby tom

WARRIORS (toms, and she-cats without kits)

OAKFUR—small brown tom
APPRENTICE, SMOKEPAW

CEDARHEART—dark gray tom

ROWANCLAW—ginger tom

TAWNYPELT—tortoiseshell she-cat with green eyes

QUEENS (she-cats expecting or nursing kits)

TALLPOPPY—long-legged light brown tabby she-cat

ELDERS (former warriors and queens, now retired)

BOULDER—skinny gray tom

WINDCLAN

LEADER **ONESTAR**—brown tabby tom

DEPUTY **ASHFOOT**—gray she-cat

MEDICINE CAT **BARKFACE**—short-tailed brown tom

WARRIORS (toms, and she-cats without kits)

TORNEAR—tabby tom

WEBFOOT—dark gray tabby tom

CROWFEATHER—dark gray tom

OWLWHISKER—light brown tabby tom

NIGHTCLOUD—black she-cat

WEASELFUR—ginger tom with white paws

QUEENS (she-cats expecting or nursing kits)

WHITETAIL—small white she-cat

ELDERS (former warriors and queens, now retired)

MORNINGFLOWER—tortoiseshell queen

RUSHTAIL—light brown tom

RIVERCLAN

LEADER LEOPARDSTAR—unusually spotted golden tabby she-cat

DEPUTY MISTYFOOT—gray she-cat with blue eyes

MEDICINE CAT MOTHWING—dappled golden she-cat
APPRENTICE, WILLOWPAW

WARRIORS (toms, and she-cats without kits)

BLACKCLAW—smoky black tom
APPRENTICE, BEECHPAW

VOLETOOTH—small brown tabby tom

SWALLOWTAIL—dark tabby she-cat

STONESTREAM—gray tom

REEDWHISKER—black tom
APPRENTICE, RIPPLEPAW

QUEENS (she-cats expecting or nursing kits)

MOSSPELT—tortoiseshell she-cat with blue eyes

DAWNFLOWER—pale gray she-cat

THE TRIBE OF RUSHING WATER

BROOK WHERE SMALL FISH SWIM (BROOK)—brown tabby she-cat

STORMFUR—dark gray tom with amber eyes

OTHER ANIMALS

SMOKY—muscular gray-and-white tom who lives in a barn at the horseplace

FLOSS—small gray-and-white she-cat who lives at the horseplace

PIP—black-and-white terrier who lives with Twolegs near the horseplace

MIDNIGHT—a stargazing badger who lives by the sea

Hareview Campsite

Sanctuary
Cottage

Sadler Woods

Littlepine Road

Littlepine
Sailing
Center

Littlepine
Island

River Alba

Whitchurch Road

CHAPTER 1

"Keep still, Birchpaw! If you don't stop wriggling, I'll have Dustpelt sit on you!" Leafpool retrieved the fallen moss with a hiss and held it over the apprentice's eye once more.

"It stings!" Birchpaw protested.

"What, worse than a badger's claws?" Leafpool meowed skeptically. She squeezed the moss between her pads and a bead of green juice dropped into the center of Birchpaw's half-closed eye. Birchpaw winced but Leafpool quickly placed her paw on top of his eyelid, keeping it closed while the juice treated the infection.

Inevitably, memories of the badger attack flooded back to her: the sight of her Clanmates battling for their lives when she and Crowfeather had stood, horrorstruck, at the entrance to the hollow; the sound of small furred bodies thudding into the ground, tossed by gigantic black-and-white paws; the snarls of the badgers rumbling beneath the shrieks of warriors. Birchpaw had been lucky to escape with nothing more serious than a clawed eye. Sootfur had been killed, and so had Cinderpelt the medicine cat, desperately protecting Sorreltail as she gave birth to her kits. Leafpool felt a fresh wave of grief,

sharp as ever, when she thought of her mentor dying without her. Cinderpelt must have been terrified for the future of
ThunderClan without a medicine cat, yet she still refused to
leave Sorreltail's side.

I came back, Cinderpelt, and I stayed, Leafpool whispered fiercely,
hoping that her mentor could hear her in StarClan.

"Talking to yourself, eh?" Brackenfur mewed, appearing in
the entrance to the den.

Leafpool shook the memories clear from her mind. "Just
remembering something important," she replied. "Is everything okay, Brackenfur?"

"Er, can I go now?" Birchpaw chirped, looking up at her
with his injured eye closed and weeping with juice.

Leafpool nodded. "Of course, but you're still not allowed
out of the hollow! I don't want any brambles poking you in
that eye before it's fully healed."

Birchpaw trotted out, muttering under his breath. Brackenfur flicked the apprentice with his tail-tip as he passed. "Some
cats need to remember how lucky they were to survive that
battle," he grunted.

Leafpool bowed her head. "And those who fell will not be
forgotten."

Brackenfur ducked to enter the den. Like most of Leafpool's Clanmates, he glanced nervously up at the roof as if
he was wondering how the weight of the cliffs above them
was supported. "Sorreltail sent me," he meowed. "Cinderkit's
picked up a couple of fleas and she wondered if you had anything that might soothe the bites."

Leafpool pictured the tiny gray she-cat scratching at her fluffy pelt. "I'm sure I can help," she purred. "Tell Sorreltail I'll bring something over before sunhigh."

Brackenfur narrowed his eyes. "There's no rush. You look tired, Leafpool. Is there anything I can do?"

Leafpool shook her head. "I'm fine. It's always busy after a battle, and a nursery full of kits doesn't help!" She paused. "Not that I don't rejoice at every kit born to ThunderClan," she added.

Brackenfur's gaze softened. "They are all precious," he agreed. He padded out of the den and Leafpool followed him as far as the entrance, where she stood in a shaft of watery sunlight. On the opposite side of the clearing, her sister Squirrelflight was sharing a mouse with Brambleclaw, her dark ginger body curled into his. Leafpool felt a twist of concern in her belly. It looked like Squirrelflight had finally made her choice between their Clanmate Ashfur and the broad-shouldered dark tabby. Leafpool wouldn't miss the tension between the warriors while Squirrelflight had been making up her mind, but she wished with all her heart that her sister had chosen differently. How could Leafpool tell her that she had dreamed of the Dark Forest and seen Tigerstar mentoring Brambleclaw in secret, training his son in the most terrible ways to kill and maim an enemy? However often Leafpool told herself that Brambleclaw was a loyal ThunderClan warrior, no cat could deny that his father was one of the most dangerous cats ever to live in the Clans.

And yet there had been the vision of stars over the lake,

when Leafpool had been walking alone at sunset. Two starry shapes, unmistakably Squirrelflight and Brambleclaw, padding side by side across the sky, tails entwined. What could that mean except that these two warriors were destined to be together? Reluctantly, Leafpool had told her sister what she had seen; it was not the duty of a medicine cat to choose which omens and visions to keep secret. Leafpool knew that this had helped Squirrelflight decide between Brambleclaw and Ashfur. And when Leafpool treated Brambleclaw for injuries that could only have come from fighting in his dreams with his Dark Forest father, she said nothing to her sister. She just hoped that Brambleclaw would make his own decision to leave his connection with Tigerstar behind, and learn only from what his living Clanmates could teach him.

Cinderkit's flea bites were easily treated with some soothing marigold leaves rubbed into her cobweb-soft fur. The tiny cat squirmed so much that Leafpool suspected her littermates would receive a good dose as well. Sorreltail blinked gratefully at her, happily worn out by nursing and keeping her little family in order. Leafpool breathed in the sweet, milky scent of the nursery and let it comfort her for a moment. She held on to the memory of it as she settled into her nest that night. The den still seemed too empty without Cinderpelt sleeping beside her, the shadows cold and thick against the rough stone walls. Leafpool tucked her nose under her tail and took a deep breath. Tonight she wanted to walk in the Dark Forest again. She needed to know if Brambleclaw was still being mentored by his father.

She woke in a dense green forest, dimly lit by an unseen moon and stirred by a whispering breeze. She felt the familiar shudder of horror at the thought of dead cats unwanted by StarClan hiding in the bushes, watching her with angry yellow eyes. But she forced herself to walk along the path that curved between the mossy trunks, convinced she could hear her heartbeat echoing among the trees.

Suddenly Leafpool stopped. Three cats stood a little way ahead with their backs to her. She recognized two of them at once—but these weren't Dark Forest warriors. Their fur glittered with starlight, and silver beams pooled around their paws as if they were standing in water. One of them turned to face Leafpool, and she felt her heart lift with joy. *Bluestar!*

"Come out, Leafpool," the StarClan cat meowed. "We've been waiting for you."

Leafpool walked forward until she could smell the scent of wind and stars on the old leader's pelt.

"You took your time," grunted Yellowfang.

Leafpool didn't know the third cat, a broad-shouldered golden tabby. He dipped his head to her. "Greetings, Leafpool. My name is Lionheart. I was with Bluestar when your father Firestar first came to the forest."

"I'm honored to meet you," Leafpool meowed. "But where am I? Why have you brought me here?" She hadn't dreamed of this place before, yet it couldn't be the Dark Forest, not if StarClan cats were here.

"Come," Bluestar ordered, turning to follow the path

deeper into the forest.

It led to a moonlit clearing, and the trees that had seemed so sinister before now looked graceful and welcoming, filled with the scents of prey. In the clear sky, three tiny stars gleamed more brightly than the others, throbbing with silver light.

"Bluestar, what's that?" Leafpool whispered.

Bluestar didn't reply. Instead, she walked into the center of the clearing and gestured with her tail for Leafpool to sit. Leafpool looked up once more, but the three stars had vanished.

"Do you have a sign for me?" she asked.

"Not exactly," Bluestar answered. "But we wanted to tell you that the path of your life will twist in ways yet hidden to you."

"Yes." Yellowfang sounded tense, as if there was more she wanted to say but some unspoken promise prevented her. "You will tread a path that few medicine cats have before."

Leafpool felt a stab of alarm. "What do you mean?"

"There are cats you have yet to meet," Bluestar meowed. "But their paws will shape your future."

What does that mean?

Lionheart rested his tail on her shoulder and his scent drifted around her, brave and reassuring. "We have come to give you strength," he murmured.

"Whatever happens, remember that we are always with you," Bluestar mewed.

Her blue eyes glittered with concern and kindness, but

Leafpool still had no idea what any of this meant. Her life was set in stone now, like her den beneath the cliffs. She would be ThunderClan's medicine cat until it was her turn to walk with these cats in StarClan. What she had with Crowfeather . . . all that was over, forgotten, a part of her life that would fade in time to nothing.

"I don't understand," she whispered. "Can't you tell me more?"

Bluestar shook her head. "Even StarClan can't see everything that will happen. The path ahead of you vanishes into shadow—but we will walk with you every paw step of the way, I promise."

Leafpool let herself be comforted by Bluestar's words. If StarClan walked alongside her, nothing terrible could happen. When she had left her Clan to be with Crowfeather, she had felt as if her ancestors had abandoned her forever. But she had followed her heart back to ThunderClan, and now they were beside her again, protecting her, guiding her, keeping her safe.

I made the right decision—no, the only *decision—when I came back to the hollow. Nothing will threaten my place in ThunderClan again.*

CHAPTER 2

❧

The moss beneath Leafpool's paws crunched with frost as she slipped into Firestar's den. One moon had passed since her dream of the three little stars, and leaf-fall was giving way to the coldest season. Leafpool fluffed up her fur and reminded herself to tell Whitepaw to bring fresh moss up to the Highledge. Firestar had to be kept warm and dry while he recovered from losing a life.

Leafpool shuddered as she recalled the blood-drenched events of the previous day, when she had found her father with a Twoleg trap around his neck, and Brambleclaw standing over the body of Hawkfrost, dead in the lake. It had been many moons since StarClan had sent her the strange, unknowable warning: *Before there is peace, blood will spill blood and the lake will run red.* That day had come when Hawkfrost tried to kill the leader of ThunderClan by luring him into a trap set for foxes. Brambleclaw had saved Firestar's life by digging up the wooden stake that held the trap, and then fighting Hawkfrost to the death—his own half brother, another son of Tigerstar. Brambleclaw was the blood that spilled blood. Leafpool's vision of a circle of thorns protecting ThunderClan, and Firestar's decision to make Brambleclaw deputy in place of Graystripe, seemed to carry the weight of StarClan now.

"Is that you, Leafpool?" Firestar croaked from the shadows.

"Hush, don't talk," Leafpool ordered. She bent over her father's nest and sniffed. There was no sign of infection, thank StarClan, and the wound left by the trap around Firestar's neck was shallow and would quickly heal. His throat would be sore for some time, but Leafpool had brought her last stock of honey to soothe it, along with a poppy seed to help him rest.

"Eat this," she meowed, unfolding the leaf wrap she had brought to reveal the sticky pool of honey topped with a tiny black seed.

"I'm fine," Firestar protested. He propped himself up, his ginger pelt gray in the half-light. "Don't fuss."

"I'll fuss as much as I have to," Leafpool retorted. "You lost a life yesterday, don't forget."

Her father's green eyes gleamed. "I won't forget, don't worry. But I have a Clan to lead. Our Clanmates need to see that I am okay, and there are patrols to organize."

"Brambleclaw has already sent out the hunting patrols," Leafpool told him. "I have told everyone that you're fine, just resting. Now, lie down, or I'll send Mousefur to tell you stories until you fall asleep."

Firestar gave a faint purr as he curled up among the feathers that lined his nest. "The poppy seed can do that for me, thanks. All right, Leafpool, I'll do what you say." He blinked fondly at her. "I need to remember that you're not just my daughter, you're my medicine cat, too."

Yes, thought Leafpool as she picked her way down the rocky slope after watching Firestar lap up the honey and poppy seed. *I am ThunderClan's medicine cat. Nothing else matters but my duty to my Clanmates.* She started running through a list of late-season herbs she wanted to find before the frost nipped the delicate leaves, and wondered if there was any honey left in the old bees' nest near the top of the ridge. A flash of white fur coming out of the apprentices' den caught her eye.

"Whitepaw!" Leafpool called, stepping down to the solid earthen floor of the clearing. "Please could you fetch some more moss for Firestar's nest? Make sure it's completely dry."

"Sure!" The apprentice nodded. "I can do that before training." She whisked around and pushed her way through the thorns that protected the entrance to the hollow.

"Are you stealing my apprentice?" came a warm voice behind Leafpool.

She turned to see Brackenfur watching her. "Only for a moment," she promised. "Firestar's bedding is a little frosty this morning."

The golden tabby narrowed his eyes. "How is he?"

"Fine," mewed Leafpool. "But losing a life is a bigger deal than Firestar makes out, so I've told him to stay in his nest today."

Brackenfur nodded. "Quite right. Brambleclaw can manage the patrols."

Leafpool studied the warrior. "Do you think Firestar made the right decision to declare Graystripe dead and appoint Brambleclaw in his place?"

The warrior flicked his tail. "A Clan without a deputy is . . . an odd thing. I always felt that it made us vulnerable." He bent down and touched his muzzle to the top of Leafpool's head. "But there are some absences that leave us even more unprotected. I'm glad you came back, Leafpool. Without a medicine cat, I don't think ThunderClan would survive."

Leafpool was saved from having to reply by a flurry of paw steps from the nursery.

"Brackenfur!" squeaked Berrykit. "Watch this fighting move that Thornclaw taught me!" He skidded to halt in front of the warrior. "I don't need to wait another moon before I become an apprentice," he chirped. "I can defend my Clan *now*!" He squatted on his haunches and glared at an ant scuttling across the ground, then sprang into the air with his front legs outstretched. He landed in a heap of creamy fur while the ant darted unscathed beneath a stone.

"You're almost ready, little one," Brackenfur meowed, picking up Berrykit by the scruff of his neck and setting him on his paws again. "Keep practicing!"

Daisy appeared at the entrance to the nursery, her cream fur ruffled. "Berrykit! Stop bothering Brackenfur! Come here so I can finish washing you!"

Berrykit's littermates Hazelkit and Mousekit popped their heads out beside their mother. "Yes, Berrykit," mewed Hazelkit. "You're so naughty, Firestar is going to feed you to the badgers!"

Daisy looked horrified. "Firestar would never do such a thing! Go back inside, you two, it's far too cold out here." She ushered her kits back into the nursery.

"Daisy seems a bit overwhelmed," Leafpool commented with an amused purr.

Brackenfur sent Berrykit on his way with a gentle nudge. "The nursery's pretty crowded with Sorreltail's kits as well. I don't remember having this many kits at the start of leaf-bare before."

Leafpool nodded. "At least Daisy's kits will be able to help with hunting soon."

Brackenfur tipped his head on one side. "Help—or hinder," he purred. Then he straightened up. "But if StarClan has given us the gift of so many kits, our ancestors must know that we are able to take care of them. That is our duty, after all." He strode away, calling to Ashfur that they would take their apprentices out as soon as Whitepaw returned.

There was a rustle of branches at the entrance to the nursery and four tiny bundles hopped out. "Can't catch me!" squealed Molekit, charging across the clearing on his stumpy legs.

"Bet I can!" puffed his sister Honeykit as she raced after him.

Poppykit and Cinderkit followed more slowly, placing each paw delicately on the frosty grass. "Ooh, it's cold!" mewed Poppykit, fluffing up her tortoiseshell fur.

Cinderkit looked around, and Leafpool felt the little cat's pale blue gaze rest on her. "Look, it's Leafpool!" Cinderkit chirped. She trotted over to the medicine cat, her short gray tail straight up in the air. "How's Firestar?" she mewed. "We heard there was a terrible accident."

"Yes, an accident," Leafpool echoed. Wise Sorreltail was keeping the true horror of the events from her babies. "He's doing well," she purred. "He'll stay in his nest for one day, then he'll be up and about again."

"Good," mewed Cinderkit. "A Clan needs its leader."

Leafpool stared at the tiny cat. What was it about her that seemed so different from other kits? Sometimes she sounded so much older than a moon, and Leafpool had watched her gaze at her Clanmates as if she was looking from far, far away, with the knowledge of a cat in StarClan. Also, there was something familiar about her scent, more than the milky comfort of the nursery and Sorreltail's warm smell. Leafpool was about to bend down and sniff Cinderkit's pelt again when Sorreltail squeezed out of the nursery, her belly still loose and swollen from the birth.

"Kits!" she called. "Don't bother the warriors!"

"We're not!" squeaked Honeykit. "Me and Molekit are practicing our running."

"Yeah, and I'm still faster than you," her brother insisted. He stretched out one front paw. "Look, my legs are longer!"

"But mine are quicker!" yowled Honeykit, hurtling away in a blur of light brown fur.

Sorreltail winced as her daughter almost knocked White-paw off her feet. The apprentice was half hidden behind a bundle of moss that she had dragged through the entrance.

"Oh Honeykit, watch where you're going!" Sorreltail chided. She turned to Leafpool and rolled her eyes. "I don't know how StarClan thought I could cope with four of them!"

But her voice was warm and full of love.

Leafpool caught her breath as her belly tightened around a powerful squirming sensation. It was not the first time she had felt it, but it still made her flinch. She had figured out what the vision of three tiny stars meant half a moon ago. Bluestar, Yellowfang, Lionheart: They had all known the shadowed path that Leafpool was about to tread. And now it was as if the kits inside Leafpool were challenging her to stop lying to herself, to admit their existence and start preparing for the future.

My kits!

Not just Leafpool's kits—Crowfeather's too. And they would arrive within the next moon. *Oh, what am I going to do?*

"Are you all right?" Sorreltail was peering at her. "Do you feel ill?"

Leafpool turned away. She didn't want Sorreltail to look at her too closely; if any cat knew what an expecting she-cat looked like, it was this experienced queen. "I'm fine," she panted. "Just a little bellyache. Must have been that tough old shrew I ate yesterday." She glanced around and saw Brambleclaw's tail whisking into the warriors' den. His hunting patrol had returned. "I must go check Brambleclaw's wounds," Leafpool meowed, hurrying away. She felt Sorreltail's gaze boring into her but she didn't turn around.

Brambleclaw was lying in his nest, licking his pads. His claws were battered from digging up the fox trap and he was covered in scratches dealt by Hawkfrost, but he had insisted on going out on patrol as usual. He looked tired, though, and

Leafpool could tell by the way he held himself that he was in pain.

He brought this upon himself! I saw him in the Dark Forest with Tigerstar and Hawkfrost! They must have plotted together to catch Firestar in the trap. Leafpool couldn't explain why Brambleclaw had decided to free Firestar and kill Hawkfrost; she assumed something had gone wrong with the plan. *But I saw the circle of thorns surrounding the hollow, keeping us safe! Why can't I trust Brambleclaw now?*

"Let me see your paws," she mewed, bending over him.

With a grunt, Brambleclaw shifted and raised each foot in turn. Some of his claws were dangerously loose, and Leafpool suspected one would fall out next time he pounced on something, but there was no smell of infection. "They'd heal more quickly if you rested," she commented. Brambleclaw shrugged. "I'll send Whitepaw over with some marigold juice," Leafpool went on. "Rub it into each pad, and also the wounds in your pelt. If you have trouble sleeping, I can give you a poppy seed."

"I don't need that," Brambleclaw meowed. Leafpool turned away, eager to leave the cramped, musty space and her troubled feelings about the injured warrior.

She felt Brambleclaw's amber gaze burning into her pelt. "You can trust me now, Leafpool," he mewed.

Leafpool looked back at him. "It's not my role to judge you."

"I know you saw me in the Dark Forest with Tigerstar and Hawkfrost."

Leafpool flinched. "I can't pretend it didn't happen," she whispered.

Brambleclaw shook his head. "No, and I'm not going to

deny it. But I promise that it won't happen again. Yesterday changed everything. Hawkfrost is dead—dead because of *me*! And I know where my loyalty lies now. I am the deputy of ThunderClan, and my Clan is the only thing that matters."

Suddenly the kits writhed, pushing against Leafpool's flanks so hard that she staggered.

Brambleclaw sat up. "Leafpool, what's wrong?"

"Nothing," Leafpool hissed through gritted teeth. "I . . . I swallowed some mouse bile by mistake when I was treating Mousefur's ticks, that's all."

"You look like you need some fresh air," Brambleclaw meowed. "Go on, I'm fine here. Send Whitepaw with the marigold juice when you're feeling better. And get the apprentices to deal with ticks!"

Leafpool stumbled out of the den, gulping the cold, clean air as if it were water. Berrykit, Hazelkit, and Mousekit were lined up in the center of the clearing, taking turns pouncing on a stick.

"Got you, ShadowClan warrior!" Mousekit spat, baring his tiny white teeth.

Berrykit braced his front paws in the middle of the twig and pushed down until it snapped. "Death to the enemy!" he squealed.

Hazelkit was distracted by their father, Spiderleg, walking past. "This is the real enemy!" she chirped, making a grab for the black warrior's tail.

Spiderleg dropped the piece of fresh-kill he was carrying and spun around. "What are you doing?" he snapped, flicking his tail out of the way.

Hazelkit's shoulders drooped. "Only playing," she mewed.

Daisy looked out of the nursery. "Don't disturb your father!" she called. Spiderleg grunted and picked up his prey again. Leafpool saw Daisy narrow her eyes as the long-limbed black tom walked away.

Crowfeather would always be willing to play with our kits. The thought flew into Leafpool's mind before she could stop it. She pictured the dark gray warrior surrounded by three tiny shapes, letting them pounce on his tail and nibble his whiskers. In her mind, the background was blurry, and she couldn't tell whether he was framed by cliffs or the open moor where WindClan made their home. But what did it matter where they lived, as long as their kits were happy?

CHAPTER 3

♣

Leafpool flattened her ears, feeling fury and shame battle inside her. Stop! Why are you thinking like this? You cannot have these kits!

She had already betrayed ThunderClan once by leaving them when the badgers attacked. When Cinderpelt died because Leafpool had chosen to go away with Crowfeather, Leafpool had made a vow to StarClan that she would never abandon her duties. *Wherever you are, Cinderpelt, if you can hear me, I promise that I will never leave our Clan again.*

In her belly, her kits thrashed in protest. *What about us?* they seemed to be saying. Leafpool was about to twist around and press her muzzle against her side when she realized that Daisy was watching her. She forced herself to stand up straight and trotted over to the Highledge. There was only one place she could go to think clearly.

"Firestar, I need to visit the Moonpool."

The ThunderClan leader looked surprised. "Really? Can't it wait until the half-moon? Or is there something you're not telling me?"

"Of course there isn't," Leafpool lied. "But it is important."

"Then you must go," mewed Firestar. He stretched his

forepaws over the side of his nest. "Brightheart can take care of Brambleclaw's wounds while you're gone." Leafpool opened her mouth to speak but he continued, with a glint in his eye, "And I promise to stay in my den for the rest of today. Although I presume I'm allowed to poke my head out for some fresh air?"

Leafpool purred. "Only your head, nothing more!" The thought of being able to go to the Moonpool made her dizzy with relief. The StarClan warriors would show her the way forward, remind her that she was not alone and that everything would be all right.

Firestar flicked his ears. "You must leave now if you want to reach the Moonpool before darkness. Go well, and be safe."

Leafpool blinked gratefully at him. "Thank you, Firestar. I will return as soon as I can."

She ran down the tumble of rocks to the clearing, careful not to let the weight of the kits unbalance her. She found Brightheart stocking the fresh-kill pile and told her she would be away for a day, no more. Brightheart agreed to check Brambleclaw's injuries, though there was a flash of alarm in her single blue eye.

"Is everything all right, Leafpool? Has there been an omen?"

"Everything's going to be fine," Leafpool told her.

Squirrelflight dragged a blackbird up to the pile. "Are you going somewhere?"

"To the Moonpool. I need to speak with StarClan."

Squirrelflight looked up at the dark gray sky. "There's a

storm on the way. Are you sure you should go alone?"

"Of course," Leafpool meowed. "StarClan will light my path."

Her sister nodded to the blackbird. "Do you want something to eat before you go?"

"No, I want to be there by nightfall." Leafpool touched her muzzle to Squirrelflight's and turned away before the she-cats could ask any more questions. In spite of the heaviness inside her belly, her steps felt light and quick. StarClan would show her what she must do!

The storm hit just as Leafpool started the rocky climb up to the hollow where the Moonpool lay. Freezing wind buffeted her fur and flung sharp pellets of hail at her until her skin was soaked and sore. Leafpool lowered her head and plodded on, sinking her claws into the mud between the rocks so the wind wouldn't blow her off the path. Inside her, the kits seemed to curl up in fear.

Don't be scared, little ones. I will keep you safe.

Leafpool was trembling so much from cold and exhaustion when she reached the top of the hollow that her paws could hardly carry her down the print-marked spiral path. She stumbled to the edge of the Moonpool, ruffled and black in the half-light, and let her body fold onto the hard stone. Waves splashed against her muzzle. Too tired to utter a prayer to StarClan, Leafpool plunged into sleep.

She opened her eyes in a warm green forest, with sunlight slicing between the branches. There was the scent of prey on the air, and the rustle of a small furry animal in a nearby patch of ferns. Leafpool looked around for the StarClan warriors she hoped to see—and saw a slender dark gray cat watching her with his head on one side.

"Your turn, Leafpool," he prompted. He nudged a ball of moss with his forepaw. "Remember what I showed you about pouncing."

Crowfeather! Then she was not in StarClan, but back in a memory of the time she had spent with the WindClan warrior, in the woods beyond the ThunderClan border.

Crowfeather flicked his tail. "Don't be afraid of some moss!" he teased. "Rabbits have teeth and claws to fight back with, but this won't hurt you."

Leafpool crouched down and crept toward the moss. She flattened her ears, shifted her weight onto her haunches, and sprang forward with her legs outstretched. At the very last moment, Crowfeather rolled the ball of moss away with his paw and Leafpool's claws grasped at thin air.

"Oh no!" Crowfeather purred. "It escaped!"

Leafpool whirled around and jumped onto the moss, ripping it to shreds. "Take that!" she hissed. "You won't get away from me!" She looked up at the dark gray tom, laughter bubbling inside her. "I haven't played this game since I was a kit!" she mewed.

Crowfeather narrowed his eyes. "I can tell!"

Leafpool launched herself at him, knocking him onto the fallen leaves. "Think I can't hunt, hmmm? I can catch you anytime I want!" She found herself standing over him, gazing down into his blue eyes.

"I'd never run away from you," Crowfeather whispered. "Ow!"

Leafpool jumped backward. "Did I hurt you?"

Crowfeather was sitting up and licking at the base of his spine. "No, I think I lay on a thistle."

"Let me look." Leafpool pushed his muzzle away and parted the hair on his back. "There's a tiny prickle stuck in you. Hold still . . ." She bent closer and gripped the end of the thorn in her teeth. It slid free easily, and Leafpool rubbed the spot with her paw. "There, you'll live!"

Crowfeather nuzzled her cheek. "Thank StarClan I had a medicine cat to save me!"

"Let's climb a tree!" Leafpool suggested. She walked over to a moss-covered oak and stared up at the branches.

Crowfeather padded over to join her. "I don't see why we can't stay on the ground," he muttered. "We're cats, not squirrels!"

"Come on," Leafpool urged. "You know it's not as hard as it looks, and the view from the top is worth it!" She jumped up to the lowest branch and used her front paws to haul herself onto the next one. Crowfeather followed, moving more carefully than Leafpool, but light-footed and nimble thanks to his slender frame. The branches were strong and dry, with deeply-ridged bark that made it easy to grip with their claws. Leafpool was hardly out of breath when she reached the top of the oak and broke through the leaves. Crowfeather popped out beside her, clinging so hard to the slender branch that

Leafpool felt it sway beneath them.

"It's okay," she mewed. "I won't let you fall."

Crowfeather blinked. "Neither of us has wings, Leafpool, so you'll have to forgive me if I don't like how high up we are."

"But look how far we can see!"

They were on the other side of the ridge from the lake, out of sight of any of the Clan territories. In front of them, the land unrolled in dips and curves all the way to the dark line of mountains on the horizon. Here and there, Twoleg dens clustered in small reddish groups, but mostly the view was empty.

Leafpool shuffled closer to Crowfeather and leaned her head against his shoulder. His pelt smelled of grass and the breeze, with a faint hint of rabbit underneath. "There is so much land beyond our homes," she whispered.

Crowfeather rubbed his chin on the top of her head. "Somewhere out there is a place we can be together all the time. You know that, don't you, Leafpool?"

Still tucked against him, she nodded. "I wonder if we'll ever find it," she murmured.

She felt the dark gray cat tense beside her. "I would give my last breath trying," he vowed.

Suddenly a gust of wind rocked the top of the tree. In a heartbeat, Crowfeather was flung off the branch. Leafpool shrieked in horror as his body plunged downward. She tried to jump down after him, but the wind was so fierce that the branch leaped and bucked beneath her. She clung on, flattening her ears, as rain pelted against her and the forest and the view disappeared in swirling darkness.

"Help!" she wailed. "Crowfeather!"

The branch under her paws vanished and her claws scraped against cold stone. The wind faded and Leafpool realized she was standing beside the Moonpool. A pair of eyes gleamed in the shadows and a familiar scent wreathed around her.

"Spottedleaf!" she mewed in relief.

The tortoiseshell she-cat walked forward. Her pelt glowed with starlight and her eyes were like tiny yellow moons.

Leafpool felt her kits cold and unmoving in her belly. Had the journey through the storm harmed them? "Are my kits all right?" she begged.

"Yes, they are well," Spottedleaf meowed. Her voice cracked with sorrow. "Oh, Leafpool, what you have done? You foolish cat!"

Leafpool flinched, feeling the lash of Spottedleaf's tongue like a blow. "But I . . ."

"You can't make excuses," Spottedleaf warned. "It's too late for that, don't you think?"

"Spottedleaf, hush!" A thick-furred gray cat lumbered across the stone. Her flattened muzzle and stained teeth shone with the same light as her Clanmate. "Leafpool knows what she has done."

Spottedleaf narrowed her eyes. "If you can see a way out of this, you're a wiser cat than I am, Yellowfang."

The old medicine cat twitched one matted ear. "Wisdom comes in many shapes. Now, leave us alone." She pointed into the shadows with her nose. Spottedleaf glanced once more at Leafpool, then padded away.

Leafpool crouched on the ground, not daring to move. She waited for Yellowfang to tell her how reckless she had been, how she had dishonored medicine cats everywhere. But to her surprise, she felt a rough tongue licking her head. Shaking, Leafpool let herself relax against the old she-cat.

"Oh little one," Yellowfang rasped, "I'm so sorry."

"It's hardly your fault," Leafpool pointed out, her voice muffled by Yellowfang's fur.

"You know, you're not the first medicine cat to have this happen," the old cat mewed.

"Really?" Leafpool was disbelieving.

Yellowfang nodded, her chin brushing Leafpool's ears. "It happened to me, a long time ago."

Leafpool sat up so quickly that her head banged against Yellowfang's muzzle. "What?"

The gray-furred she-cat sighed and turned away to sit at the edge of the Moonpool. The water was still now, black and starlit like the sky. "Have you heard of Brokenstar?" she asked.

"Of course," mewed Leafpool. "Leader of ShadowClan before Nightstar and Blackstar. He tried to destroy Thunder-Clan with the help of rogues."

Yellowfang nodded. "He was my son."

Leafpool nearly fell over. "Did any cat know?"

"Never. It was a terrible mistake, and I was punished by my secret every day of my life."

"Is . . . is that what's going to happen with my kits?" Leaf-pool whispered. "Are they a terrible mistake, too?"

Yellowfang closed her rheumy eyes. "Never say that. Life

is always precious. It is what we fight for so hard, with every breath we take."

"But medicine cats are forbidden to have kits. What I have done is wrong." Leafpool crouched on the stone, feeling the chill seep into her paws.

"Wrong according to one code, but there are other ways to judge what we do," Yellowfang rasped. "We are not allowed to have kits because we are supposed to love all our Clanmates equally, and the first Clan cats were afraid that we could treat our own kin ahead of any others. But when your kits are born, Leafpool, you will learn that your heart has space in it to love more than you could possibly imagine. Loving your kits does not mean you have less love for your Clan."

"Then the code should be different?" Leafpool mewed hopefully.

Yellowfang lashed her tail. "I did not say that. The code of the medicine cats is there to remind us of our duties. We cannot change it, any more than we can change the seasons."

Leafpool felt a faint stirring in her belly, and she curled her tail protectively around her flank. "Is there any chance my Clanmates will accept these kits?"

"ThunderClan lives and breathes the warrior code. I cannot promise they will forgive you. But your Clanmates have suffered so much these past few moons, nothing should matter more to you than staying with them." The old cat's gaze softened. "Your kits need not follow the same path as mine. If they believe that they are wanted and loved from the moment they take their first breath, they will have a chance to grow into strong, loyal, kind warriors." She looked down at her paws. "My mistake was to give Brokenstar to a cat who did not love him, who resented every mouthful of milk he took from her."

"Please help me!" Leafpool begged. "I want to serve my Clan, but I cannot make these kits disappear!"

Yellowfang stood up and started to walk back to the shadows. "You'll have to be smarter than I was, that's all."

Leafpool opened her mouth to protest. But there was a rush of wind and darkness, and when she opened her eyes she was lying beside the Moonpool with her babies wriggling inside her as if they were tired of lying on the cold ground. Leafpool heaved herself to her paws. StarClan had spoken clearly: Her duty was to remain as ThunderClan's medicine cat. But how, when there was no way to keep these kits secret?

Leafpool knew she had to confide in a living cat. And there was only one she could think of: a cat from whom love and happiness spilled out. Surely there would be enough to spare for some helpless kits? And this was the cat Leafpool had been closest to all her life, even when they were far apart. . . .

CHAPTER 4

"Squirrelflight, do you have a moment? I need to speak with you."

The dark ginger she-cat turned and looked at Leafpool. "Can't it wait?" Her pelt was ruffled and her green eyes shone with temper. "Brambleclaw wants me to fetch soaked moss for the nursery, even though it's an apprentice task. He hasn't stopped giving out orders since Firestar made him deputy!"

"I could come with you," Leafpool offered.

Squirrelflight twitched her ears. "Okay, if there's really nothing more important you need to do."

They passed Mousefur on the way to the entrance. The elderly she-cat eyed Leafpool's belly. "Plenty of mice at the Moonpool, was there? You're looking plump, Leafpool!"

Leafpool flinched and tried to tuck in her flanks. "StarClan has been generous with prey this leaf-bare," she mewed, speeding up.

Once they had pushed their way through the thorns, Squirrelflight looked at Leafpool. "Wow, that was rude of Mousefur! She's right, though. Have you been taking more than your fair share?" Her tone was gentle and amused, but Leafpool felt hot beneath her pelt.

"I'd never do that," she meowed. She plunged into the ferns and headed down the slope toward the lake. The cool fronds brushed against her sides and made her feel calm again. Behind her, Squirrelflight was muttering.

"Who does Brambleclaw think he is, treating me like I'm still wet behind my ears? Toms are so much trouble! You don't know how lucky you are, Leafpool, not having to worry about things like that." She broke off as she drew alongside her sister. "Well, I know there was Crowfeather . . ."

Leafpool didn't say anything. They emerged from the trees onto the edge of the lakeshore. Pebbles crunched under their paws, and in front of them stretched the lake, flat and silver.

Squirrelflight trotted ahead. "There's a good clump of moss up here," she called. "It won't take long to soak some and take it back to the camp. I'm tempted to put it in Brambleclaw's nest," she added under her breath.

Leafpool waited until her sister had stopped by a fallen tree and was prodding at the thick growth of moss. Her heart was pounding and her pelt felt strange and prickly. Inside her, the kits were still, as if they were waiting. *I have no choice,* Leafpool reminded herself.

"I need your help, Squirrelflight," she began.

The ginger she-cat paused and looked up. "Sure. Do you want me to fetch some herbs for you?" She pulled a face. "You don't need me to collect mouse bile, do you?"

"No, nothing like that."

Squirrelflight's eyes widened. "Do you want me to take a message to Crowfeather? Leafpool, you know I can't do that!"

Leafpool winced and closed her eyes for a moment. *This is something Crowfeather must never find out!*

Stones rolled beneath Squirrelflight's paws as she shifted her weight. "What is it, Leafpool? It's obviously important." She let out a sigh. "I always used to know what you were thinking, but recently—since . . . since the Crowfeather thing—it's as if you're hiding from me. Is something wrong? What is so terrible that you can't tell me? I'm your sister!"

Leafpool gazed out across the lake. Three tiny dots of light were dancing on the water, even though the sky above was gray with clouds.

"I'm expecting kits."

"You're *what*?" Squirrelflight jumped down from the fallen tree and faced her sister. "Are they Crowfeather's?"

"Of course they are," Leafpool snapped.

"Yes, of course." Squirrelflight stared at her in dismay. "Are you going to leave again? I'll miss you so much! Who'll be our medicine cat instead?"

Leafpool lifted her head. "I am ThunderClan's medicine cat," she meowed. "Nothing is more important than that. Squirrelflight, you have to help me find a way to raise these kits and still serve my Clan!"

Squirrelflight took a step back. "That's impossible!"

"Without me, ThunderClan won't have a medicine cat," Leafpool insisted. "There's not enough time to train an apprentice, and there are still wounds to be treated from the badger fight!"

Squirrelflight's eyes were troubled. "Other cats can take

over your duties. Brightheart knows about herbs, doesn't she? You don't have to be a medicine cat, Leafpool. Everyone will get used to the idea eventually. It's not like our Clanmates don't know about you and Crowfeather."

"ThunderClan needs *me* to be their medicine cat. I cannot have these kits!"

Squirrelflight looked at Leafpool's swollen belly. "I don't think you have a choice right now." She moved closer and Leafpool felt the warmth of her sister's breath against her cheek. "I'll help you as much as I can, I promise," Squirrelflight murmured. "Everything will be okay."

Leafpool looked at the tiny points of light being tossed on the lake, fragile and churned by the waves. *Oh, Squirrelflight, you don't understand. Nothing will ever be okay again.*

CHAPTER 5

Leafpool looked up as Berrykit limped into the nursery. "What is it this time?" she mewed.

Hazelkit's head popped up behind her brother. "He stood on a giant thistle!" she squeaked. "His paw is full of prickles!"

Berrykit miserably held up his forepaw. He screwed up his eyes and twisted his head away. "Will I ever be able to hunt?" he whimpered.

Leafpool studied the tiny pink foot. She could just see the tip of a thorn, no bigger than a mouse's whisker, in one of the pads. "I think you'll be okay," she meowed.

"Can I come in?" called a voice from the entrance. It was Brightheart, rolling a bundle of cobwebs in front of her. "Here you are," she puffed, tucking them into a little cleft in the stone wall. "I found loads under a piece of old bark by the shore."

"Thanks," mewed Leafpool. "While you're here, would you like to extract a gigantic thorn from this brave little warrior?"

Brightheart blinked. "Sure, if you want me to." She squinted down at Berrykit's paw. "Wow, that's huge! Okay, hold still."

Berrykit leaned against Hazelkit as Brightheart bent over his foot and nipped out the prickle. She spat it onto a leaf and straightened up. "All done," she declared.

"Did it hurt?" Hazelkit asked.

Berrykit nodded. "A bit. But I'm nearly a warrior, so I don't mind. Thanks, Brightheart!" With a flick of his stumpy tail, he trotted out of the den with his sister.

Brightheart watched them leave, then turned to Leafpool. "Is there something you want to tell me?" she meowed, her single eye wide with concern. In the half-light of the den, the ginger patches of fur glowed against her white pelt.

Leafpool flinched. "What do you mean?"

"So far today I've treated an infected tick wound on Mousefur, sorted out the last of our yarrow stocks, collected cobwebs, and now dealt with the smallest thorn I've ever seen. You know I never mind helping you, Leafpool, but any cat would think you wanted me to be your apprentice!"

"How would you feel about that?" Leafpool mewed quietly.

Brightheart purred. "I'm flattered to be asked, but what about Cloudtail and Whitepaw? I am a mother and a mate, and I don't want to give that up. No, Leafpool, you made a brave decision to follow your destiny, especially after the . . . the Crowfeather incident. But I am very happy as I am. I love helping you and I hope that never changes, but you'll have to look to these new litters of kits for an apprentice. With so many of them, it won't be hard!"

She ducked under the brambles at the entrance and vanished into the cold sunshine. Leafpool stood in the middle of her den. She had never felt more alone in her life. Then her kits stirred inside her, and she reminded herself that the problem was that she *wasn't* alone. She felt a flash of anger toward her unborn kits. *Why did you have to come? Your father doesn't even know you exist. You're going to ruin everything!*

Three sunrises passed. Sleepless and feverish with fear, Leafpool watched each one appear over the tops of the trees. She felt exhausted, weighed down by her belly, and frightened to spend much time out of her den in case her Clanmates realized what was going on. In particular she hid from Mousefur, sending Brightheart to the elders' den to check the old she-cat's infection. They hadn't discussed the issue of a new apprentice again.

Leafpool was counting out her stock of poppy seeds when there was a commotion in the clearing. She stuck her head out and saw Cloudtail carrying Whitepaw's still, pale body on his shoulders. The rest of the dawn patrol clustered around them.

Thornclaw broke away and yowled, "Leafpool, come quick! Whitepaw is hurt!"

Brightheart flew out of the warriors' den. "What's going on?" She helped Cloudtail lower their daughter to the ground. "Whitepaw! Wake up!"

Leafpool ran over. "Stand back, Brightheart," she mewed gently. "Let me see her."

Brightheart stepped away and pressed herself against Cloudtail. "Our baby!" she whimpered.

The little white cat lay very still, her breathing shallow and her heartbeat weak. Leafpool looked up at Brackenfur, who was staring at his apprentice in distress. "Tell me exactly what happened," she ordered.

The golden brown warrior narrowed his eyes. "She was practicing for her final assessment. A hare crossed the Wind-Clan border and Whitepaw went for it. She caught it, but it struggled and got away. By the time I reached her, she was like this." His voice shook.

Sorreltail padded up behind him, having heard the commotion from the nursery, and rested her tail on his shoulder to comfort him. "It wasn't your fault," she murmured.

Leafpool traced the outline of Whitepaw's body with her paws, feeling for broken bones. There was a swelling on Whitepaw's jaw which felt hot to the touch. "Did the hare strike her face?"

Thornclaw nodded. "Yes, I think so."

"That's what has knocked her out," Leafpool mewed. "I'm guessing it was a large animal?"

"Massive," Brackenfur confirmed. "I can't believe Whitepaw thought she could take it."

Brightheart let out a gasp. "My poor brave kit!"

Leafpool continued her examination. She hoped Whitepaw would wake up on her own, but she needed to check if there were any other injuries. Her legs seemed fine but there was something wrong with the angle of her tail. . . .

"I think she's dislocated her tail," Leafpool announced.

Cloudtail blinked. "Is that possible?"

"It's rare, but I've heard of it happening." Leafpool prodded the base of Whitepaw's spine, feeling the joint crunch. Whitepaw stirred.

"She's waking up!" cried Brightheart. "Does that mean she's in pain?"

Leafpool nodded. "Putting her tail back will hurt a lot."

"Then you have to give her something to sleep through it!" Brightheart insisted. "Shall I fetch poppy seeds?"

Leafpool thought for a moment. Poppy seeds would make Whitepaw sleep more deeply, and if she had already been knocked out, would that be dangerous? She wanted the apprentice to wake up as soon as possible and indicate if she was in pain anywhere else. "No," she meowed at last. "The pain won't last long, and if it helps to rouse Whitepaw, that might be a good thing." Brightheart let out a yelp of dismay but Leafpool ignored her. "Thornclaw, fetch a stick and put it between Whitepaw's jaws in case she bites down. Brackenfur, hold her hindquarters steady like this." She demonstrated by placing her paws firmly on Whitepaw's haunches. The little cat let out a murmur.

Brackenfur gritted his teeth and followed Leafpool's directions. "You'll have to be quite strong," Leafpool warned. "Her tail might not go back easily."

She realized her paws were trembling. She tried to picture the skeletons of shrews and rabbits that Cinderpelt had used to demonstrate the way bones fitted together. For a moment she hesitated, terrified that she was going to damage the apprentice even more.

Brackenfur murmured in her ear, "I know you can do this, Leafpool. Go on."

Leafpool took a deep breath and curled one paw over

Whitepaw's tail, close to the tip. She rested her other paw on the base of the little cat's spine. With Brackenfur holding the haunches steady, Leafpool began to twist the tail. Whitepaw's eyes stayed shut but she let out a dreadful screech. Brightheart lurched forward but Cloudtail held her back. Brackenfur grunted with the effort of holding Whitepaw still. Leafpool kept up the pressure until she felt a tiny click underneath Whitepaw's fur. Suddenly the tail relaxed in her paw and Whitepaw gave a small sigh.

"You did it!" breathed Brightheart.

Whitepaw shivered and opened her eyes. "Where am I?" she mewed.

"You're safe," Brightheart told her. She ran her paw over Whitepaw's head. "Leafpool has fixed your tail."

"My mouth hurts," Whitepaw whimpered. The swelling on her jaw was making it difficult for her to speak.

"Perhaps next time you see a hare you'll let it run away," Leafpool mewed. "You'll have a nasty bump there for a little while, but I can give you something to help with the pain. Thornclaw, Brackenfur, carry Whitepaw into my den. I'll send Birchpaw to fetch clean moss and feathers for her nest."

Thornclaw carefully eased Whitepaw onto her mentor's shoulders and with Brightheart holding her steady, they made their way to the cleft in the rock.

"You did very well, my dear," commented a voice behind Leafpool.

"Sandstorm!" she meowed. She hadn't realized her mother had been watching.

"I'm so proud of you," Sandstorm mewed, her green eyes glowing. "You even managed to keep Brightheart calm."

"No queen wants to see her kits in pain," Leafpool meowed.

"Of course not," Sandstorm agreed. She took a step forward and let her tail tip fall against Leafpool's flank. "Even when her kits are grown up, a she-cat is always a mother." Her breath was warm and sweet scented. "Are you all right, Leafpool?" she murmured. "You seem distracted at the moment, as if something is troubling you. You can tell me anything, you know."

No I can't! Leafpool felt a tiny quiver inside her, and suddenly she wanted to get out of the hollow, away from Sandstorm's too-close questions, from her mother's knowledge of what an expecting she-cat looked and smelled like. "I need to fetch fresh stocks of yarrow," she meowed. "Tell Brightheart to stay beside Whitepaw, but she mustn't give her any poppy seeds. I won't be long."

Sandstorm nodded, looking troubled, but she didn't try to stop her. Leafpool turned to push her way out of the barrier of thorns. Without thinking, she headed up the slope toward the ridge. There was yarrow closer to the camp, beside the lake, but her paws carried her to the plants that grew along the edge of the stream on the border with WindClan. She breathed in the scents of moorland and rabbit, and felt the kits shift inside her. *Do they know this is where their father comes from?*

She had just nipped through a fleshy yarrow stalk when she heard the sounds of cats approaching on the other side of the stream. A WindClan patrol! Leafpool poked her head up to see four cats racing over the grass. Crowfeather was leading, his dark gray fur flitting like a shadow across the ground. A black she-cat ran close beside him, matching his stride.

Leafpool bolted out of the stream and ducked under a holly bush. The prickly leaves grazed her fur as she crawled out of sight. She knew she had done nothing wrong, crossed no boundaries, taken nothing that belonged to WindClan, but she wasn't ready to face her neighbors' scrutiny, not so soon. She heard the WindClan cats pause to renew scent marks, then continue on up the hill. Leafpool waited for a few moments, then wriggled out and shook bits of twig from her fur.

She returned to the stream and was dragging the bitten stalk of yarrow up the bank when a voice startled her.

"Did you think I hadn't noticed you? I'd know your scent anywhere!"

Leafpool dropped the stalk, which fell into the stream with a splash. "Crowfeather! What are you doing? Where is your patrol?"

"I sent them on to check the marks beyond the ridge." Crowfeather's blue eyes were huge and searching. "I . . . I wanted to see how you were."

Leafpool took a step back from the bank. "I'm fine. Busy, as you can see."

Suddenly Crowfeather leaped across the stream. His scent wafted over Leafpool and the nearness of him made her want to press against his shoulder and feel the warmth of his pelt. "I have missed you," he whispered, so close she could feel his breath on her muzzle. "I need you with me. I wish things could be different."

"I wish that too," Leafpool mewed. "More than you could possibly know." She pictured Whitepaw's frail body lying in the clearing, Mousefur's seeping tick wound, Berrykit's pricked foot. These were the cats that really needed her. She straightened up. "But we can't change anything, Crowfeather. It's over. I am ThunderClan's medicine cat, until the day I join StarClan."

She felt Crowfeather pull away and stare at her. *Did he think he could go back to the way things were? Whatever happens now is my destiny, and mine alone. He cannot be part of it!* "I think you should leave," she meowed. "Your patrol will come looking for you soon. Do you want them to doubt your loyalty all over again?"

Crowfeather blinked. "I thought we didn't care what our Clanmates believed about us."

"Well, I do," Leafpool meowed. "Go back to your Clan, Crowfeather. I won't let you ruin everything again."

It was as if she had struck the WindClan warrior a physical blow. He flinched away with hurt in his eyes. "If that's what you really want," he murmured.

"It is," Leafpool growled. Inside her, the kits squirmed so fiercely that Leafpool was convinced Crowfeather would see. *Can they hear me sending their father away? Oh, little ones, what choice do I have? If I lose my place in ThunderClan, we will have nothing!*

Crowfeather jumped over the stream. He gazed back at her and opened his mouth to speak but the sound of rapid paw steps made them look up the hill. His patrol was racing toward them. Leafpool whisked around and dived back under the holly bush. She peeped out to see the patrol circling around Crowfeather. The black she-cat pressed close to him, twining her tail with his. When she spoke, Leafpool recognized her as Nightcloud, a WindClan warrior who had never been friendly toward ThunderClan.

"Is everything okay?" Nightcloud was asking. "Who were you talking to?"

"No one important," Crowfeather grunted, and Leafpool felt her heart crack. "Come on, let's finish the patrol."

The WindClan cats bounded away. Leafpool crawled out of her hiding place. *No one important? Well, it looks as if Nightcloud is the important one now.* Had Crowfeather lied about wanting to go back to the way things were? His life seemed to have moved on already, and his Clanmates didn't look like they doubted his loyalty. Leafpool was alone with her kits—by choice or accident.

The StarClan cats said they couldn't tell me what to do, but Yellowfang must know something that might help. I'll go back to her, remind her that she lived through this herself, and beg for advice. I cannot do this on my own!

CHAPTER 6

❧

Brightheart stayed with Whitepaw all night, which made the den a little crowded, but Leafpool was glad of the help when the apprentice kept waking in pain from her jaw and the dull ache in her tail. She still didn't dare give Whitepaw any poppy seeds, so Brightheart curled herself around her daughter and licked the top of her head, urging her back to sleep. By sunrise both cats were dozing, so Leafpool tiptoed out of the den to fetch them something from the fresh-kill pile in case they woke up hungry.

Squirrelflight and Brambleclaw were just returning with the dawn patrol, purring in amusement at something Rainwhisker had said. It looked like their quarrel had been long forgotten. Leafpool joined her sister as Brambleclaw bounded up the Highledge to report to Firestar.

"Will you come to the Moonpool with me?" Leafpool asked. "I need to speak with StarClan and I don't want to go alone." Leafpool risked a glance at her cumbersome belly. "Obviously."

Squirrelflight nodded. "All right, I'll come. Do you want to go now?"

"If we can. Brightheart can take care of Whitepaw for today."

"Let me tell Firestar and Brambleclaw first." Squirrelflight trotted up the rocks and vanished into the leader's den. Leafpool felt the kits sagging inside her and thought with dread of the long trek up to the Moonpool.

Squirrelflight reappeared. "That's all fine. Come on, then." She looked up at the sky. It was cloudy, but as pale as a dove's wing. "At least we shouldn't get wet."

She was right, it didn't rain, but the journey was harder than Leafpool had ever found it before. Every stone seemed to roll away from her paws, every bramble reached out to snag her fur, and the weight of her belly made her gasp for breath. Squirrelflight slowed her pace to walk beside her, boosting her up the rocks and urging her on when all Leafpool wanted to do was lie down and rest.

At last they reached the path that led down to the Moonpool. Squirrelflight stared into the hollow in astonishment. Dusk was falling, and pricks of starlight were starting to appear on the still, silver water. "It's beautiful!" she whispered.

Unlike in the old forest, apprentices no longer visited the medicine cats' special place as part of their training. This was Squirrelflight's first sight of the Moonpool, and Leafpool felt a flush of delight at her sister's reaction. "Isn't it?" she agreed. "Can you feel the marks in the path?"

Squirrelflight rubbed her paws over the dimpled stone and nodded.

"Those are the paw prints of all the cats who have come here before us," Leafpool explained. "We are not the first cats to know of this special place."

"Wow," Squirrelflight breathed. "I feel so honored to be here."

"I know what you mean," meowed Leafpool. "Follow me. I need to lie at the water's edge." She padded down the spiral path with her sister close behind her. The stars sparkled more brightly in the pool as they approached. Leafpool sank with a grunt of relief onto the cold stone.

"What happens now?" Squirrelflight asked, sitting down and looking around.

"I will share tongues with StarClan in my sleep. You should sleep too, if you can. It's a long walk home."

Squirrelflight settled down, grumbling about the hardness of the ground. Gradually her breathing slowed. Leafpool nudged a little closer to soak up the warmth of her sister's fur, then closed her eyes. She opened them to find Yellowfang standing over her. The old cat's gray pelt was as ruffled as ever, and her breath rasped so loudly that it echoed off the walls of the hollow.

"Back again?" Yellowfang grunted.

Leafpool struggled to her paws. "Please help me, Yellowfang. Everything seems so dark. I can't find a way out of this anywhere."

The old cat sat down with a sigh. "I'm sorry you feel that way, Leafpool. If only you had thought about the consequences of what you were doing."

"Well, I didn't!" Leafpool flashed back. "I can say I'm sorry until the lake runs dry, but that won't change a thing. Please help me decide what to do! There's no one else I can ask!"

To her surprise, Yellowfang didn't reply. Instead she leaned over and prodded Squirrelflight with one paw. Squirrelflight lifted her head blearily.

"Is it time to leave? I only just closed my eyes." Her gaze fell on Yellowfang. "Oh! You're from StarClan, aren't you?"

Yellowfang twitched her ears, which glowed with starlight. "It would seem so. Do you know who I am?"

Squirrelflight put her head on one side. "I'd guess you are Yellowfang. I've heard many stories about you." She studied the old cat's matted, dusty pelt and her nose twitched. "I'd know you anywhere."

"I am flattered," Yellowfang commented dryly.

Squirrelflight stood up and looked from Yellowfang to Leafpool and back again. "Why am I here? Is there a way I can help Leafpool raise her kits?"

"Yes," mewed Yellowfang. "You can take them and raise them as your own."

Squirrelflight looked horrified. "What? How could I do that? I would have to lie to Firestar, to all my Clanmates, to *Brambleclaw*!"

The old medicine cat blinked. "If a lie is what it takes to save these kits, so be it."

Squirrelflight paced in a tight circle. "I'm sorry. I just can't see how I could do this. It's too much."

"I can't make you do anything that you don't want to,"

Yellowfang rasped. "I understand why you don't want such a huge responsibility—not that I could appreciate it, of course, being a medicine cat."

Leafpool stiffened. So Yellowfang wasn't going to tell Squirrelflight about her own terrible history?

"But I have watched you, Squirrelflight," Yellowfang continued, her voice barely louder than the wind against the stone. "I know you would make an excellent mother." Her cloudy yellow gaze drifted to the Moonpool, which was being whipped into little waves by the breeze. Her ears pricked, as if she had seen something in the water. She blinked, then turned back to Squirrelflight. "I am so sorry," she whispered.

Squirrelflight stared at her, huge-eyed. "Sorry about what?"

The old she-cat sighed. "I wish that the stars had not sent this message to me to pass on. But it is my duty. Squirrelflight, you will never have kits of your own."

Leafpool gulped. *What?*

Her sister rocked backward on her haunches. "Are you sure? How can you possibly know that?"

"Are you questioning StarClan?" Yellowfang hissed. Then she let her fur lie flat again. "Leafpool is offering you your only chance to be a mother. And Brambleclaw will be a great father. One day he will be the leader of ThunderClan! He needs kits to follow in his paw steps, don't you think?"

Leafpool held her breath. Squirrelflight stood up and walked to the edge of the Moonpool, where she gazed at the starlight rippling on the surface. Yellowfang followed her. "I know how difficult this is to hear. Come and rest. You will see things more clearly when you wake up." She guided Squirrelflight back to the warm patch of stone where she had been lying before. Squirrelflight curled up, as silent and obedient as a kit, and let Yellowfang soothe her to sleep with long, smooth licks across her head.

Leafpool waited until her sister was fast asleep, then stood up. "StarClan has never seen the future in the Moonpool before," she meowed quietly. "Were you telling the truth?"

Yellowfang kept her gaze fixed on Squirrelflight's head. "The truth is that Squirrelflight will make a far better mother for these kits than you will, Leafpool. That is the only thing which matters now."

Leafpool tried to speak but a feather-soft darkness tugged at her, pulling her back into sleep. She lay down and let her eyes close as Yellowfang's glowing shape faded away. When Leafpool woke, Squirrelflight was standing beside the Moonpool. Without looking around, she mewed, "Do you remember our dream?"

"Yes," Leafpool whispered. Her legs were trembling. *Was Squirrelflight really going to take these kits from her?* If it meant they could stay in ThunderClan and she could watch them grow, while still serving as a medicine cat, perhaps it was the only answer.

Squirrelflight turned to face her, and her eyes were soft with sadness. "I love you, Leafpool, and I will keep my promise to help you. But I can't lie to Brambleclaw for the rest of his life, nor to Firestar, Sandstorm and all our Clanmates. I'm so sorry, but I can't do this for you."

CHAPTER 7

The sky had lightened as much as it was going to by the time Leaf-pool and Squirrelflight reached the hollow. Leafpool felt dizzy with fatigue, and had been leaning on her sister's shoulder for most of the journey. She had to walk into the clearing on her own, though. She couldn't risk any of her Clanmates seeing how weak and breathless she was. She headed straight for her den, and was relieved to find Whitepaw sleeping peacefully.

Brightheart was sitting beside her daughter, rolling up the newly dried yarrow leaves. "She's in less pain today," she commented. She peered at Leafpool. "You look worn out! You needn't have traveled back overnight. I could have seen to Whitepaw today."

Leafpool sank down into her nest. "I know, but we didn't want to sleep on the mountain. Why don't you go get something to eat now?"

The she-cat glanced at her once more, then padded out of the den. Leafpool stretched out as flat as she could with her belly propped awkwardly beside her. *No more journeys to the Moonpool, little ones. StarClan has done as much as it can for us. Perhaps Yellowfang was right, and giving you to Squirrelflight was the only way to keep us here. But if Squirrelflight doesn't want to, then we will have to find our own path.*

She smoothed her paw over the uncomfortable swelling. She knew the kits would come in the next quarter-moon. She would have to leave the camp in time to find a safe place to give birth. After that, she had no idea what would happen. If her Clanmates refused to accept her kits, she would have to give up her place in ThunderClan forever. Other cats had left, so Leafpool knew she could survive. It would be hard to hunt for food while the kits were still nursing, but Leafpool could cope with going hungry for a while. She would eat as much as she could from the fresh-kill pile before she left, and hope that none of her Clanmates were watching too closely.

By the following sunrise, Whitepaw was sitting up in her nest and complaining strongly about not being allowed out of the den. It was the best sign so far of her recovery. Brightheart knew better than to fuss over her daughter, and instead surveyed her from a distance, offering food and soaked moss in between the complaints.

Leafpool beckoned Brightheart farther into the cave with a twitch of her tail. "Would you mind if I left the camp for a while?" she asked.

Brightheart's single eye stretched wide. "Is something wrong?"

"I . . . I have to go in search of an herb that doesn't grow in our territory. StarClan told me to go when I visited the Moonpool."

"Are we going to be struck by greencough this leaf-bare?"

Brightheart mewed worriedly.

Leafpool shook her head. "Not that I have heard. Will you take care of my duties while I'm gone?"

"Of course," the she-cat mewed. "But don't stay away too long, Leafpool. We need you here."

Firestar was less easy to convince. "Is StarClan sure that we need this herb?"

"Completely." Leafpool felt her pelt crawl. She hated lying to any of her Clanmates but especially her father, who trusted her to interpret the signs from their ancestors. She wondered if StarClan would forgive her for using them falsely.

"Then you'll have to go, of course," Firestar meowed. "Did StarClan say how long it might take to find this plant?"

Leafpool swallowed. "I might be away for more than a moon."

The ginger tom blinked. "A moon? This herb must be very important."

Sandstorm entered the leader's den in time to overhear. "Do you have to go, Leafpool? Couldn't it wait until after leaf-bare?" Her voice was gentle, but the words burned into Leafpool's fur. *Does she know why I have to leave?*

"No, it can't wait," she insisted. She gazed at her father. "StarClan wouldn't send me away if there was any danger to my Clanmates. I promise I will come back as soon as I can."

Firestar twitched his tail. "And you have to go alone, do you?"

Leafpool nodded, but at that moment Squirrelflight burst

into the den. "No, she doesn't! I'm going with her!"

Leafpool stared at her sister. Squirrelflight continued, "Is it true, what Brightheart said? That you're leaving Thunder-Clan?"

"Only for a while," Leafpool whispered.

"Then I'll come with you," Squirrelflight meowed.

"I'd be happier if you weren't alone," Firestar admitted.

"So would I," Sandstorm murmured.

"You may go if you take Squirrelflight with you," Firestar meowed, as if that was his final decision.

Leafpool glanced at her sister, whose jaw jutted in determination, and nodded. "Very well. Thank you, Firestar."

He rested his muzzle briefly on top of her head, then watched her walk out of the den. At the bottom of the stones, Leafpool turned to Squirrelflight. "You know why I'm going, don't you?"

Squirrelflight nodded. "Yes, and I am keeping my promise to help you however I can."

"Have you told Brambleclaw?"

"That I'm going away with you for a while? Yes." Squirrel-flight curled her lip. "He tried to persuade me to stay here and let Thornclaw or Rainwhisker go instead, but I said that you had asked for me."

Leafpool suddenly felt exhausted by the lies, the half-truths, the weight of the secret that dragged in her belly. "I'm glad you are coming," she murmured.

Squirrelflight touched Leafpool's ear with the tip of her tail. "I could never let you go through this alone."

* * *

They left just before sunhigh, not that the sun was visible through the dense yellow clouds that hung above the tops of the trees. Brambleclaw curled his tail with Squirrelflight's and seemed to be trying to persuade her to change her mind. But Squirrelflight shrugged him off.

"I'm sure you can organize the patrols without me," she teased. But her voice was high-pitched with tension, and Leafpool knew that her sister was frightened of what lay ahead. There was nothing she could say to reassure Squirrelflight. The future yawned before her like a bottomless chasm. The path ahead of her led straight into the dark.

They headed up to the ridge above the hollow and crossed over the ThunderClan border as soon as they could. Now that they were on their way, Leafpool had a strange urge inside her to get as far from her home as she could, as if the whispers of her Clanmates could still be heard all around her. In spite of her swollen belly, she walked quickly, and Squirrelflight sometimes had to trot to keep up.

"What's the hurry?" she panted.

Leafpool just looked at her. Squirrelflight ducked her head with embarrassment. "Okay, let's keep going."

The dense undergrowth and fresh young trees that Leafpool associated with ThunderClan territory gave way to sparser, older trees, their trunks silvery and scaled with lichen. The bracken thinned out and soft grass lay underpaw. They could have moved faster here, but Leafpool's paws were starting to ache and instead she slowed down. Squirrelflight said nothing, just matched her pace and stayed close enough to support Leafpool with her shoulder when the medicine cat stumbled.

Peering through the lake toward the trees, Leafpool figured they were almost level with ShadowClan territory by now. She hoped the breeze wouldn't carry their scent across the border. They were skirting a thicket of elderberry bushes when Squirrelflight let out a soft cry.

"Look! There's an old Twoleg nest!" She ran forward and slipped inside the tumbledown heap of reddish stones. Leafpool studied it. If Twolegs had ever lived here, it had been a long time ago. There were holes in the roof, and ivy sprouted from the stones as if the den were trying to grow itself a pelt.

Squirrelflight reappeared at the entrance. "We could shelter here for the night," she mewed. "It's dry inside, and there's a good smell of mouse."

Leafpool padded over and peered into the den. It was filled with shadows but it felt warm without the constant tug of the wind. Squirrelflight trotted past her and started nosing through a pile of old straw. "You know, this would make a great place to have your kits. It's clean enough and dry, there's plenty of prey, and we're not too far from the Clans if anything goes wrong."

Leafpool cut her off with a hiss. "We cannot ask any Clan cat for help! And this is much too close to the territories; we might be seen or heard. No, we can't stay here."

With a sense of panic swelling inside her, and her kits writhing in distress, she ran away from the abandoned den.

Squirrelflight followed without trying to argue. Leafpool was grateful for her sister's silence. She couldn't explain the strange, fierce feelings that surged inside her the closer it came to her kits arriving. All she knew was that the urge to follow her instincts was too strong to fight.

The trees toward the lake grew thinner and Leafpool glimpsed the stretch of open grass where Twolegs came during greenleaf. The cats reached a narrow, steep-banked stream which bubbled down to the shore. Squirrelflight paused on the bank.

"I guess you don't feel like jumping across?" she mewed.

Leafpool shook her head, too breathless to speak.

Squirrelflight narrowed her eyes. "You can't go much further. Come on, we'll head deeper into the woods and find somewhere to spend the night." She turned and led the way along the stream. As the trees thickened around them, the sounds of birds and rustling prey died away, and Leafpool felt as if they were the only living creatures in the forest. It started to rain, gently at first but then harder, until the cats were drenched to the skin. Leafpool shivered uncontrollably, and the sound of her chattering teeth competed with the raindrops that spattered around them.

Suddenly Squirrelflight halted and scented the air. "I smell rabbit," she announced. She veered away from the edge of the stream and plunged into the dripping ferns. "Follow me, Leafpool," she called over her shoulder. "I'm not leaving you on your own!"

Leafpool was too tired and uncomfortable to argue. She

stumbled behind her sister along the faint trail of scent. They emerged from the ferns in a sandy clearing dotted with holes. Rabbit burrows! Leafpool saw Squirrelflight lick her lips in anticipation of the hunt.

But there was another scent here, stronger than rabbit, only half disguised by the rain. Not rabbit but . . .

"Fox!" gasped Squirrelflight, whirling around. "Quick, let's get out of here!"

It was too late. In front of them the bracken shook violently and tore apart to reveal—not a fox, but the pointed, striped face of a badger, little eyes gleaming and jaws parted to reveal slavering yellow teeth. It growled when it saw the cats.

Squirrelflight jumped in front of Leafpool. "Wait until it attacks me, then run!" she hissed.

Leafpool crouched down, ready to flee. Her kits squirmed in her stomach as if they could feel her terror. Leafpool felt such a surge of love for her babies that she rocked on her paws. She glared at the badger and felt her lip curl in fury. If she couldn't get away, then she would stay and fight. Badgers held no fear for her now.

You will not harm my kits!

CHAPTER 8

♣

The badger took one step forward and lowered its head, ready to charge. Suddenly there was a ferocious roar behind them and Leafpool glanced around to see a big red fox explode from the nearest burrow. For a moment Leafpool waited to be crushed between fox and badger. Then there was a rush of stinking air as the fox leaped over her head and launched itself at the black-and-white intruder. Squirrelflight threw herself against Leafpool and bundled her into the nearest burrow. Around them, the ground shook and sand fell from the walls as the two animals battled outside. The she-cats crawled deeper into the burrow and curled into a corner, huge-eyed with terror, too frightened to speak.

At last they heard the fox bark in triumph, and the sound of the badger lumbering away. Leafpool began to stand up but Squirrelflight stopped her. "Wait," she urged in a whisper. "We won't be able to find shelter in the dark, and it's still raining. It's dry inside, and the tunnel is too small for the fox to follow us down. I think we should stay here for the night."

Leafpool stared at her sister in alarm. Sleep next to a fox hole? Had Squirrelflight lost her mind? But then she saw the exhaustion in her sister's eyes, and knew that Squirrelflight couldn't walk another step. From the scent of blood drifting down the burrow, she guessed that the fox had been badly hurt, hopefully enough to make it lose any interest in hunting a couple of cats. "Okay," she meowed, lying down again. "Let's get some rest."

Squirrelflight fell asleep almost at once and began to snore gently, just audible above the patter of rain overhead. The kits in Leafpool's belly were wide awake, wriggling and wrestling to change position, and sleep seemed a long way off. With a grunt, Leafpool hauled herself to her paws. If she stayed here, tossing and twitching, she would disturb Squirrelflight. A cold breeze whispered down the burrow, making Leafpool reluctant to go outside. Instead she turned deeper into the tunnel, carefully testing with her whiskers to see where the walls were.

A tiny beam of moonlight shone through a hole in the roof ahead of her, casting a silvery gleam onto the sand below. Leafpool padded forward and found herself at the opening to a much larger burrow. The scent of fox almost sent her fleeing back to the open air, but she steadied herself and peered into the half-light. The big fox was here, smelling of blood and anger, but fast asleep now. Her body was curled around three cubs, each not much larger than a kit. In spite of her wounds, the she-fox had tucked them close to her belly, and as one of the cubs stirred, she reached out and nudged it back to the warmth of her fur.

Leafpool felt a strange sensation of joy swell inside her. *I know how this fox feels. Even asleep, she is still their mother. Soon I will have babies of my own to guard with my life, to love with every beat of my heart.* With one more look at the she-fox, this time with a mix of admiration and envy, Leafpool turned and tiptoed back to her sister.

"Leafpool, wake up! It's light outside. We should leave before the fox scents us." Squirrelflight prodded Leafpool with her paw.

Leafpool rolled over and opened her eyes. Her kits had settled at last and she had gone to sleep dreaming of gentle foxes and milk-scented dens. She stood up, and gasped as her belly swung below her.

Squirrelflight jumped to her side. "What's wrong?"

Leafpool found her balance and took a deep breath. "I think the kits will come today," she mewed.

She waited for her sister to panic, but instead Squirrelflight looked calm and determined. "Okay. Well, you can't have them here! We need to get you as far from this fox hole as possible and find some shelter." She helped Leafpool up the sandy tunnel and into the cold, clear air. It had stopped raining, and the forest was quiet save for dripping leaves.

Leafpool could hear Squirrelflight's belly rumbling with hunger but she was relieved when her sister didn't suggest stopping to hunt. Leafpool didn't think she could eat a mouthful. She just wanted to find a safe place to have her babies. Squirrelflight sniffed at a clump of ferns and stuck her head inside.

"It looks dry in here," she called, her voice muffled.

"Not if it rains again," Leafpool replied. She staggered on, almost falling when a bramble snagged her fur.

"What about underneath this thicket?" Squirrelflight suggested as she helped Leafpool free from the prickly tendril.

"Do you want my kits to be full of thorns?" Leafpool meowed.

Squirrelflight said nothing, just walked on. "How about next to that fallen tree?" She pointed with her tail to an oak that lay on its side.

Leafpool wrinkled her nose. "It smells bad." She could tell Squirrelflight was about to explode. Then she stumbled to a halt as a spasm of pain gripped her belly. "Oh! I think they're coming!"

In an instant Squirrelflight was pressed against her. "Not yet, Leafpool! We have to find somewhere safe for them."

Leafpool looked up and saw a gnarled tree in front of them, so old and twisted that she couldn't tell if it had been an oak or an elm to begin with. It was smothered in ivy, and a dark shadow that ran down its length showed that it had been hollowed out by a blast of lightning many moons ago. She felt a pull toward it as if it had reached out and grabbed the scruff of her neck.

"That is the place," she whispered as another wave of agony rippled through her. "That is where my kits will be born."

CHAPTER 9

Leafpool dragged herself into the hollow tree and collapsed onto the leaf mulch with a groan. She was dimly aware of Squirrelflight fluttering around her, shoving more dried leaves beneath her and placing a bundle of dripping moss near her head. Leafpool felt as if the whole world had shrunk to the dimensions of her body, a world that was full of scarlet pain and throbbing fear. There was a pulling sensation underneath her tail and Leafpool cried out in alarm.

"Tell me what I should do!" Squirrelflight hissed in Leafpool's ear. "I can see a kit coming!"

Leafpool gritted her teeth against the next pulse of agony. "Wait until it is free, then nip open the sac around its body. Push it toward me so I can lick it." She yelped at a wave of sharp stabbing pain across her belly. She lifted her head and saw a small, slime-covered black shape slither out onto the leaves. Squirrelflight tugged away the transparent sac that covered its head and Leafpool stiffened as a wail pierced the air.

Squirrelflight nudged the kit closer to Leafpool's belly and Leafpool curled herself around it. Her world expanded just enough to enclose this beautiful, perfect kit. She started to lick its fur clean as she felt its tiny mouth latch onto her. Then she writhed as another spasm racked her body, stronger than any before. She waited for the wave of pain to die away as the kit shifted inside her, but the throbbing continued. In the red mist of agony, Leafpool felt herself begin to panic.

Something's wrong!

"I can see another kit!" Squirrelflight called. "But it's not moving! Push harder!"

Leafpool had no breath to speak. She tried to press her paws against her belly, manipulate the kit the way she would if she were helping a queen in the nursery. But her legs flopped weakly to the ground. She felt Squirrelflight trying to help, prodding and nudging with her own paws, but she hadn't been trained, and Leafpool had no strength to tell her sister what to do. Dark shadows clustered around her and she felt herself ebbing away. She knew that cats could die if a kit got stuck. *Help me, StarClan . . .*

Then the air stirred beside her, and a new, familiar scent filled the hollow tree. Leafpool felt strong paws pressing down on her flanks, and the kit inside her started to turn. She opened her eyes and saw the faint outline of a starlit cat, gray-furred and flat-muzzled. *Yellowfang!*

Squirrelflight was standing beside Leafpool, huge-eyed and gaping.

"Make yourself useful," Yellowfang ordered, and her voice sounded like the wind between the stars. "Give Leafpool some water, and rub some warmth into that black kit."

Squirrelflight rolled the moss closer to Leafpool so she

could drink, then started pummelling the tiny shape beside her belly until the little cat squeaked. Leafpool felt Yellowfang shove a stick between her teeth.

"This is going to hurt," the old cat grunted. She leaned on Leafpool's belly with a force that made her shriek in protest. "Have a little faith," Yellowfang hissed.

With a wrench, the kit was born, a huge golden tabby tom with broad shoulders and a deafening yowl. Squirrelflight dragged him beside the black kit and Leafpool stared down at the tom in disbelief. *My son!* She felt him start to suckle and let her head fall onto the leaves. She had never been so exhausted in her life. She felt as if she had been turned inside out, and wanted nothing more than to sleep for a moon.

But Yellowfang shook her roughly awake. "Stay with us, Leafpool," she rasped. "There's one more kit to be born."

"I can't," Leafpool whimpered without opening her eyes. "I'm not strong enough."

"You have to be," Squirrelflight told her, her amber eyes fierce in the darkness. "Come on!" She propped Leafpool's head against her shoulder and held her close as yet another spasm rolled through Leafpool's body. This time the kit slipped out easily, a pale gray tabby even smaller than its littermates.

"Another tom," Yellowfang announced, efficiently peeling off the sac and delivering the mewling bundle to Leafpool's belly. "Two sons and a daughter. Congratulations, Leafpool." There was warmth in her voice, and Leafpool caught a spark of emotion glistening in the old cat's eyes.

"Thank you," she whispered. She bent over her babies and started licking the stickiness from their fur.

Above her, she heard Yellowfang telling Squirrelflight that they both needed to get some rest, then Squirrelflight could fetch prey and more water. "Wait for the kits' eyes to open before you go back to the hollow," she mewed. There was a pause. "*If* you go back."

As she slipped into the stillness of sleep, Leafpool thought she might stay in this hollow tree forever. *Everything that matters to me in the world is here.*

She woke to a strong, meaty scent under her nose. Blinking open her eyes, she saw Squirrelflight pushing a shrew toward her. "You haven't eaten for two sunrises," her sister meowed. "Come on, share this with me."

Leafpool half sat up, aware of an empty feeling in her belly. She looked down and saw her three kits curled tightly against her, fast asleep. Her heart swelled with love, more fierce than anything she had felt before. *I would die for you,* she thought. The hollow was cold and there was a strange white light filtering through the narrow entrance. Leafpool craned her neck and saw thick flakes drifting down from the sky to settle on the forest floor.

"It's snowing!" Squirrelflight mewed. "It'll make hunting more difficult, but at least it will hide our scent." She watched Leafpool tuck into the shrew. The black she-kit wriggled free from her brothers and wailed when she felt cold air on her pelt. At once Leafpool stopped eating and tucked her daughter gently back into her belly fur.

"See?" Squirrelflight purred. "You know exactly what to do! I knew you'd be a brilliant mother."

There was a ring of sadness in her voice, and Leafpool recalled Yellowfang's prophecy that Squirrelflight would never have kits of her own. She felt a stab of guilt that she had ever doubted these kits should be born. They were a blessing, like Brackenfur had said. *Thank you, StarClan*, she whispered.

Squirrelflight curled her body around Leafpool's, blocking out the draft from the entrance. Leafpool felt her sister's breath warm on the back of her neck as they drifted into sleep. A slight shift in the air made Leafpool open her eyes. Outside the forest was still and silent under its pelt of snow. She could hear the tiny breathing sounds of her kits, muffled against her belly, and steady snores from Squirrelflight. And something else . . .

A glittering outline appeared in a shaft of starlight. Warm eyes glowed from the shadows, and Leafpool detected a faint, half-remembered scent. Not Yellowfang this time. *Feathertail!*

The pale silver she-cat stepped forward and looked down at the kits. Her purrs rumbled against the hollow tree, and Squirrelflight stirred. Leafpool felt her sister stiffen in surprise.

"Feathertail!" she gasped. She scrambled to her paws and tried to press herself against the starlit shape, her tail curled over her back in delight. "I never thought I'd see you here! Have you come to see Leafpool's kits? Aren't they amazing?" Squirrelflight broke away and leaned down over Leafpool.

Very gently, she moved the kits into view one by one. "A black she-cat and two toms, this golden tabby and this gray. I've never seen anything more beautiful in my life." Her voice cracked.

Feathertail's blue eyes brimmed with love. "They are perfect. Crowfeather would be so proud."

With a jolt, Leafpool remembered that Feathertail had been Crowfeather's mate first. Had she come all the way from the Tribe of Endless Hunting to tell Leafpool that Crowfeather deserved to know he had become a father? As if she could tell what Leafpool was thinking, Feathertail shook her head.

"These kits are more precious than you could possibly know," she mewed softly. "Cats will speak of them for many seasons to come. They must stay in ThunderClan, for all the Clans' sakes, with a mother and father who can be proud of them, who can share them with their Clanmates to be raised as strong, loyal warriors."

Leafpool opened her mouth to protest that this was impossible, her Clanmates would never accept Crowfeather as their father, and might reject her too, knowing that their medicine cat had destroyed the code. But Feathertail was looking at Squirrelflight.

"I know how much Leafpool loves these kits," she murmured. "But you must be their mother and raise them in ThunderClan with your head held high."

Squirrelflight stared at the starlit she-cat. "How can you do this?" she whispered. "You are asking me to lie to every cat I love."

Feathertail ran her paw very lightly over the backs of the sleeping kits. "Because I love these kits as much as you do. They are Crowfeather's: How could I not? I want them to have the best life, not one lived outside the Clans, in shame and exile."

"Do you wish they were yours?" Squirrelflight whispered.

The silver cat blinked without looking up. "That was never meant to be. The destiny of these kits begins now, and you have the power to change everything, Squirrelflight. Please believe me when I say that Leafpool's kits *must* stay in ThunderClan."

She began to fade until the bark of the hollow tree could be seen behind her. Squirrelflight gazed at Leafpool, and the medicine cat saw water glistening in her sister's eyes. "Feathertail was right," Squirrelflight whispered. "I do love these kits, and I want them to have the best life they can—whatever lies ahead for them." She took a deep breath. "I will raise them as mine and Brambleclaw's, as true cats of ThunderClan."

Leafpool closed her eyes. *It is the best for my babies,* she told herself. "Thank you," she murmured.

At that moment the golden tabby wriggled and started mewling. Leafpool nudged him toward her belly but he didn't seem interested in feeding; he just wanted to test his voice. His sister burrowed deeper into Leafpool's fur with a squeak, while the pale gray tom raised his head, eyes still tightly shut, as if he was trying to figure out where the noise was coming from.

"I need to give them names," Leafpool purred, marveling

at the way these tiny cats already seemed so different, so strong and full of life. She studied the golden tom. His neck was ringed with thick fluff, and his mouth opened wide to reveal thorn-prick white teeth. "He looks like a lion!" she commented. "I think I'll call him Lionkit."

Squirrelflight nodded. "The she-cat is as dark as holly bark. Maybe Hollykit for her?"

Leafpool hesitated. *My daughter is the image of Crowfeather. Shouldn't she be named after her father, even if he never knows the truth?*

Her sister was watching her closely. "Leafpool," she mewed, as gently as the snow falling outside. "I am going to raise these kits as my own. Surely I should have a say in their names?"

Leafpool felt a pain inside her belly that was sharper than birth pangs. *My precious kits!* A few snowflakes drifted down through the hollow tree and settled on Lionkit's fur. Leafpool battled the urge to cover the kits with her body, protect them from snow, rain, hail, badgers, foxes, anything that might harm one hair on their pelts. Then the scent of Feathertail drifted around her, and she knew their path had already been chosen. Whatever she felt, however many regrets the future held, the only thing that mattered was creating the best life for these three perfect babies.

Squirrelflight pressed her muzzle against Leafpool's shoulder. "ThunderClan needs you to be their medicine cat," she mewed. "I will love these kits as if they were my own. I already do! I will never take them from the Clan, you will see them all the time, and they will know you are my kin so they will always be close to you. Remember what Feathertail said: These kits deserve parents who can be proud of them, who can raise them among their Clanmates as fine warriors. Brambleclaw and I can do that. And the secret of their birth will die with me, I promise."

But I am their mother! Leafpool wailed silently. In her heart, she knew Squirrelflight was right. She could not raise these kits, their mother a medicine cat, their father a WindClan warrior who seemed to have found a new mate already.

"Hollykit is a good name," she mewed numbly.

CHAPTER 10

Sunrises rolled past in a snow-bright haze. The kits grew faster than Leafpool thought possible, and almost overnight the hollow tree seemed too small to contain them. After five days, she and Squirrelflight ushered the little cats outside. They stumbled into the thick snow on tiny legs with their tails stuck straight out behind them. Lionkit and Hollykit had already opened their eyes—amber and green, reminding Leafpool of newleaf and warmth and the certainty that the snow would not stay forever.

The smallest kit was still unnamed and his eyes were tight shut. As Leafpool went to fish him out of a snowdrift, he blinked and Leafpool was dazzled by a flash of brilliant blue. "Like a jay's wing!" she gasped.

Squirrelflight bounded over, snow clinging to her belly fur, and looked down at the tom. "Then we should call him Jaykit, don't you think?"

Leafpool nodded. *And one day you will be Jayfeather, like your father.*

Jaykit ran in a circle and blundered straight back into the snowdrift. Squirrelflight hooked him out with an amused purr. "You can watch where you're going now that your eyes are open!" she teased.

Lionkit squeaked and Jaykit tottered in the direction of the sound. Leafpool looked around for her daughter. She was wrestling with a leaf, biting it with her tiny teeth and clawing at the edges. "Come on, fierce little warrior," Leafpool called. "Back to the nest to warm up!"

The kits only stayed still long enough for Leafpool to lick their fur clean before they tumbled out of the nest and started exploring the inside of the tree. Lionkit found the dry clump of moss that Leafpool had drunk from during the birth, and he started rolling it around with angry little growls in his throat. Hollykit watched for a moment, her head on one side, before running over to join him. Bits of moss flew up as they tussled with their prey.

Leafpool noticed Jaykit marching across the den. Suddenly he slipped on a wet leaf and bumped his nose against the bark wall. Leafpool was ready to comfort him, but the little cat shook his head, then changed direction and headed for the moss game instead. Hollykit stopped playing and sat back to let him have a turn shredding the ball. There wasn't much left but a few scraps once Lionkit had finished shaking it in his teeth. Leafpool felt a rush of love for her brave, strong son and her gentle, thoughtful daughter. But there was a special place in her heart for her smallest kit, who seemed oddly vulnerable compared with his littermates.

Half a moon passed. The snow began to thaw and the

she-cats basked in an unexpected and welcome patch of sunshine outside the hollow tree. In front of them, Lionkit, Hollykit, and Jaykit were pushing fronds of dead bracken into a pile, then leaping off a grassy tussock into the middle.

"I can jump the highest! Watch me!" mewed Lionkit. He sprang into the air with his sturdy forelegs outstretched and plunged into the ferns.

"And me!" squeaked Jaykit. He leaped off the tussock and there was a muffled yelp as he landed squarely on his brother, who was still wriggling free.

"Jaykit, look out!" Hollykit piped. She was purring with amusement. "You're so silly!"

The little toms scrambled out of the bracken with their fur full of spiky brown prickles.

"I think we've just seen some flying hedgehogs," joked Squirrelflight. "Come here, you two. Let's clean you up."

Lionkit ignored her. "That was fun! Let's do it again!" He scampered back to the tussock.

"Wait for me!" Jaykit chirped.

Leafpool shook her head. "They have so much energy!" she exclaimed.

"They're growing fast," Squirrelflight agreed. There was a pause, and it seemed to Leafpool as if the whole forest was waiting. "You know we should take them back," Squirrelflight mewed.

Leafpool closed her eyes. "I wish we didn't have to," she whispered. "They're so happy here."

"I know. But we don't have a choice. If we stay here any

longer, the kits might remember too much . . ."

Leafpool stared at her kits as if she would never see them again. *Will they remember this time?* she wondered. *Will there always be some part of them that knows the truth?* She knew that Squirrelflight would love them, but what about Brambleclaw? And through Brambleclaw, Tigerstar? *Does he know that these kits have been born?* Leafpool stared at Lionkit in alarm. *Will Tigerstar lure him to the Dark Forest as well?*

Suddenly there was a wail, and Leafpool realized Jaykit had vanished. Lionkit and Hollykit were standing on top of the tussock with their backs to the she-cats, looking down.

"Jaykit fell in a hole!" Lionkit called. "I think he's stuck."

"Jaykit's a mouse-brain!" mewed Hollykit.

"Hush," Leafpool chided, bounding over to take a look. The little gray tom had vanished into the gap where a sapling had stood before being wrenched out of the soil by a storm. Only the tips of his ears were visible against the brown earth.

"Help!" he wailed.

Leafpool braced her hindpaws in the loose soil and leaned down into the hole. "Wriggle this way, Jaykit," she panted. She felt his feather-soft fur brush against her muzzle, and reached down to grip his scruff in her teeth. With a heave, she dragged herself backward and hauled him out of the hole.

Jaykit crouched down and shook himself, sending earth flying. He gazed up at Leafpool with eyes as clear as the sky. "Thank you for rescuing me!" he chirped. "That was a really big adventure, wasn't it?"

"Yes it was," purred Leafpool. She looked into her son's

eyes. They were so beautiful, and yet . . .

She looked over her shoulder. "There's a big leaf over there, Jaykit," she mewed. "Please could you fetch it for me so I can wipe the mud off my fur?"

"I'll get it!" Hollykit offered, jumping down from the tussock.

"It's okay, Jaykit can manage," Leafpool meowed. She watched as her son trotted away from her. He paused when his paws crunched onto the edge of a dead leaf.

"Is this the one?" he called.

"Find the biggest leaf you can, please!" Leafpool told him.

Jaykit lowered his muzzle and brushed his whiskers over the leaf under his paws. He moved sideways and did the same to the next leaf. With a satisfied grunt, he picked up the second leaf and carried it back to Leafpool, almost tripping over the bottom edge.

"Thank you, little one," Leafpool praised him. "That will get me very clean." She watched him trot back to his littermates.

"What was all that about?" Squirrelflight asked. "Are you getting him ready for apprentice duties?"

Leafpool shook her head. "He didn't choose the biggest leaf," she murmured. "And did you see the way he only stopped when he was standing on them, and how he measured the size of the leaves with his whiskers?"

Squirrelflight looked curiously at her. "Am I missing something?"

Leafpool took a deep breath. "I think Jaykit is blind."

"Blind? Are you sure?"

Leafpool nodded. Squirrelflight stared at the gray kit as he bundled against Lionkit, growling like the tiniest badger. Lionkit turned and batted him very gently with his paw.

"Poor little thing," Squirrelflight murmured. "What sort of life will he have?"

"The same as his littermates, of course," Leafpool snapped.

Squirrelflight's eyes were troubled. "But blind cats can't be warriors! Longtail had to join the elders' den as soon as he lost his sight. What place is there in a Clan for a cat who cannot see?"

"There is an equal place for Jaykit as any of these kits!" Leafpool hissed. "I will make sure of it, even if you won't. Look at him! He doesn't know there is anything different about him!"

The she-cats watched the three kits tumbling on the damp grass. When Jaykit rolled too close to a patch of brambles, Hollykit nudged him away from the thorns, then pounced on his tail with a squeal.

"His littermates already know how to look after him," Leafpool pointed out. Her heart ached. *Be brave, my little son. I will always walk beside you, I promise.*

CHAPTER 11

They left the hollow tree at the next sunrise. It was cold and calm, but drifts of snow still lay under the trees in the densest parts of the woods. The kits started out full of enthusiasm, but quickly became tired when their stumpy legs sank into the snow and their fur grew clogged and heavy. Leafpool felt exhausted too, uncomfortably full of milk and with a stabbing ache deep in her belly. Squirrelflight darted from one to the other, hoisting the kits out of clumps of snow and nudging Jaykit when he sat down and refused to move.

At sunhigh Leafpool found a sheltered patch of ferns and ordered the kits to rest. Squirrelflight darted into the undergrowth to look for prey. Hollykit and Jaykit snuggled into Leafpool's belly for warmth and milk but Lionkit sat bolt upright, his sun-colored eyes curious.

"Where are we going?" he mewed.

"To the place where ThunderClan lives," Leafpool told him. "In a big hollow full of warm dens and places for you to play. There will be lots of other cats there, and a big lake to cool your paws when it gets hot."

For a moment Lionkit looked doubtful. "But I liked living

in the hollow tree."

"I know you did. But you're getting too big to stay there forever! You are a ThunderClan cat, Lionkit, and you need to join your Clanmates."

"Will they like me?"

"They will love you," Leafpool purred.

Squirrelflight returned with a rather scrawny vole, which she shared with Leafpool. When they had crunched the last of the bones, Leafpool gently untangled her kits from her fur. "Come on, little ones. Time to go."

"I don't want to walk anymore," Jaykit wailed. "My paws hurt!"

"Climb onto my shoulders," Squirrelflight meowed, crouching down so he could scramble on. "I'll carry you for a while."

"That's not fair!" grumbled Hollykit. "Just because Jaykit can't see, it doesn't mean his legs don't work!"

"But his legs are much shorter than ours," Lionkit pointed out, looking down at his fluffy forepaws. "We can manage better than he can in the snow. Race you to that tree, Hollykit!"

Leafpool watched her son and daughter scamper ahead, throwing up specks of snow from their tiny paws. *They are so close already, my three beautiful kits. As long as they have one another, they can survive anything.*

They followed the steep-banked stream until they could see the open stretch of grass leading down to the lake, then turned and headed along the ridge above the ThunderClan boundary. The snow had melted here and all three kits trotted along, sniffing the new scents.

"We'll have to cross the border soon," Squirrelflight mewed.

Leafpool nodded. She felt sick with dread. One small paw step would change everything, plunge her back into her life as a medicine cat, when she had barely become a mother. She slowed down, her paws as heavy as rocks, and Squirrelflight kept pace with her, resting her tail lightly on Leafpool's back.

Lionkit had scrambled onto a fallen tree. "I can see the lake from here!" he yowled. "It's as big as the world!"

"Let me see!" panted Hollykit, trying to haul herself up. Her scrabbling paws knocked Lionkit off balance and he fell off the trunk with a yelp.

Leafpool was about to run over to him when she stopped. She looked at Squirrelflight. "You go," she mewed. "They need to learn that you are their mother." The words stuck like thorns in her throat and the trees blurred around her.

Squirrelflight's gaze was warm and full of sorrow. "Are you sure?" she asked quietly. "I know what we agreed, but you can still change your mind. I will do everything I can to help you, whatever you decide."

Leafpool leaned against her sister's shoulder for a moment. *I wish everything were different! Oh, my kits, I am so sorry!* Then she straightened up. "I am sure. Be good to them. Love them more than life."

"I will," Squirrelflight promised.

Leafpool rubbed some of her milk scent onto Squirrelflight's fur, then watched as her sister trotted over to the tree trunk to rescue Lionkit, who was unharmed but squeaking indignantly on the other side. As Squirrelflight pulled Lionkit clear of the ferns, Jaykit and Hollykit clustered around her.

"Can you help us all climb up?" they mewed. "We want to see the lake!"

Squirrelflight curled her tail around them. "Of course I can, my darlings," she purred. "One at a time, no pushing!"

Leafpool forced herself to turn away and walk into the undergrowth. She needed to find some herbs that would stop her milk. There was a patch of wild parsley growing close to the border. Nosing carefully through the bracken, she found the frost-nipped plants and picked the leaves. Some she ate at once, wincing at the sharp taste, and the rest she rolled up to carry back to her den. *I am the ThunderClan medicine cat,* she told herself. *My sister has had three kits, and I could not be more delighted.*

They crossed the border close to one of the tunnel entrances and began to descend the slope toward the hollow. Hollykit stopped by the tunnel and peered in, her fur flattened by the cold wind.

"Stay away from there!" Squirrelflight warned. "It's not safe for cats to go inside."

Lionkit scrunched up his nose. "Who'd want to? It's all dark and scary!"

Jaykit was sniffing a clump of moss. "I can smell cats!" he squeaked.

"That's right, little one," Squirrelflight mewed. "Those are your Clanmates."

Hollykit trotted over and butted Squirrelflight's belly. "I'm hungry! Where's all the milk gone? You smell the same, but I can't find anything to eat!"

Leafpool watched as Squirrelflight stroked Hollykit with her tail. "I'm sorry, poppet. My milk has gone, but there's a lovely cat called Daisy who will have plenty for you."

Hollykit pouted. "But I want your milk!"

Leafpool's belly ached with a pain more fierce than the birth of her kits. She hung back as Squirrelflight led them down the narrow path beside the hollow. She couldn't risk the kits picking up the milk-scent that still clung to her. When she noticed a deep patch of snow among the roots of a tree, she stopped and rolled in it to clean off the last traces of kit scent. Then she rubbed herself against a patch of damp ferns, covering her fur in sharp green flavors as further disguise.

In the distance, she could hear Squirrelflight telling the kits about ThunderClan, how they would grow up to be great warriors, strong and skilled at hunting and fighting.

"I know how to fight already!" Lionkit boasted. "Watch this!" He launched himself at a branch that lay on the fallen leaves, then stumbled back as a twig poked him in the eye. "Ow!"

"Come on, little warrior," Squirrelflight meowed. "Let's see if we can get you home in one piece!"

"Why aren't you walking with us anymore?" piped a small voice beside Leafpool.

She jumped and looked down at Jaykit's dazzling blue eyes.

"I . . . I had to fetch some herbs," she explained after putting the leaf wrap on the ground. "I'm the medicine cat for Thunder-Clan, you see."

Jaykit put his head on one side. "You were in the hollow tree, weren't you?"

"That's right. I am your mother's sister. I came to look after her while she gave birth to you."

"Why didn't she stay in the Clan to have us?" Jaykit asked.

Leafpool's heart began to beat faster. "Because we had to go on a journey together," she meowed. "And you came unexpectedly. But it's my duty to care for all of our Clanmates when they are sick or in trouble, so it's lucky I was there to look after your mother."

Jaykit blinked his beautiful eyes. "Does that mean you can make me see?" he mewed. "Hollykit and Lionkit can see things, I know. And I guess you and my mother can. Why not me?"

Leafpool felt her heart crack. "I don't know," she whispered. "I'm so sorry. I can't make you see. I would if I could, I promise."

Jaykit shrugged his tiny shoulders. "Okay," he chirped. He spun around and scampered down the slope, following exactly in the paw steps of his littermates. He grabbed at Hollykit's tail as he passed, and she squealed.

The barrier of thorns loomed up in front of them. Squirrel-flight hesitated, and Leafpool saw her take a deep breath. She knew she was asking so much of her sister, not least that she spend the rest of her life lying to the cat she had so recently chosen to be her mate. *I know these kits are worth it! Remember what Feathertail said, that their destiny will shape the future of all the Clans.*

Squirrelflight looked down at the little cats beside her. "Are you ready to meet your Clanmates?" she asked. "And your father?"

Three small heads nodded vigorously.

"When can I start being a warrior?" Lionkit squeaked.

Squirrelflight licked his head. "Soon enough," she promised. She looked over her shoulder at Leafpool. "This is it," she murmured.

"Thank you," Leafpool whispered.

Squirrelflight led her kits into the thorns, holding the prickly tendrils aside with her body. Lionkit and Hollykit walked either side of Jaykit to guide him through. The branches stirred around them, swallowing them up. There was a moment of silence as they emerged into the clearing, then Leafpool heard a chorus of voices.

"Squirrelflight! You're back!"

"With kits? I didn't even know you were expecting!"

"Thank StarClan Leafpool was with you! Are you all well? They look fine!"

"Brambleclaw, look! You're a father!"

Leafpool stood outside the barrier of thorns and closed her eyes. Three tiny shapes filled her mind, three pairs of eyes—amber, green and blue—glowed from the shadows.

Live well, my darlings. You will always be in my heart.

WARRIORS

DOVEWING'S
SILENCE

For RAH

ALLEGIANCES

THUNDERCLAN

LEADER   **BRAMBLESTAR**—dark brown tabby tom with amber eyes

DEPUTY   **SQUIRRELFLIGHT**—dark ginger she-cat with green eyes

MEDICINE CATS   **JAYFEATHER**—gray tabby tom with blind blue eyes

     LEAFPOOL—light brown tabby she-cat with amber eyes

WARRIORS   (toms and she-cats without kits)

     GRAYSTRIPE—long-haired gray tom

     DUSTPELT—dark brown tabby tom

     SANDSTORM—pale ginger she-cat with green eyes

     BRACKENFUR—golden-brown tabby tom

     CLOUDTAIL—long-haired white tom with blue eyes

     BRIGHTHEART—white she-cat with ginger patches

     MILLIE—striped gray tabby she-cat with blue eyes

     THORNCLAW—golden-brown tabby tom

     SPIDERLEG—long-limbed black tom with brown underbelly and amber eyes

     BIRCHFALL—light brown tabby tom

     WHITEWING—white she-cat with green eyes

     HAZELTAIL—small gray-and-white she-cat

BERRYNOSE—cream-colored tom

MOUSEWHISKER—gray-and-white tom

CINDERHEART—gray tabby she-cat

IVYPOOL—silver-and-white tabby she-cat with dark blue eyes

LIONBLAZE—golden tabby tom with amber eyes

FOXLEAP—reddish tabby tom
APPRENTICE, CHERRYPAW (ginger she-cat)

DOVEWING—pale gray she-cat with blue eyes

ROSEPETAL—dark cream she-cat
APPRENTICE, MOLEPAW (brown-and-cream tom)

POPPYFROST—tortoiseshell she-cat

BRIARLIGHT—dark brown she-cat with sky-colored eyes, paralyzed in her hindquarters

BLOSSOMFALL—tortoiseshell-and-white she-cat

TOADSTEP—black-and-white tom

BUMBLESTRIPE—very pale gray tom with black stripes

QUEENS (she-cats expecting or nursing kits)

DAISY—cream, long-furred cat from the horseplace

SORRELTAIL—tortoiseshell-and-white she-cat with amber eyes (mother to Lilykit, a dark tabby she-kit with white patches, and Seedkit, a very pale ginger she-kit)

WHITEWATER—white she-cat with long fur, blind in one eye

RATSCAR—brown tom with long scar across his back

OAKFUR—small brown tom

SMOKEFOOT—black tom

KINKFUR—tabby she-cat, with long fur that sticks out at all angles

IVYTAIL—black, white, and tortoiseshell she-cat

WINDCLAN

LEADER   **ONESTAR**—brown tabby tom

DEPUTY   **HARESPRING**—brown-and-white tom
APPRENTICE, SLIGHTPAW (black tom with flash of white on his chest)

MEDICINE CAT   **KESTRELFLIGHT**—mottled gray tom

WARRIORS   **CROWFEATHER**—dark gray tom
APPRENTICE, FEATHERPAW (gray tabby she-cat)

NIGHTCLOUD—black she-cat
APPRENTICE, HOOTPAW (dark gray tom)

GORSETAIL—very pale gray-and-white tom with blue eyes

WEASELFUR—ginger tom with white paws

LEAFTAIL—dark tabby tom, amber eyes
APPRENTICE, OATPAW (pale brown tabby tom)

EMBERFOOT—gray tom with two dark paws

HEATHERTAIL—light brown tabby she-cat with blue eyes

BREEZEPELT—black tom with amber eyes

FURZEPELT—gray-and-white she-cat

CROUCHFOOT—ginger tom

LARKWING—pale brown tabby she-cat

QUEENS   **SEDGEWHISKER**—light brown tabby she-cat

ELDERS   **WHISKERNOSE**—light brown tom

WHITETAIL—small white she-cat

RIVERCLAN

LEADER   **MISTYSTAR**—gray she-cat with blue eyes

DEPUTY   **REEDWHISKER**—black tom
APPRENTICE, LIZARDPAW (light brown tom)

MEDICINE CATS   **MOTHWING**—dappled golden she-cat

WILLOWSHINE—gray tabby she-cat

WARRIORS   **MINTFUR**—light gray tabby tom

MINNOWTAIL—dark gray she-cat

MALLOWNOSE—light brown tabby tom
APPRENTICE, HAVENPAW (black-and-white she-cat)

GRASSPELT—light brown tom

DUSKFUR—brown tabby she-cat

MOSSPELT—tortoiseshell she-cat with blue eyes
APPRENTICE, PERCHPAW (gray-and-white she-cat)

SHIMMERPELT—silver she-cat

LAKEHEART—gray tabby she-cat

HERONWING—dark gray-and-black tom

QUEENS

ICEWING—white she-cat with blue eyes

PETALFUR—gray-and-white she-cat

ELDERS

POUNCEFOOT—ginger-and-white tom

PEBBLEFOOT—mottled gray tom

RUSHTAIL—light brown tabby tom

CATS OUTSIDE CLANS

SMOKY—muscular gray-and-white tom who lives in a barn at the horseplace

CORIANDER—tortoiseshell-and-white she-cat who lives with Smoky

Hareview Campsite

Sanctuary
Cottage

Sadler Woods

Littlepine Road

Littlepine
Sailing
Center

Littlepine
Island

River Alba

Whitchurch Road

CHAPTER 1

Dovewing stood very still in the center of the camp as silence crashed over the forest. From the corner of her eye she saw two pale shapes, a badger with a long striped nose and a hairless cat with swollen blind eyes. They nodded to her, then walked out of the hollow. For a moment Dovewing wanted to chase after them, to haul them back and demand to know what happened next.

Midnight! Rock! How can you leave us like this? The Dark Forest may have been defeated but we have lost everything!

The quiet beneath the trees was broken by a muffled sob. Sandstorm was crouching beside Firestar's unmoving body, which still lay at the foot of the lightning-scorched tree.

"We have lost everything," Dovewing whispered out loud.

She watched Leafpool press a wad of cobweb onto a bite wound on Cinderheart's flank; Lionblaze stood over them, the tip of his tail twitching anxiously, until Leafpool sent him away to fetch marigold and tansy from the medicine cats' den.

Millie touched Dovewing's shoulder with her muzzle. "Are you hurt?" she mewed.

Dovewing shook her head. In truth, she had no idea what

wounds she had suffered in the terrible blood-soaked skir-
mishes; she felt numb from her nose to her claws, and her ears
were still buzzing from the sounds of the battle.

"Then come help us," Millie prompted. She steered Dovewing gently over to the edge of the clearing where the bodies
of Hollyleaf, Mousefur, and Ferncloud were being arranged.
Dustpelt was staring down at Ferncloud, his dark tabby coat
matted with blood and patchy where tufts of fur had been
ripped out.

"You need to see Leafpool," Icecloud prompted him, paus-
ing as she carefully straightened Ferncloud's feather-soft tail.
"I'll stay here."

"I will never leave Ferncloud's side again," Dustpelt snarled.
He slammed his paw onto the ground, his claw-tips scoring
the soil. "I should have been with her. She should never have
been left to fight Brokenstar alone. She was nothing but a
scrap of prey for him!"

Icecloud glanced up at him with a glint of anger in her pale
blue gaze. "My mother gave her life to protect the nursery. She
died the death of a warrior. Don't take that away from her."

Spiderleg limped up and rested his tail on his father's shoulder. "I'm sure Leafpool can come see you while you're here,"
he told Dustpelt. "We should all be with her now. Birchfall
has taken Foxleap to the medicine den, then he and Leafpool
will join us."

Dovewing felt a stab of grief for her father. Poor Birchfall.
Ferncloud was his mother as well as Icecloud's and Foxleap's.
He would feel her loss hard.

Dovewing jumped as Whitewing appeared beside her. The white she-cat's pelt was streaked scarlet with blood, and Dovewing opened her mouth to protest that she should be in the medicine cats' den. Her mother quickly shook her head. "It's not mine," she meowed. "Can you help Purdy?" She gestured with her muzzle toward the old tabby tom, who was struggling to fold Mousefur's paws beneath her.

There was an invisible stone lodged in Dovewing's throat that made it impossible to speak, but she went over to Purdy and held Mousefur's leg still while he gently curled her feet under her belly as if she was sleeping. The old tom's eyes were overflowing, and his breath rasped in his chest.

Dovewing was distracted by a stir at the entrance to the hollow. Jayfeather and Brambleclaw were standing by the flattened tangle of thorns that had once protected the camp. "I'm leaving now for the Moonpool," Brambleclaw announced, his voice ringing beneath the night-black sky. "More than ever, ThunderClan needs a leader." He faltered as he gazed at the flame-colored body in the shadows. More quietly, he went on, "And now, it seems I must be that leader." He nodded to Squirrelflight, who was watching him with her green eyes brimming with sorrow. "Squirrelflight, as my deputy, I leave the Clan under your charge."

Without another word, he turned and bounded over the thorns. Jayfeather followed more slowly, his gray pelt the color of clouds in the moonlight.

Squirrelflight climbed the rocks to Highledge as if every bone in her body was in pain, and looked down at her

Clanmates. "Before we do anything else, we must see to our wounds. Check yourself carefully and go to the medicine den if you are hurt." Her voice was dull as if the battle had bled out her ability to feel anything. "The time is past for heroes," she meowed. "The Clan needs you to be strong now. So if you have any injuries at all, get them treated." She narrowed her eyes at Dustpelt, who had wrenched his gaze away from Ferncloud. "That means you too," Squirrelflight finished.

Dovewing glanced at her flanks and looked briefly at each paw but she couldn't see any wounds that needed urgent attention. She started to lick Mousefur's ears to clean them, but Purdy placed his tail-tip on her shoulder. "I can take care of her now," he mewed gruffly.

Dovewing nodded and took a step back to let the old cat shuffle closer to Mousefur's head. She closed her eyes in pain as Purdy's tongue rasped over his denmate's pelt. *What will he do without you, Mousefur?*

Beside her, a silver-and-white she-cat was picking leaf scraps from Hollyleaf's fur. Dovewing pressed her flank against her sister. "Are you okay, Ivypool?"

The silver-and-white cat nodded without looking up. "I'm alive, aren't I? Thanks to Hollyleaf." Ivypool traced her muzzle over Hollyleaf's back. "If it hadn't been for her, Hawkfrost would have killed me. Hollyleaf gave her life for mine!"

Dovewing winced at the tremor in Ivypool's voice. "Remember that Hollyleaf is watching you now," she murmured. "She will never regret what she did."

From the other side of Hollyleaf's body, Daisy nodded.

She was untangling the long black fur with her claws, teasing out the knots as gently as if Hollyleaf could feel every tug. "Hollyleaf died as a true warrior," she agreed.

Dovewing looked around at the sound of paw steps. Brackenfur was pacing across the clearing, his tail flicking. "Has anyone seen Sorreltail?" he called.

Brightheart emerged from the remains of the elders' den, the white patches on her fur glowing in the half-light. Muffled sounds of her three kits came from deep within the crushed branches.

"Is it safe to come out now?"

"Have those dead cats gone? They were bad!"

"Ow! Dewkit's treading on me!"

Brightheart glanced over her shoulder. The skin on her ravaged face was taut and red from strain. "Wait there!" she meowed. "You can come out soon, I promise." She turned back to Brackenfur. "I saw Sorreltail go into the nursery. You should try there first."

"Thanks." Brackenfur trotted toward the clump of brambles, miraculously intact thanks to Ferncloud's courage.

Dovewing shook her head, trying to clear the buzzing from her ears. *Something's wrong*, she thought. The hair along her spine rose. *I should be able to hear Sorreltail—but I can't.*

"Are you feeling all right?" Ivypool asked.

Dovewing didn't take her eyes from the nursery as she watched Brackenfur slip inside. "I'm fine," she murmured.

"*No.*"

Brackenfur's single word dropped like a stone into the

hush of the clearing. Dovewing was at the entrance to the nursery before she realized her paws were moving. Brackenfur was standing at the edge of Sorreltail's nest, looking down at his mate's unmoving body. The air was thick with the stench of blood, and Dovewing felt it sticky and liquid beneath her pads.

A tiny dark tabby head with white patches popped up from behind Sorreltail, her blue eyes huge and worried. "We can't wake her!" Lilykit squeaked. "We tried and tried but she's still asleep!"

Her sister Seedkit appeared. Her pale ginger fur was fluffed in all directions, making her look like a hedgehog. "Is she really tired from the fighting, do you think?"

"Tired . . ." Brackenfur whispered without lifting his gaze from Sorreltail's sweet face. The she-cat's eyes were lightly closed as if she had just dozed off.

"Lilykit, Seedkit, come with me," Dovewing urged, her voice coming out as a croak.

The kits scrambled over Sorreltail's body. "Sorry, Mama," Lilykit mewed when her paw slipped into Sorreltail's ear.

Dovewing tried not to flinch when she saw that the kits' belly fur was soaked with blood. She glanced sideways at Brackenfur, but he hadn't noticed. His legs had crumpled beneath him and he was curled around Sorreltail's head, pressing his muzzle against her.

"Wake up, my love," he murmured. "Our kits need you. We can't lose you now."

Dovewing nudged the kits toward the entrance. "I think

Papa is sad," Seedkit chirped. "Shall I stay and make him feel better?"

"No, let's leave him be," Dovewing urged. She followed the kits into the clearing. Several cats were waiting outside, eyes wide and anxious. Brightheart let out a gasp when she saw the bloodstained little cats. As she bounded forward, she called over her shoulder, "Cloudtail? Tell our kits to stay where they are." Her mate trotted to the remains of the elders' den while Brightheart pulled Lilykit and Seedkit to her belly with her tail and began licking their soiled fur. Over their heads, she met Dovewing's gaze with a question in her eyes. Dovewing nodded. Brightheart bent over Sorreltail's kits and drew them closer.

Squirrelflight padded over. "What's going on?"

"Sorreltail is dead," Dovewing meowed, each word dragged out with claws sharp as thorns.

Cherrypaw visibly swayed on her paws, and Whitewing closed her eyes with a grimace of pain. Squirrelflight looked baffled. "But . . . but she was fine. She didn't say anything about being hurt." The dark ginger cat looked around at her Clanmates. "Didn't anyone notice she'd been injured?"

Sandstorm walked forward, her eyes still wet with grief for Firestar. She rested her tail on Squirrelflight's shoulder. "If she was injured that badly, we couldn't have done anything to help her."

Squirrelflight lashed her tail. "We could have tried!"

There was a wail from inside the nursery. "Sorreltail! Don't leave me!"

"I'll go to him," Millie offered, slipping into the brambles. "He shouldn't be alone at this time."

Graystripe stepped forward. With a shock, Dovewing realized he looked old and tired. "The Dark Forest has claimed another victim," the warrior declared. "May Sorreltail watch over us from StarClan." He bowed his head.

Squirrelflight paced anxiously around the cats. "I told you all to check yourselves for injuries. Have you done it yet? I won't have any other cats die on me!"

Dovewing felt a stab of guilt as she licked at the scratch on her flank. She should get it treated before it got infected. She headed toward the medicine cats' den. Inside, Spiderleg was helping Leafpool pad the gaping bite wound in Foxleap's belly with crushed leaves. Foxleap lay very still, only the flickering of his eyelids proving that he was alive.

Leafpool looked up. "Are you hurt, Dovewing? Can it wait?" Her amber eyes were huge with distress.

"Sorreltail died," Dovewing meowed.

Leafpool jumped up, almost tripping over Foxleap. "What? She didn't tell me she was hurt!"

"She didn't tell anyone," Dovewing whispered. "I think she just wanted to be with her kits."

The medicine cat's shoulders slumped. "There is nothing I can do for her now. Let me finish treating Foxleap, then I'll bring some herbs and cobweb outside to treat you and anyone else that I haven't seen yet."

Dovewing padded back to the clearing. The three bodies of her fallen Clanmates were surrounded by little knots of their kin and closest friends. Ivypool was hunched beside Holly-leaf, licking the soft black fur on her shoulder. Bumblestripe was next to his father at Firestar's body. The pale gray tom caught Dovewing's eye and twitched his ears, as if offering to join her instead, but Dovewing shook her head. Graystripe needed him more right now.

Cloudtail and Berrynose were picking through the remains of the warriors' den, trying to drag out scraps of bedding. As Dovewing watched, Squirrelflight went over to them and told them to stop.

"We'll get nothing done tonight," she meowed, sounding calmer now, more like a Clan deputy. "We should all get some rest before Brambleclaw returns."

He'll be Bramblestar by then, Dovewing thought. She found a patch of clean sand close to the tree stump where apprentices loved to practice leaping and settled down. Curling her tail over her front paws, she looked up at the pale stars and tried to spot the new warriors of StarClan that had been born this night. But the stars were nothing more than cold glints of light in a depthless sky, and Dovewing felt no comfort from them. *Did we really win the battle? Because this doesn't feel like a victory.*

She pricked her ears, straining to hear how the other Clans were coping with their dead and wounded, but all she heard was a soft rushing sound like wind through leaf-heavy trees. The forest loomed around the hollow, dark and thick with shadows full of menace, and Dovewing wondered if she would ever feel safe again.

CHAPTER 2

Dovewing woke to find pale dawn light filtering through the leafless branches. She was bitterly cold, and her breath hung in clouds in the still air. All around the clearing, her Clanmates were stirring from where they had slept beneath the sky, huddled around the fallen warriors. Sorreltail's body had been brought out of the nursery during the night and laid next to Mousefur, a splash of light color against Mousefur's soft brown pelt. Brackenfur crouched beside his dead mate, his eyes closed, though Dovewing doubted he had slept for a moment.

A dark tabby shape moved through the clearing, gently rousing each cat. It was Purdy, his muzzle looking grayer than ever and his pelt ruffled with lack of rest. "Our vigil is over," he meowed quietly to his Clanmates. "These cats must be laid in the ground." When Molepaw responded with a grunt of protest, Purdy told him, "I am the only elder left. I cannot bury them alone. I need your help."

Abashed, the young brown-and-cream tom scrambled to his paws and followed Purdy across the clearing to where the dead cats lay. Others joined them: Graystripe, Rosepetal, Blossomfall, and Bumblestripe. Dovewing fell in behind them, stumbling on paws that felt as cold as stone. As she passed the tangled remnants of the elders' den, she heard muffled squeaks, loud enough to suggest that Daisy and Brightheart had made room for Sorreltail's kits in there as well and were keeping them away from the clearing for as long as they possibly could.

Bumblestripe headed for Firestar's body, and Dovewing watched her sister pad up to Hollyleaf, her shoulders hunched with grief. Dovewing followed and gently took one side of Hollyleaf's scruff in her mouth. From the corner of her eye she saw her father go up to Ferncloud. Icecloud and Spiderleg stood beside the little gray body, their heads bowed and their flanks hollow with exhaustion. As Birchfall approached, Dustpelt stepped forward, blocking Ferncloud from view.

"We can manage, Birchfall," he mewed.

The tip of Birchfall's tail twitched. "She was my mother. I want to carry her on her last journey."

Dustpelt flattened his ears. "You gave up that right when you betrayed your Clan," he growled, so softly that Dovewing could hardly hear. She let go of Hollyleaf's scruff and shook her head impatiently, trying to sharpen her senses.

To her surprise, Birchfall didn't argue. Instead he turned and walked back to the warriors' den. Dovewing opened her mouth to call after him but Ivypool caught her eye.

"Don't say anything," she warned. "Let's get this done first." She bent down and took hold of the other side of Hollyleaf's neck fur. Poppyfrost and Cloudtail gripped the loose skin on her haunches. Their eyes were dark with sorrow. Dovewing noticed Thornclaw, Mousewhisker, and Blossomfall following her father back to the den. Had their help been turned down as well? A prickle of alarm stirred beneath Dovewing's fur. *Are they being shunned by the other cats because they trained with the Dark Forest?* She was distracted as the others hefted Hollyleaf off the ground, and she had to splay her paws to take her share of the weight. Hollyleaf wasn't heavy, but her cold, stiff form was awkward and unwieldy to move, swinging between the four cats and knocking them off balance. Dustpelt and Spiderleg carried Ferncloud between them as if she weighed no more than a piece of thistledown. Icecloud walked behind with her mother's tail draped over her shoulder. Bumblestripe, Lionblaze, Cinderheart, and Purdy bore Mousefur among them, the old she-cat silenced forever, her jaws hanging slightly open as if she had something more to say. Firestar was carried by Sandstorm, Graystripe, Squirrelflight, and Millie. Dovewing heard the gray tabby she-cat murmur, "We were born as kittypets, but look at us now, my precious friend."

At first Brackenfur seemed reluctant to let anyone else touch Sorreltail, as if they might disturb her. Gently Rosepetal, Berrynose, and Whitewing pressed around the queen's body and lifted her as carefully as if she were a newborn kit. Brackenfur stooped to cradle Sorreltail's chin on the back of his neck. His grief clung like mist to his ruffled pelt and Dovewing had to look away.

Leafpool led the sad procession out of the hollow and into the oldest part of the woods in ThunderClan territory, between the camp and the lakeshore, where oak trees grew twisted and silver with age. The ground here was soft and thick with moss, making it easier to dig. The cats laid down their precious burdens in a row and stepped back to let Leafpool stand over each fallen warrior and send them on their journey to StarClan.

They are already there, thought Dovewing, recalling the glittering shapes she had seen filing out of the battle-torn camp. She glanced around, looking for the cats who had returned to the warriors' den. Toadstep and Hazeltail had joined the procession of fallen cats but there was no sign of the others. "Birchfall isn't here!" she whispered to Ivypool. "Do you think we should fetch him?"

Her sister looked at her with anger in her eyes. "Our father isn't here because he knows he wouldn't be welcome. Every cat knows that Birchfall fought on the side of the Dark Forest. Same for Thornclaw, Mousewhisker, and Blossomfall. They are traitors. As am I, to some of our Clanmates."

"That's so unfair!" Dovewing protested under her breath. "All of those cats switched allegiance thanks to you."

Ivypool bent her silver-and-white head. "Our sins are not easily forgiven, not when the battle lost us so many cats. Hollyleaf only died because she saved me from Hawkfrost." Her whole body shuddered. "Perhaps it should be me lying there instead."

Dovewing stepped closer to her sister and wrapped her tail over Ivypool's flank. "Never say that!" she hissed. "Hollyleaf knew what she was doing. She died as a true warrior, don't forget."

Leafpool finished the words of the ceremony, wishing each cat a safe and swift journey to their starry ancestors and promising to see them again. She walked slowly along the line of dead cats, touching her muzzle to each still, cool head. She paused longest beside Hollyleaf, her lips moving as she whispered one last message to her daughter. Dovewing found herself instinctively pricking her ears to listen, then turned away. Whatever Leafpool was saying, it wasn't for anyone but Hollyleaf to hear. Dovewing hoped the black she-cat was listening, wherever she was.

Squirrelflight joined Leafpool beside Hollyleaf and stood in silence for a moment. The deputy's eyes were closed and her shoulders were hunched with pain. Then she opened her eyes and raised her head. "Only we know the debt that we owe to these cats. It is up to each of us to make sure that their deaths were not in vain." She looked down at Firestar and reached out with her front paw to touch his cheek. "Sleep well, my father," she whispered.

Purdy stepped forward. "Don't dig the holes too close together," he rasped. "They must be at least one fox-length deep. For safety, like," he added, shuffling his paws. "Oh, an' if the hole starts fillin' with water, leave it an' dig another further up the slope."

"Thank you for sharing your knowledge with us, Purdy," Squirrelflight meowed. "Is there anything else?"

The old tabby cat twitched his ears. "Well, Mousefur used to like watchin' the sun go down over the lake. She said it looked like the water was on fire." His voice trailed off and he swallowed. "So I was goin' to bury her where she'd still get a good view. P'raps over there." He nodded toward a grassy mound with a clear line of sight to the lake. "I know she's not really here, but it feels like the right place for her."

Sandstorm moved beside him and ran her tail over his bony spine. "It's a lovely idea, Purdy. Of course we can do that."

Dovewing blinked away the moisture that was gathering in her eyes. "Come on," she mewed to Ivypool. "Let's find a place for Hollyleaf."

The cats began to move quietly through the trees, choosing soft but well-drained spots for each hole. Poppyfrost stopped beside a young holly bush growing beside the mound that Purdy had selected for Mousefur. "What about here?" she called over her shoulder.

Cloudtail walked over and prodded the soil with his paw. "Yes, this should be okay." He started to scrape away the leaf mulch, pushing it further under the tree. Dovewing and Ivypool went over to join him and began to scoop up the earth. On top of the mound, she heard Bumblestripe, Cinderheart, and Lionblaze marking a space for Mousefur.

"Make it a bit longer," Purdy ordered. "Give 'er room to stretch out."

Silence fell among the trees, apart from the sounds of digging and an occasional grunt of effort. Dovewing's fur felt hot and prickly but she kept going, even though damp earth was wedged uncomfortably beneath her claws and her eyes stung from bits of dirt that flicked up from Ivypool's paws. Poppyfrost and Cloudtail worked at the other end of the hole, cramped against the holly bush but uncomplaining even when sharp-pointed leaves pricked their skin.

"Ow!" There was an exclamation followed by a muffled curse from somewhere above Dovewing's head. She looked up and saw Lionblaze holding up his front paw. Blood dripped from a broken claw.

Cinderheart bounded over to him. "What happened?"

Lionblaze shook his paws, scattering scarlet drops onto the moss. "I caught it on a root," he meowed. "I'm okay."

Cinderheart tipped her head on one side. "Are you sure?" Her voice was heavy with meaning, and Dovewing understood. Lionblaze wasn't supposed to get hurt like other cats. It was the power that made him invincible in battle. If the Dark Forest cats couldn't injure him, why should a harmless tree root?

Lionblaze turned back to the hole. "I told you, it's nothing," he growled, his voice muffled by flying earth.

Dovewing started digging again. *It doesn't mean anything*, she told herself. *Lionblaze is exhausted from the battle. He can't protect himself like he usually does.* The buzzing in her ears drowned out the sound of her paws scrabbling in the dirt until Dovewing could hear nothing except her own breathing.

At last the five cats had been laid in their earthy nests and covered over. Purdy checked each one carefully to make sure that no scent clung to the top layer of leaves. "We don't want to attract anything that might be hungry," he explained. Dovewing felt a rush of affection for the old cat. At this moment, no one would ever think he wasn't Clanborn, and had never been a warrior.

The cats trailed back to the hollow and sank down in the clearing, too exhausted to fetch anything from the fresh-kill pile. It was well-stocked with two sparrows and a squirrel; Dovewing guessed that Birchfall and the others had gone hunting. A gesture of reconciliation, she wondered? But she noticed that none of the cats who had been involved in the burials made any effort to thank their Clanmates, or even speak to them. Dovewing winced as Dustpelt walked straight past Birchfall without looking at him. *He's your son!* she wanted to yowl. *He's not your enemy!*

Night was falling and cats were just starting to stir in search of their temporary nests when the sound of paw steps came from the entrance to the hollow and Bramblestar leaped over the flattened brambles. Jayfeather followed more cautiously, picking his way through the tendrils.

Dovewing stared at the new ThunderClan leader. His dark brown coat looked glossier than before, as if lit by starshine, and his amber eyes glowed. Was that because he had been given nine lives? Dovewing strained to hear the whispers of StarClan warriors around him, but there was nothing but the sound of her Clanmates moving tiredly through the camp. She scolded herself for being fanciful.

Squirrelflight limped over to meet Bramblestar in the center of the hollow. "Welcome back," she purred, dipping her head. She seemed to be in awe of him too.

Bramblestar looked around and narrowed his eyes when

he saw Birchfall, Thornclaw, Mousewhisker, and Blossomfall sitting at the edge of the clearing, a little distance off from the other cats. "What's going on?" he mewed. "Haven't you all been burying the others today?"

Squirrelflight moved closer to Bramblestar. She spoke close to his ear, the flicking of her tail-tip betraying her discomfort. Dovewing leaned toward them, straining to hear what the deputy was saying.

"I don't think that's a conversation for your ears," meowed a voice behind her.

Dovewing jumped and looked around to see her mother watching her with concern in her pale blue eyes. "You . . . you said you can hear things," Whitewing went on. "Even when you're not close enough to listen like other cats."

Dovewing nodded. To her surprise, Whitewing sighed and stroked Dovewing's shoulder with her tail. "That must feel very strange," she murmured. "Do you ever get any peace? I wish you had told me sooner. I might have been able to help."

"It was part of a prophecy," Dovewing mewed, feeling very uncomfortable. "I was given this power to help the Clans against the Dark Forest. It's okay, I promise."

Her mother straightened up, still looking troubled. "If you ever want to talk to me about it, I'm always here." She nodded toward Bramblestar and Squirrelflight. "And I still think that even if you *can* hear something, it doesn't mean that you *should*."

Dovewing glanced down at her paws. "It's okay," she mewed. "I can't make out what they're saying anyway. My ears haven't stopped buzzing from the battle yet, and my head hurts."

"Why don't you go and see if Jayfeather can give you something for that?" Whitewing prompted. "All the injuries have been treated now. There's no need for you to be in pain."

Dovewing padded to the entrance to the medicine den and peered through the screen of brambles. "Jayfeather? May I come in?"

The medicine cat's head appeared through the fronds. His fur stood on end and his face was taut with tension. "Is it urgent?" he snapped. "Leafpool's asleep and I'm in the middle of changing Foxleap's dressings."

"How is he?" Dovewing asked, her belly tightening.

Jayfeather looked over his shoulder at the warrior, who was a faint hunched shape inside the den. Briarlight was propped on her forelegs beside him, licking his ears. "Not good," Jayfeather replied. "Now, what do you want?"

"It's okay, it can wait," Dovewing meowed. She started to back away. "I'll come back tomorrow if I need to."

Jayfeather vanished back into the den, leaving Dovewing staring at the quivering brambles. She was used to Jayfeather's short temper and brisk manner, but this was different. He seemed . . . frightened. But what could be more terrifying than the attack from the Dark Forest? The battle had been won. Surely there was nothing left to be scared of?

CHAPTER 3

"Ouch! Mind my eyes!"

"Sorry!" Dovewing dropped her end of the bramble and backed off to let Bumblestripe scramble clear. They were working on the collapsed wall of the warriors' den. Dustpelt was supposed to be supervising but he had vanished; Dovewing guessed he was visiting Ferncloud's burial place. It had only been two sunrises since they buried the cats who fell in the battle, and neither Dustpelt nor Brackenfur seemed willing to leave their mates alone in their cold earthen nests. None of their Clanmates had challenged them on it; there was nothing but compassion for their unspeakable grief.

The cats who had fought briefly on the side of the Dark Forest, however, were still being treated as if they had green-cough. They had taken to sleeping separately in a space behind the elders' den. Last night Ivypool had joined them, and Dovewing wondered if her sister felt guilty because she seemed to be treated more favorably by the cats who had seen her take on Hawkfrost. Dovewing's pelt pricked at the injustice of the situation, and she waited for Bramblestar to say something but he was busy with Squirrelflight, organizing patrols to hunt for food and repair the dens.

Bumblestripe nudged Dovewing. "It's all right, I think I escaped with my sight," he joked. "Come on, help me untangle this ivy." They started to unravel the knot of dark green leaves. All the cats were trying to salvage as much of the dens as they could to save having to find fresh leafy branches so late in the season.

Suddenly Cinderheart, who was working on the other side of the wall, let out a soft mew. "Blackstar's here!"

Dovewing peered around the den and saw the ShadowClan leader hobble into the clearing with his deputy Rowanclaw close beside him—so close, in fact, that their shoulders were touching, as if Rowanclaw was holding his leader upright.

Bumblestripe put down the ivy and came to stand beside Dovewing. "I wonder what he wants?"

There was no suspicion in his tone; in fact, none of the ThunderClan cats who had stopped working to watch the new arrivals were bristling with hostility. *The Dark Forest has changed everything*, Dovewing mused, recalling a time not so long ago when these visitors would have been treated with distrust. Now they hadn't even been challenged as they slowly entered the hollow.

"Blackstar! Come and sit down." Bramblestar bounded down the rocks from Highledge and showed the ShadowClan leader a space on the grass where he could rest his trembling legs.

"Great StarClan, Blackstar looks so old he's barely alive!" Cinderheart commented under her breath beside Dovewing.

Squirrelflight joined them from the nursery, where she had been helping Daisy amuse all the kits while Brightheart was out on a hunting patrol. "Is everything well in ShadowClan?" Squirrelflight asked, exchanging nods with Rowanclaw.

"We are fine," Blackstar rasped, so faintly that Dovewing barely heard. *It's been two days since the battle; why can't I hear anything yet?* she thought in frustration.

Blackstar seemed to be having trouble speaking due to the wheezing in his chest, so Rowanclaw took over. "We have to come to talk to you about the Dark Forest cats who still walk among us," he announced.

Dovewing flinched. What Dark Forest cats? She looked around and saw her Clanmates bristling.

"As you know," Rowanclaw went on, "the Dark Forest attack was helped in part by warriors from the living Clans." He paused and glanced around the clearing as if he wanted to name those cats right now. "Some of them survived the battle. We need to decide what should be done to them."

Bramblestar shifted his paws. "I agree this is something to think about, but I assumed each Clan leader would decide alone. It involves our own Clanmates, after all."

Blackstar struggled to his paws and lashed his tail. "We are still bound by our alliance during the Great Battle!" he hissed. "This is a problem faced by all the Clans, and therefore we should deal with it together. There cannot be any inequity between us."

"Whoa!" Bumblestripe breathed in Dovewing's ear. "He does know the battle is over, right? We're not allied with ShadowClan now!"

Bramblestar let his gaze travel around the hollow, ending up on the four cats who were apart from the rest, clearing trampled brambles from one side of the entrance. "Very well, Blackstar," he meowed. "Perhaps it's right that we should agree on a course of action together. Shall we meet on the island tomorrow night?"

Blackstar nodded. "I'll send word to RiverClan and WindClan, if you'll permit my warriors to travel along your lakeshore."

"Of course," mewed Bramblestar. He stood up and padded beside the ancient white cat as he started to leave. "Thank you for coming, Blackstar. Get some rest before we meet on the island."

Blackstar just grunted. Rowanclaw dipped his head to Bramblestar and guided his leader through the remains of the barrier, then ushered him into the trees.

Dovewing's fur had risen along her spine, and Bumblestripe smoothed it down with his muzzle. "Calm down," he mewed. "You're not in trouble!"

"But Ivypool could be!" Dovewing snapped. "And my father! These cats can't be punished for believing the lies that the Dark Forest warriors told them!"

Bumblestripe started to unravel the ivy knot once more. "We can't forget what happened, Dovewing. Perhaps they need some sort of punishment just to make sure they understand that what they did was wrong."

"Blossomfall is your sister," Dovewing mewed softly. "Do you really think she'd do anything to betray her Clan?"

The gray tom didn't look up from the strand of ivy. "Training in the Dark Forest was never part of the warrior code," he muttered.

"Nor was dead cats coming back to life to attack us!" Dovewing reached out with one front paw and rested it on Bumblestripe's shoulder. "Our Clanmates made a terrible decision, but when it mattered, they were loyal to us, and us alone."

Bumblestripe finally looked at her, his eyes troubled. "You really believe that."

Dovewing nodded. "Ivypool is my littermate, just as Blossomfall is yours. I would trust my sister with my life. Don't you feel the same way?

There was a pause, then Bumblestripe nodded. "Thanks, Dovewing," he whispered.

Before Dovewing could say anything else, Bramblestar spoke just behind her.

"Dovewing, may I speak with you?"

Dovewing nearly jumped into the air. How had she missed him walking up to her?

"I'd like you to come with me to meet the other leaders," Bramblestar meowed. "Jayfeather will be with me, of course, and the cats who were trained by the Dark Forest, but I think you and Lionblaze should be present as well. You both know more about what the Dark Forest planned than many of us." He blinked. "Because of the prophecy, right?"

Dovewing nodded mutely.

"Good." Bramblestar turned away. "We'll leave at dusk

tomorrow. Make sure you get some rest during the day."

Dovewing didn't go back to helping Bumblestripe at once. Instead she stood very still, listening to the whispers around her. The rest of ThunderClan seemed excited at the prospect of choosing a punishment for the traitors among them. Dovewing felt a wave of impatience at their stupidity. *Can't you see that these are loyal warriors who made one mistake? Are you all so perfect yourselves?*

Then she tilted her head and tried to pick up what was being said in ShadowClan. Were those cats equally thrilled? But all she heard was the rustle of branches as Bumblestripe and Cinderheart worked beside her, and a burst of squealing from the elders' den as one of the kits stepped on a thorn. When she tried to picture the neighboring camp, her mind was clouded and fuzzy, as if it were filled with mist. Dovewing felt a cold trickle of fear seep into her fur. *Why can't I hear and see like I used to? Has something happened to me?*

She looked at Ivypool, who was salvaging clean moss from a bundle that had been dragged out of the nursery. Her sister had more than enough to worry about without Dovewing adding her concerns about her senses. Jayfeather was too busy with Foxleap and the other wounded cats, and Lionblaze was constantly out on patrol. Dovewing recalled his broken claw during the burial, and winced. She could no longer hear, and Lionblaze was able to suffer injuries.

Has something happened to all our powers?

CHAPTER 4
❧

A faint three-quarter moon showed over the tops of the pine trees as the cats filed across the tree-bridge to the island. Dovewing stayed close to Ivypool, trying to comfort her sister without saying anything. Ivypool walked with her head high and her tail kinked confidently over her back, but Dovewing knew she was scared of what might be said at this meeting. Bramblestar and Jayfeather led the ThunderClan patrol, and Birchfall, Thornclaw, Mousewhisker, and Blossomfall brought up the rear. The four cats radiated tension and the fur bristled along their spines; Dovewing wished they would relax and not look as if they had something to be ashamed of.

Blackstar was already seated at the foot of the oak tree, flanked by his medicine cat, Littlecloud. Both cats looked frail and thin against the sturdy trunk. Their Clanmates Tigerheart and Ratscar sat a tail-length off, ears twitching. Bramblestar stopped halfway across the clearing and gestured with his tail to his Clanmates, inviting them to sit down. "We'll stay here," he mewed quietly. Dovewing felt a stab of relief that he was staying with them rather than leaving to sit with Blackstar.

Onestar arrived before the ThunderClan cats had finished settling. He was accompanied by his medicine cat, Kestrelflight, and Breezepelt. The black warrior's eyes flashed defiantly. *He clearly doesn't think he's done anything wrong*, Dovewing thought.

The three Clans waited in silence, listening to the rustle of ferns as the last cats approached. Mistystar emerged first from the bracken followed closely by Mothwing and Icewing. Dovewing blinked. ThunderClan had brought by far the most cats! What did that say about their loyalty to the warrior code?

Bramblestar seemed to guess what his Clanmates were thinking. "The other Clans lost cats who fought with the Dark Forest," he murmured. "All of you survived, which is why there are more of us here."

It didn't make Dovewing feel much better. She felt warmth on her pelt, and turned to see Tigerheart gazing at her. She looked away quickly. That was one complication she didn't need.

Onestar spoke first. "Why are Lionblaze and Dovewing here?" he asked. "They weren't part of the Dark Forest, were they?"

"No," Bramblestar replied. "But they know as much about the involvement of our Clanmates in the Dark Forest as I do." He stepped into the space between the four Clans and looked around at the other leaders. "We must pay attention to the truth of what happened and why these cats behaved as they did. The battle is over; they are no longer our enemies."

His fur was ruffled and Dovewing knew that in spite of

what he'd said, he was troubled by the presence of so many ThunderClan cats. Whatever penalty was chosen, Thunder-Clan would be the most affected. The atmosphere in the clearing crackled with tension. It felt strange to have the leaders standing among the other cats, and the warriors who had been associated with the Dark Forest bristled as if they were ready to defend themselves with tooth and claw.

Mistystar raised her head. "As you know, Beetlewhisker and Hollowflight were killed in the battle, so they cannot answer for anything they have done. Icewing knows her loyalty was tested by the Dark Forest, and that she failed. But she has learned from this and I do not doubt her now. She has always been a good warrior. I would like to give her the chance to be one again."

"The same goes for Breezepelt," Onestar declared. "We suffered great losses during the battle. Why should I want to punish one of my few remaining warriors? We need Breeze-pelt on patrol, not wasted because of something that has finished."

"But they broke the warrior code!" Blackstar protested. He looked at Tigerheart and Ratscar, and his eyes were full of sorrow. "They betrayed the Clan, their leader, and them-selves. How can this go unpunished?"

Onestar let his gaze rest on the ThunderClan cats. "I sup-pose we have to face the fact that some of our Clanmates were recruited by the Dark Forest, for whatever reason. Some Clans more than others," he added meaningfully.

Dovewing felt her pelt burn with indignation. Bramblestar

opened his mouth to speak but Mistystar interrupted him. "There must be a way to move forward without further weakening our Clans," she meowed. "None of us can spare more warriors, so exile is not an option."

Dovewing blinked. *Exile!* She hadn't even thought that would be a possibility. She shifted closer to Ivypool. "You have to tell them what happened," she whispered in her sister's ear. "How Hawkfrost recruited you. You weren't being disloyal to your Clan! They have to understand that!"

Bramblestar overheard and nodded. "Go on, Ivypool. Please."

The gray-and-white warrior looked daunted as she moved into the center of the clearing, but when she spoke her voice was steady. "I think it would help to understand why some of us joined the Dark Forest," she began. Onestar and Blackstar bristled but Ivypool kept talking. "It wasn't because we hated our Clanmates, or didn't believe in the warrior code. We thought we were learning more skills that would help the Clans. Cats from the Dark Forest sought us out in our dreams and . . . and used our most personal reasons for offering a different way to train." She glanced at Dovewing, who blinked. *Was I one of those reasons?* she wondered in alarm. Around her, Birchfall and the others were nodding.

"Hawkfrost approached me," Ivypool went on. "He made me believe that the best thing I could do for ThunderClan would be to train with Dark Forest warriors. I would be braver, better at fighting, more loyal to my Clanmates. He made me feel . . . important." She paused for a moment, then continued. "I overheard Hawkfrost and Tigerstar planning to attack the Clans. I told my Clanmates, and became a spy, reporting everything I learned about the Dark Forest. I knew other cats from the Clans were being trained, but to avoid suspicion I didn't say anything to them." She looked over her shoulder at her father. "Only when the battle began did I tell them the truth, and they instantly followed me back to our Clanmates to fight alongside them. They never intended to be disloyal. Like me, they thought they were being given a chance to be better warriors."

Breezepelt was looking smug and Dovewing felt an urge to rake his ears. She was sure he hadn't wanted to be a better WindClan warrior. He had wanted power and strength, that was all. Birchfall leaned toward Dovewing as if he could read her thoughts. "If one of us is to be forgiven, all must be forgiven," he mewed.

Blackstar heaved himself to his paws. "You have spoken well," he rasped. "It's Ivypool, isn't it?" He peered at her, his eyes cloudy. "But I saw my own Clanmates attack each other. How was that being loyal, or a better warrior?"

"We were promised a different way to serve our Clan," Ivypool insisted.

"I believe you," Mistystar meowed. "Thank you, Ivypool."

Onestar traced his forepaw in the dust. "I don't need to know why Breezepelt made his choices. I only need to trust him from now on. Which I do."

Blackstar shook his great white head. "I don't know if I can agree with this." He avoided looking at Tigerheart and

Ratscar, who were staring at him in dismay. Dovewing felt a pang of alarm. What would happen to Tigerheart? She knew he was loyal to ShadowClan.

"It seems we all feel differently about these cats," Blackstar went on. He sounded confused, as if he couldn't understand why the alliance between the four Clans had melted away.

"With good reason," Bramblestar meowed. He looked at Breezepelt. "There is at least one warrior here who attacked ThunderClan cats alongside the Dark Forest warriors. I cannot see that as anything but a betrayal of the warrior code."

"Breezepelt never turned against his own Clanmates," Onestar mewed. "That is the essence of the warrior code, surely? And he is my warrior, so it is up to me what happens to him."

Mistystar nodded. "I agree that we should each be responsible for our own Clanmates. We know our warriors best, after all."

Blackstar flattened his ears. "But we must follow a single course of action! Otherwise how will it be fair?"

"ShadowClan does not get to decide anything on behalf of WindClan!" Onestar spat.

"The Clans got along better when we were united against the Dark Forest," murmured Thornclaw. "Peace has brought out the old quarrels."

Mothwing walked out from behind Mistystar and stood in the center of the cats with starlight gleaming on her pelt. "I suggest that each of these cats swears a new oath of loyalty to the warrior code," she meowed. "They walked a different path for a while, but now they must return to the way things were. They do not need to be punished—none of our Clans should suffer more pain—but we deserve to have some clear sign that we can trust them again."

Dovewing breathed out in relief. It seemed the obvious solution, and from the nods of the Clan leaders, it looked as if they agreed. Ratscar flicked his patchy brown tail. "This oath . . . do we have to swear it now? In front of cats who have nothing to do with us?"

"No," Bramblestar meowed. "I think this is a matter for each Clan to deal with on its own. What do you think, Blackstar?" he added.

The old cat waited for a moment before replying. "I will see that it is done as soon as we return to our camp," he mewed.

Onestar dipped his head. "As will I."

Dovewing felt another flash of anger toward Breezepelt. She had seen his furious attacks on her Clanmates. There was nothing noble about him! He didn't deserve forgiveness from anyone. *At least my father and Ivypool will be accepted back into ThunderClan now,* she thought. *We have too much to do repairing the camp and building up our strength before leaf-bare to worry about what went on before the Great Battle.*

The cats began to file out of the clearing. Tigerheart drew level with Dovewing and caught her eye, a swarm of questions in his gaze. Dovewing turned her head away. He was part of the past, just like the battle with the Dark Forest.

CHAPTER 5

✤

"Let all cats old enough to catch their own prey gather together!"

Bramblestar's words were still echoing around the cliffs when cats started appearing from half-built dens and thickets of bramble. It was too early even for the dawn patrols to have gone out; the moon was still visible against the pale gray sun. Dovewing looked up at the dark tabby cat standing on Highledge and wondered how it felt to summon the Clan as their leader. If Bramblestar was daunted by his new position, he showed no sign.

When all the cats were standing in the clearing, yawning and ruffled with sleep, Bramblestar walked halfway down the tumble of rocks. "It has been decided by the leaders of all four Clans that any cat who fought on the side of the Dark Forest in the Great Battle must swear a new oath of loyalty to the warrior code." A murmur rippled through the Clan. Bramblestar raised his tail for silence. "After this, the past will be forgotten in favor of looking toward our future. This Clan must be united if we are to survive our losses, and the leafbare that lies ahead. Is that understood?" He gazed down at the cats, and Dovewing noticed a few of them flattening their ears, including Dustpelt and Berrynose.

"You are asking us to forgive a great deal," Dustpelt meowed, and there were nods around him.

"No ThunderClan cat finished the battle fighting for the Dark Forest," Bramblestar pointed out. "When they learned the truth about their new allies, they showed nothing but loyalty to the Clans. There is little to forgive, in my opinion."

Dustpelt didn't look satisfied, and Berrynose hissed something into Poppyfrost's ear. Dovewing looked at her father. Birchfall, Thornclaw, Mousewhisker, Blossomfall, and Ivypool were standing at one side of the cats, tails clamped down with tension.

"I hope this works," Bumblestripe muttered. Dovewing rested her tail-tip on his shoulder. *I hope so too.*

Bramblestar nodded to the five cats. "Come," he invited, walking down the rocks until he stood in the clearing. The warriors lined up in front of them. Bramblestar looked nervous for the first time, and Dovewing realized that nothing had been decided about the form this ceremony should take. How would Bramblestar know what to say?

"Warriors of ThunderClan," he began, "only you know the true reason you let yourself be persuaded to join the Dark Forest cats. That reason, whatever it was, no longer matters. The only thing of importance is that you are loyal to ThunderClan and to the warrior code, to the exclusion of everything else. Whatever might be promised to you," he added with a note of stone in his voice.

The five cats nodded. Bramblestar thought for a moment,

then continued. "Repeat after me: I am a true warrior of ThunderClan, loyal to my Clanmates and to the code from this moment forward until it is my time to join StarClan."

Birchfall started speaking first, then the others joined, a little clumsily and bristling with discomfort. Dovewing felt a stab of indignation that Ivypool had to swear along with the others. She had risked her life spying on the Dark Forest! What greater proof of her loyalty did Bramblestar need?

When the cats had stumbled to the end of the oath, Bramblestar swished his tail. "Let that be an end to the divisions within this Clan," he declared. "You all know what you have to do to make ThunderClan strong again. Carry on, and may StarClan light your path." He twitched his ears as a signal for the meeting to break up. Most cats headed back to their dens to wash and sort out patrols, but a few stayed clustered in a group, Berrynose and Dustpelt among them.

"Are we really supposed to forgive and forget?" Berrynose protested. "If they hadn't given away all our secrets, the Dark Forest might never have attacked!"

Dovewing couldn't believe that any of her Clanmates would think this was true, but Poppyfrost was nodding. "Those cats need to prove they can be trusted," she growled. She glanced around fearfully as if she thought Birchfall might be inviting Dark Forest cats into the camp at that very moment.

Dustpelt leaned forward and said something Dovewing couldn't hear. She curled her lip in anger. *My ears!* She felt a physical pain inside her head. *What is wrong with me?* She had to speak with Lionblaze and Jayfeather, find out if they were losing their powers too. She spotted Lionblaze walking toward her and opened her mouth to ask if she could speak with him alone. Then Cinderheart bounded across the clearing.

"Lionblaze! I told you to rest today! You can't go out on patrol until your claw heals."

Dovewing realized that Lionblaze was limping, favoring the paw that had been injured while digging. "It's fine," he growled. "Stop bugging me about it."

Cinderheart narrowed her eyes. "Don't take it out on me," she warned, flicking her tail. "You should see Jayfeather if it's infected."

"I don't have time now," Lionblaze grunted. "We have to hunt while the weather holds." He looked up at the sky, which was bulging with dark gray clouds, so low they almost touched the tops of the trees.

"I'll come with you," Dovewing offered. Perhaps this would give them a chance to talk.

"Well, you're not going without me," Cinderheart meowed. "Come on, let's tell Squirrelflight what we're doing."

She bounded across the clearing to where the deputy was standing. Lionblaze looked at Dovewing. "Are you okay?"

"No, I . . ."

Dovewing broke off as Ivypool emerged from the warriors' den. "Hey! Are you going on patrol? Can I come?" She trotted over, her fur fluffed out. "Anything to warm up! This wind is bitter."

"Sure," mewed Lionblaze. Cinderheart returned and they headed out of the camp, Lionblaze in the lead. Dovewing watched him stumble over a loose bramble and wince. She'd never seen him with a lasting injury like this.

They reached a clump of bracken above the hollow and separated to track prey. Dovewing picked up the faint scent of a mouse and crept along the trail, nose to the ground, letting the ferns brush over her spine. She had rounded an ash tree and was just casting around for fresh odor when there was a flurry of paws behind her and Ivypool lunged past, landing on a squirrel.

The gray-and-white she-cat delivered a killing bite and sat up, wiping blood from her whiskers.

"Good catch!" Dovewing mewed.

Ivypool put her head on one side. "I can't believe you didn't hear the squirrel coming down the tree," she purred. "It almost landed on your head! Have you got moss in your ears?"

Dovewing felt hot with embarrassment. "I . . . I was following a mouse trail."

Her sister stood up and started scraping leaf mulch over her prey. "Better go and catch it then!" she meowed, but there was a note of tension in her voice that Dovewing didn't miss. *Has Ivypool realized that I'm losing my powers?*

She marched into the bracken, feeling a sense of relief as the fronds closed up behind her. She soon picked up the scent of mouse again and caught the little creature as it nibbled on a seed pod. "Thank you, StarClan, for bringing food to us," she murmured over the tiny brown body.

She hunted around for another trace of prey but hadn't found anything by the time Lionblaze called them back to the path. A pigeon lay at his paws and Cinderheart stood beside him with a pair of baby voles in her mouth. Dovewing felt embarrassed by her puny contribution, especially when Ivypool puffed her way out of the bracken, dragging the squirrel.

Lionblaze nodded approvingly. "If the weather's turning colder, we need all the fresh-kill we can get," he meowed. "Good work, everyone."

They headed back to the camp. Lionblaze fell behind even though the muscles on his shoulders were tense with the effort of not limping. Dovewing slowed to keep level with him. When Cinderheart and Ivypool had vanished around a corner, she put down her mouse and turned to face the golden tabby.

"Lionblaze, I need to talk to you."

Reluctantly, he put down his pigeon and waited.

Dovewing took a deep breath. "Do you think we're losing our powers?" Ignoring the flash of anger in his eyes, she kept going. "I can't hear or see like I used to. You've been injured by a tree root, for StarClan's sake! And Jayfeather seems really scared of something. Could he be losing the power to walk in other cats' dreams?"

Lionblaze drew one massive paw over the pale-feathered breast of the dead pigeon. "The Great Battle took a lot out of all of us," he meowed. "None of us know how long it will take to recover."

"But this isn't a battle wound!" Dovewing protested. "This is something else, something that has changed inside me! I can't describe it exactly, but I know I'm different."

Lionblaze kept his gaze fixed on the bird at his feet. "Talk to Jayfeather if you're worried. He knows more about this than we do. We're part of a prophecy, remember? I don't see how that could change."

Dovewing wanted to challenge him but he picked up the pigeon, making it clear their conversation was over. Lurching awkwardly on his infected paw, he trotted along the path and vanished into the bracken. Dovewing scooped up her mouse and followed, letting her tail trail miserably in the dirt.

"Jayfeather!" Dovewing shivered as a cold gust of wind whipped up her fur at the foot of the cliff. She moved closer to the bramble fronds as if they offered some shelter. "Jayfeather, I have to talk to you!"

"Really? Right now?" came the impatient reply.

Dovewing braced herself. "Yes, now."

"You'd better come in then. But don't touch anything!"

She pushed through the brambles and stopped, waiting for her eyes to adjust to the dim light inside the cave. The sandy floor was covered with piles of herbs, some fresh and green-smelling, others wizened and dried into tiny black curls. Jayfeather was crouched beside Foxleap, who lay on his side in a moss-lined nest, his eyes closed. The medicine cat was peeling a dressing of leaves away from the warrior's belly.

Dovewing took a step back. The stench that came from the wound was overpowering. "Great StarClan!" she whispered.

"Exactly," Jayfeather commented dryly. Without moving his head, he reached out with one paw and expertly scooped up a wad of recently chewed leaves. "What do you want?" he muttered as he began to press the leaves against the open pus-filled wound.

Dovewing tried not to gag. "Can Foxleap feel that?" she asked.

"StarClan be thanked, no," Jayfeather replied. "I keep him dosed with poppy seeds to make him sleep, and he rarely stirs. I want him to stay like this until the wound starts to heal. Is something wrong, Dovewing? As you can see, I'm quite busy. Leafpool's out collecting herbs, since Brightheart is taking care of Sorreltail's kits in the nursery, and Briarlight has gone into the forest with Daisy to stretch her legs."

Dovewing moved closer. "I think something has happened to me since the Great Battle," she began. "My senses have changed. I mean, they're gone. I can see and hear like other cats, but that's all. And Lionblaze has injured his paw, which never used to happen. So I wanted to know if you had noticed anything different about your powers."

Jayfeather froze, his paws motionless on Foxleap's injury. Then his ears twitched. "Dovewing, this can wait. Let me do my duty to Foxleap, and to the other cats that need me to treat them. You're not in pain, are you?"

Dovewing shook her head, until she remembered that Jayfeather couldn't see her. "No," she meowed.

"Then I don't see how I can help you. I have to concentrate on my responsibilities to this Clan." His voice rose and one of his front paws curled up in anger. "Foxleap cannot die! We have lost too many cats already! Why does StarClan keep punishing us like this?"

Dovewing stared at the medicine cat in shock. "You can't say that! We defeated the Dark Forest cats! We won the battle!"

"Really?" snarled Jayfeather. "It doesn't feel that way to me. All I've done is watch my Clanmates die because there was nothing I could do to help them."

"You can't bring cats back to life," Dovewing whispered.

"Then what is the use of having any power at all?" Jayfeather hissed. He bent closer to Foxleap's belly, running his paw over the dressing. "Go away, Dovewing. Talk to me when I'm not trying to save a warrior's life. Right now, there is nothing more important than that."

Dovewing staggered out of the cave and stood at the edge of the clearing, letting the wind cool her scorched pelt. Something was terribly wrong with Jayfeather, that was for sure. Was it simply that the Clan had lost so many cats? Or did he know something about their powers?

"Dovewing?" called a voice from the elder thicket. It was Purdy, peering through rheumy eyes. Now that the nursery had been repaired, Daisy and Brightheart had taken the kits out of the elders' den. "I think I've got a tick on my back, an' I can't reach it," the old tom grumbled.

"Okay, I'll take a look," Dovewing mewed. With so few apprentices in the camp, the warriors were sharing duties among themselves. Dovewing knew it was Berrynose's turn to deal with Purdy but he was out on patrol, and since she was here, she wasn't going to refuse to help. She followed the tom into the den and waited for him to settle stiffly in his nest.

"Oh, that chill's got into my bones," he griped as he folded his legs under him.

"Do you want me to find some feathers for your nest?" Dovewing offered.

Purdy blinked. "Only if you've got time. I know you're all stretched, with so many cats still recoverin'."

Dovewing ran her paw over his bony spine, searching for the tick. "Most of us are okay now. Only Foxleap is still in danger." Purdy grunted as she rubbed against the tick. "Found it!" she declared. "I'll put some mouse bile on that and it'll be gone in a flash." She started to leave but Purdy beckoned her back with his chin.

"That can wait a while," he rasped. "Talk to me first. It's so empty in here without Mousefur." He stared at the abandoned nest, cold and dusty but still imprinted with the shape of Mousefur's body. "I miss her so much, you know," he murmured. "She was a grouchy old fox at times, but she had the best heart. At least she died protectin' her Clan. It's what she would have wanted."

"It is," Dovewing agreed.

"So why does everyone still look so miserable?" Purdy snorted, propping himself up on his front legs. "I go outside an' it's like we're still buryin' our Clanmates. Have they forgot we drove those blighters out? No Dark Forest cats around here, are there?"

Dovewing wasn't sure what to say. "I . . . think we're all

aware of what has been lost," she stammered.

"And what about what we won?" the old cat demanded. "Did Mousefur, did any of 'em, die for nothing? It's an insult to their memory, that's what it is, to act like we lost everything." He slumped back into his nest with a cough. "Sorry, young 'un. I was forgettin' myself."

"No, it's okay, Purdy," Dovewing mewed. She reached out her paw and smoothed the tom's untidy black pelt. "You're right. We did win, and we should honor our fallen Clanmates by knowing they didn't die in vain. Now, let me fetch that mouse bile for you."

She stood up and squeezed out of the den. Sharp drops of rain splashed onto her pelt, and she ducked her head as she ran back to Jayfeather's den. She hoped he wouldn't mind if she helped herself to some bile. As she neared the opening to the cave, a terrible moaning sound stopped her in her tracks.

"Foxleap, no! Not now! I've done everything I could! Oh StarClan, why can't you let me help these cats?"

Dovewing nearly retched at the raw grief in Jayfeather's voice. Foxleap must have died—and Jayfeather was left in agony. What about Dustpelt? First his mate, now his son, lost to the Dark Forest. How would he ever recover? Dovewing rocked on her paws as Leafpool brushed past her, shedding leaves from her jaws.

"Jayfeather! What's wrong?" The she-cat pushed through the brambles and Dovewing heard a wail. "Oh no! Foxleap!"

"StarClan wanted him more than we did," Jayfeather growled. Leafpool began to murmur comforting words to him and Dovewing turned away, reeling with despair. She almost bumped into Graystripe, who was heading to the fresh-kill pile, his fur blown the wrong way by the wind.

When the big warrior looked down at her in surprise, Dovewing spat, "The Dark Forest is not finished with us. Foxleap is dead!"

CHAPTER 6

"Hargh! Hargh-argh! Sorry," Sandstorm *spluttered before* another bout of coughing racked her body. *"Hargh-argh-argh!"*

Bumblestripe stirred beside Dovewing. "I feel sorry for her, but none of us are getting any sleep," he murmured, his breath warm on her neck. "Maybe she should see Jayfeather."

"I'm sure she's thought of that," Dovewing muttered back. Her eyes were gritty from lack of sleep and she wished Sandstorm would be quiet too, but she felt nothing but sympathy for the poor she-cat, who had kept them awake for three nights in a row now.

A dark shape brushed past Dovewing's muzzle. "Have some soaked moss, Sandstorm," urged Poppyfrost. There was a soft squelching sound as she placed it beside the she-cat's nest. "That might help."

"Thanks," Sandstorm croaked. "I'm so sorry, everyone." Dovewing listened to her sucking on the moss, then a merciful silence descended on the den and she drifted into sleep.

It seemed as if Dovewing had only closed her eyes for a moment before Squirrelflight was standing over her, prodding her with a paw. "Come on, sleepy hedgehog! I want you to lead the dawn border patrol."

Dovewing stumbled groggily to her paws and followed the deputy out into the frost-sharp morning. Almost a whole moon had passed since the Great Battle and leaf-bare had fallen over the forest like a pelt of ice. Dovewing shivered as her breath made clouds in the air.

Toadstep joined her, squinting in the early light. "I can't remember the last time I got a full night's sleep," he muttered. "I'm going to take Sandstorm to Jayfeather myself if she doesn't see him today."

Dovewing didn't have the energy to argue. After listening to Squirrelflight's instructions, she led Toadstep, Hazeltail, and Rosepetal out of the newly rebuilt entrance and down to the lakeside border with WindClan. The moor was empty and quiet, draped with mist, and the patrol returned to the camp without spotting any trace of rival warriors. The clearing was full of cats sharing prey, stretching cold limbs, and talking quietly. Sandstorm stood in a corner, her back hunched in another coughing fit.

"Bramblestar!" Berrynose called to the Clan leader. "Can you ask Sandstorm to sleep in the elders' den tonight? She can't keep us awake every night, or we'll never be able to keep up with the patrols."

Dovewing noticed Purdy's ears perk up.

Bramblestar looked questioningly at Sandstorm. "What do you think? Would that give you a better chance to recover, if you're not worried about waking the other warriors? I know we're planning to build a second warriors' den to give you all more room, but that won't be finished for another quarter moon."

There was a flash of defiance in Sandstorm's green eyes. "It's just a touch of whitecough!" she croaked. "Are you saying that I'm only fit to be an elder now? I still have moons in me to serve my Clanmates!"

There was a harsh note of fear beneath her words that gave Dovewing a stab of empathy. *I know how she feels. Whatever's wrong with my senses, it's making me feel useless as well!* She hadn't made a decent catch for the fresh-kill pile in days, and her ears ached from straining over the boundaries when she was on border patrol. A tiny voice in her mind whispered, *What if your powers never come back?*, but Dovewing pushed it away. *How can I serve my Clan if I'm deaf and blind?*

Bramblestar padded over to the ginger she-cat and pressed his muzzle against her shoulder. "No cat is asking you to retire," he assured her. "I just want you to be as fit as possible for leaf-bare. And if you're keeping the other cats awake, you need to think about them as well."

Sandstorm lifted her head. "I'll ask the medicine cats for some honey." She sniffed. "I'll be fine. And why don't I sleep in the apprentices' den, since that's empty? That way I won't disturb anyone."

Purdy's shoulders slumped and Dovewing wondered if she should offer to sleep in Mousefur's old nest beside him. He must be feeling cold on his own, now that the frost had taken hold. Before she could say anything, Berrynose stepped forward.

"The warriors' den is kind of cramped," he mewed to Bramblestar. "Poppyfrost and I would be happy to sleep in with Purdy, if he'll have us."

The old tabby cat's eyes lit up. "Glad to give you room," he meowed. "I'd better go and sort out some nests." He bustled off, his tail straight up.

"That was kind of Berrynose and Poppyfrost," Dovewing murmured to Ivypool, who was standing beside her.

Her sister narrowed her eyes. "Do you think so? Or are they just desperate to get away from those ferocious Dark Forest cats who sleep too close to them?"

Dovewing stared at her in shock. "But it's been almost a whole moon since you swore your new oath! Surely you've been forgiven by now?"

"Not by some cats," Ivypool growled. "Haven't you seen how Dustpelt would rather wait until the fresh-kill pile has been stripped of all the best prey, rather than go up at the same time as one of us?" She padded away, her tail leaving a tiny line in the frostbitten grass.

"We'll sleep in the elders' den too," piped up Cherrypaw, nodding to her brother, Molepaw.

That makes sense, since Poppyfrost and Berrynose are their mother and father, Dovewing thought. But then she saw Molepaw glare at Birchfall, and her belly flipped over. Those cats had done nothing but serve their Clan loyally since the Great Battle. How could there be anything left to forget?

"That's fine," meowed Squirrelflight to the young cats. "I'll join Sandstorm in the apprentices' den, and that way there will be more room for the other warriors while the new den is being built." When Sandstorm started to protest, Squirrelflight blinked affectionately at her mother. "I'll be there whether you like it or not," she purred. "It's too cold for you to sleep alone."

There was a flurry of activity as the cats scattered to prepare new nests. Dovewing stayed where she was, as if her paws had frozen to the grass. Her ears were buzzing again and shadows clustered at the edges of her mind, making her heart beat faster. Dividing the warriors into separate dens felt like a terrible omen; the Clan was splitting apart, in spite of everything they had survived together. Had the Great Battle been forgotten already? Or were her Clanmates determined only to remember whose loyalty had been questioned, without recalling the courage every cat showed to drive out the Dark Forest attackers?

"Dovewing? Are you all right?" Whitewing was peering at her with a concerned look in her eyes.

Dovewing shook herself, sending drops of mist flying from her pelt. "I'm fine."

"Why don't you help me fetch some moss?" Whitewing suggested. "It feels like ages since I spent any time with you!"

They squeezed through the new barrier of thorns, which seemed denser and pricklier than before, and trotted down the slope toward the lake. Their route to the best moss took them past the place where the dead cats had been buried and Dovewing slowed down to look at the peaceful mounds of soil, each one silvered with a thin coating of ice. "Can you see what is happening to us?" she whispered. "Do you feel as if you died for nothing?"

"Oh little one, you don't really think that, do you?" mewed Whitewing.

Dovewing jumped; she hadn't heard her mother come up. *Of course I didn't hear! I can't hear* anything! She took a deep breath. "It feels as if everything has gotten worse since the Great Battle," she confessed. "The warriors who were involved with the Dark Forest are being treated worse than rogues, and no one seems to remember that the cats lying here gave their lives so that we could win the battle." She couldn't bring herself to talk about her senses; that was something she had to deal with alone.

Whitewing rested her tail on Dovewing's spine. "All battles leave deep wounds, whether you can see them or not. And wounds take time to heal. You know that, Dovewing. Don't give up hope." She turned and headed down toward the lake, which was shining gray and still through the trunks.

Dovewing watched her walk away. She thought of Foxleap, dying from infection in the medicine den. *But some wounds never heal, whatever you do.*

It was the night of the Gathering. A huge white moon hung above the hollow, turning the cats to silver and casting sharp-edged shadows across the ground. This would be the first Gathering since the Great Battle, the first chance to see how the Clans they had fought alongside were faring, and yet the mood among the ThunderClan cats was somber, even reluctant. Berrynose was muttering to Toadstep, close enough for Dovewing to hear.

"I can't believe Bramblestar wants to take Blossomfall and Thornclaw with us. Does he want to draw attention to the traitors in our own Clan?"

Toadstep flicked his thick black-and-white tail. "The other Clans managed to kill most of their traitors," he hissed back. "Maybe we should have done the same!"

Dovewing bounded forward. "And maybe you should realize that your Clanmates did nothing wrong when it came to fighting our enemies!" she spat.

"Dovewing! Stop! What's going on?" Squirrelflight trotted over, her fur fluffed up in alarm.

Dovewing twitched her ears, reluctant to let Toadstep and Berrynose think she was about to go running to the deputy with her complaint.

"Just a difference of opinion," Berrynose meowed. He glanced at Dovewing. "Some cats seem to believe we aren't allowed to think for ourselves."

Squirrelflight narrowed her eyes. "See that full moon up there? This is the night of the truce—and that goes for Clanmates as well as the other Clans. Come on, or we'll be late." She trotted to the entrance where Bramblestar was waiting with the rest of the Gathering patrol.

Dovewing glared at Berrynose and Toadstep, then followed the deputy. Blossomfall was waiting for her, looking troubled. "I saw what happened," the tortoiseshell-and-white warrior mewed. "Don't try to fight this battle for us. It will take time to prove our loyalty, that's all."

"It shouldn't be a battle!" Dovewing growled. "You swore the oath, and you did nothing to harm us during the Great Battle!"

"The warrior code means everything," Blossomfall reminded her. "And that's just as it should be."

They joined the other cats squeezing through the new barrier of thorns, wincing as tufts of fur got left behind on the prickles. "If this barrier doesn't soften up soon, we're all going to be bald!" muttered Graystripe.

As the cats headed down through the trees toward the shore, Dovewing trotted to catch up with Bumblestripe. They'd basked together in an unexpected burst of sunshine earlier that day, and she was feeling warm and affectionate toward him. "Wait for me!" she puffed.

The big gray-and-black tom paused and looked back at her. "Come on, little legs!" he teased.

They reached the shore with the others and turned along the stony beach. The pebbles gleamed in the moonlight, and tiny waves lapped beside them. Dovewing cast her hearing out the way she used to on these nights, listening for the preparations for departure in each of the other Clans. Were they feeling apprehensive about this Gathering, too? But her ears were full of the sound of paws crunching over stones and water washing on the shore.

Dovewing frowned and concentrated harder. *I must be able to hear something! My senses have had time to recover from the battle! I have to make Lionblaze and Jayfeather talk to me about their powers. What if we're all losing them?* Suddenly her paw was caught underneath a branch and she lurched forward. She would have fallen flat on her face if Bumblestripe hadn't shoved his shoulder underneath her to boost her back onto her feet.

"Are you okay?" he asked.

"Fine," Dovewing snapped. "I didn't see that branch in the shadows, that's all." She noticed his ears flatten with hurt and felt a stab of guilt. Even if she couldn't tell him what was going on, he didn't deserve to be treated unkindly. "Thanks for catching me!" she purred. "I'd have looked dumber than a sheep if I'd landed on my muzzle!"

"I'll always be here to catch you," Bumblestripe murmured. He nuzzled the back of her head before stepping away and they walked on in silence, close enough for their fur to brush together.

CHAPTER 7

The first thing Dovewing noticed when she reached the clearing on the island was that almost all the former Dark Forest cats were there. She wondered if it was because each leader wanted to prove that their Clan was united and loyal once more. She also thought that the other Clans seemed less hostile toward their traitorous Clanmates, but then, ThunderClan had so many more that had survived the battle. Perhaps it was easier to forgive one cat rather than several.

After spotting Breezepelt and Ratscar, Dovewing found herself searching for a familiar dark tabby pelt among the ShadowClan cats. As she watched, the warriors shifted to make room for Blackstar, who was heading for the leaders' tree, revealing Tigerheart deep in conversation with Shrewfoot. The pretty gray cat was gazing up at him as if he was telling her the greatest secret. Dovewing pushed down the pang of jealousy that twisted her belly. It was good that Tigerheart had been forgiven by his Clanmates. Any connection they had once shared was over forever. She had Bumblestripe now.

As if he had heard her thoughts, the gray-and-black tom

joined her. "Do you mind if we sit with Blossomfall?" he meowed. "I don't want her left on her own."

"Of course," Dovewing replied, feeling a rush of fondness for him. They padded over to fill the gap left beside Blossomfall and Thornclaw. Dovewing ended up next to Toadstep, and she tried not to hiss at him when he curled his lip at her.

Mistystar spoke first, her gray fur tipped with silver in a beam of moonlight. "RiverClan is well and strong after a moon of hard work. All my warriors are united in making the Clan secure and full-fed for leaf-bare, and all the seasons to come. I am pleased to report that Petalfur is expecting kits with Mallownose." She paused to glance fondly at the gray-and-white queen, who preened. "A large pike was preying on the smaller fish on our side of the lake, but Lakeheart had the brilliant idea of placing stones in the shallow water to create an area the pike couldn't enter. Thanks to this, we have protected many of the smaller fish to stock our fresh-kill pile." She dipped her head. "May StarClan light your path, all of you."

As she sat back down on the branch, Blackstar rose unsteadily to his paws. His white pelt was so pale, he looked as if he was part of StarClan already. "ShadowClan is as strong as it ever was," he wheezed, so quietly the listening cats leaned forward to hear. "We have rebuilt our dens and secured our borders. Our fresh-kill pile is full and we do not fear the leaf-bare ahead." His wide eyes suggested otherwise, and Dovewing winced as he fought for breath. "We were briefly troubled by a fox on our topmost border but my brave warriors drove it out." He sat down abruptly, his flanks heaving.

Bramblestar spoke next, then Onestar. Their speeches were similarly short and vague, with little news beyond the restoration of dens and borders, and reports of well-stocked fresh-kill piles. None of the leaders mentioned the Great Battle or the recent alliance between the four Clans, as if history had never happened. Dovewing narrowed her eyes. *Will everything be forgotten so soon? What about the cats we lost? Shouldn't we honor their memory somehow, all of us together?*

But the leaders were jumping down from the tree—or in Blackstar's case, lowering himself gently to the ground—and the cats in the clearing were already standing up, eager to leave. There would be no lingering tonight, no sharing of tongues and gossip after the serious business was done. Onestar led his warriors away first, swiftly followed by Mistystar. Bramblestar summoned ThunderClan with a flick of his tail and Dovewing found herself pressed among her Clanmates as they trotted over the tree-bridge and jumped down onto the marshy shore.

"That was weird," Lionblaze commented when they were crunching along the pebbles below the moor. "Any cat would think the most exciting thing that happened in the last moon was RiverClan losing some fish to a pike!"

Beside him, Cinderheart looked thoughtful. "Perhaps that's the best way to recover, to return to the way things were before as quickly as we can. We won the Great Battle, so nothing needs to change."

Bumblestripe twitched his ears. "Really? Do you honestly

think the Great Battle didn't change anything? Sometimes I think it has changed everything."

Dovewing agreed with him. She watched him look sadly at his sister, walking a little way ahead with Thornclaw. Would ThunderClan be divided forever because of the Dark Forest?

The sound of coughing drifted through the trees as they climbed the slope to the hollow. Jayfeather trotted ahead, as sure-footed over the moss as if he could see. "Hazeltail, why are you still out here? You should have asked someone else to stand guard." He sniffed her closely and placed his paw on her side to check her heartbeat.

The gray she-cat looked exhausted and hunched. "I'm okay," she wheezed. "It's just a cough."

"And it's not being helped by this cold air," Jayfeather snorted. "Come on, you're spending the night in the medicine den." He started to usher her through the thorns. "Bramble-star, you'll have to put someone else on guard," he called over his shoulder.

Millie stepped forward. "I'll do it," she offered. "I don't feel tired, and there's no point waking another warrior for what's left of the night."

"Thanks, Millie." Bramblestar dipped his head toward her. He looked closely at the rest of the cats. "Is anyone else feeling ill? Better to start getting treated now rather than wait until you're really sick."

"Toadstep hasn't eaten much today," Poppyfrost meowed, shooting a worried glance at the black-and-white tom.

"I wasn't hungry, that's all," he muttered.

Bramblestar narrowed his eyes. "If you don't feel hungry tomorrow, see Jayfeather, please. Now, let's get to our nests. Patrols as usual first thing."

Dovewing waited her turn to wriggle through the barrier. She heard Brightheart hiss to Cloudtail, "Why didn't you tell Bramblestar you've got a sore throat?"

"I'll see Jayfeather if it gets worse, I promise," Cloudtail mewed as he ducked into the gap.

Dovewing felt a tremor of worry. First the Dark Forest seemed to have left divisions that would never heal, and now the whole Clan was getting sick! *Oh StarClan, help us!*

Blinking sleep from her eyes, Dovewing stumbled out of the warriors' den at sunrise to see Jayfeather leaping confidently down the rocks that led to Highledge. Her heart lurched.

"Is Bramblestar sick?" she called.

Jayfeather stopped beside her and shook his head. "No, he's fine. I was just letting him know that Hazeltail will be off duties for a while." As he spoke, Bramblestar emerged from his den and trotted down to the clearing, where he arched his back in a long stretch.

The sound of coughing came from the cave at the foot of the cliffs. Jayfeather looked grim. "I think Hazeltail has greencough. She has a fever, and I don't like the way her heart is racing."

There was a gasp behind Dovewing. She turned to see Millie trotting from the entrance, having finished her post on guard. "What about Briarlight? She can't stay in your den if there's a cat with greencough in there!" She ran over to the cave. "Briarlight! Come out at once!"

There was a pause, then Briarlight's dark brown face poked through the brambles. "What's the matter?" she asked sleepily.

"I don't want you in there if Hazeltail has greencough!" Millie ordered. "We'll have to find you somewhere else to sleep."

Briarlight dragged herself out of the den with her strong front legs. As always, Dovewing felt a spasm of sadness as she saw the she-cat's haunches trailing uselessly behind her. "I wouldn't mind being somewhere a bit quieter," Briarlight admitted as she crawled into the clearing. "Poor Hazeltail hasn't stopped coughing since she arrived!" She stopped to twist and bite an itchy spot on her spine. "Besides, I don't need to stay in the medicine den now, surely? I'm not ill!"

Leafpool emerged from the cave with a bundle of soiled moss in her jaws. She put it down and looked at Jayfeather. "Briarlight's right, you know," she meowed. "We don't need to watch over her at night anymore."

Briarlight twisted around to look at Bramblestar, who had finished stretching and was licking his chest fur. "Can I sleep in the warriors' den, Bramblestar? Please?"

The leader frowned. "I'm not sure there's room," he admitted. "It's still pretty crowded in there."

By now, other cats had woken and come into the clearing, where they were stretching and arching their backs, ready for the first patrols. Purdy had emerged from his den and was listening as he smoothed his sleep-ruffled fur. "She's welcome to join us in here," he called, nodding toward the elder thicket where there were sounds of Berrynose and his family stirring.

Briarlight's head drooped. It was obvious she wanted to join the warriors in their den.

"Why don't I join you, Purdy, then Briarlight can have my nest?" Dovewing offered.

Bumblestripe came up to her looking startled. "But I'd miss sleeping next to you!"

"It won't be for long," Dovewing told him. "Squirrelflight is planning to build a second den for the warriors, remember?"

"Thanks, Dovewing!" purred Briarlight. "Can I go see my new nest now?" When Dovewing nodded, Briarlight hauled herself to the warriors' den and disappeared inside, leaving a scuffed trail on the earth.

She reappeared a moment later looking serious. "It's the right size for me, but it needs fresh bedding," she commented. "Please can I have some pigeon feathers?"

Lionblaze dipped his head. "Why yes, leader. Anything else I can bring you? The finest fresh-kill perhaps? Soaked moss?" His tone was good-humored and teasing.

Blossomfall bristled. "Briarlight has to have the softest nest," she insisted. "She can't feel thorns sticking into her, remember? If she gets a wound, it could get infected before she noticed."

Lionblaze rested his tail-tip on Blossomfall's shoulder. "It's okay, I understand. Squirrelflight, is it okay if I take a patrol to fetch bedding for Briarlight? We can go hunting straight after."

The deputy nodded. "Take Dovewing, Ivypool, and Rosepetal with you. Make sure none of the moss is damp before you line her nest. And feel free to hunt a pigeon so we can use the feathers."

Dovewing purred. This was a duty she would enjoy!

Briarlight's blue eyes shone. "Thank you! I promise I'll be useful. I can wake everyone for dawn patrols, and check nests for thorns while you're out. There's no reason I can't have duties of my own now. I am a warrior, after all!"

CHAPTER 8

The warriors enjoyed only two nights of peace after the Gathering before Toadstep started coughing. This time Dovewing struggled to feel sympathetic. *He knew he was getting sick! He should have gone to Jayfeather!*

Hazeltail was still being nursed in the medicine cats' den, but as Toadstep didn't seem quite as sick, Jayfeather and Leafpool made a nest for him in the apprentices' den with Sandstorm. Squirrelflight announced that she was moving back to the warriors' den, saying that it made sense to let the coughing cats keep themselves awake. But Dovewing saw past the deputy's lighthearted comment to the strain in her eyes, and she wondered how many more cats would succumb to the illness.

Leafpool stood over the fresh-kill pile, making sure each cat was eating properly. When Dovewing selected a rather scrawny mouse, Leafpool reached out with one paw and stopped her. "I'll have that," she meowed. "You and Bumblestripe can share this squirrel."

Dovewing looked at the plump, fluffy creature. "It's huge!" she pointed out. "We could eat that for a whole moon!"

"Share it with Purdy, then," Leafpool urged.

Dovewing dragged the squirrel over to the tree stump, trying not to sneeze as the wispy tail tickled her nose. Purdy licked his lips. "What a feast!" he commented.

"Bumblestripe, join us!" Dovewing called. The big gray tom trotted over with Sandstorm at his heels.

"Is there enough for me?" she asked hoarsely. She looked tired, and Dovewing could count her ribs along her bony sides.

"O' course!" Purdy grunted with his mouth full. He shifted to let Sandstorm take a bite from the squirrel's juicy rump. Swallowing, the old tom watched as Toadstep shuffled into the apprentices' den, followed by Jayfeather with a clump of fresh bedding. "Putting you and Toadstep together reminds me o' the time Firestar took all them sick cats to the old Twoleg den," he remarked. "That were a brave thing he did, keeping the rest of us from getting ill."

Sandstorm's eyes clouded. "It cost him a life, too," she recalled.

"Do you think we'll do that again, if more cats start coughing?" Dovewing asked as she scraped a stringy piece of meat from between her teeth.

Sandstorm shook her head. "I doubt it. I don't want to infect anyone else, but it wouldn't help to be in that drafty old den. Better for all of us to be close to the medicine cats." She looked down at her paws as if she'd lost her appetite, and Dovewing felt bad for making her think back to that terrible time of sickness.

She glanced around the clearing. Although it was sunhigh,

the sky was thick with clouds and the breeze smelled of rain. The cats huddled over their food, their fur blown all ways so that they resembled pine cones more than sleek, well-groomed warriors. A flash of movement caught Dovewing's eye. Blossomfall was slipping through the barrier, not using the usual gap but forcing a new way at one side of the entrance. The fur pricked along Dovewing's spine. Was Blossomfall trying not to be seen? She battled briefly with a stir of suspicion and cast out her senses, trying to picture the she-cat on the other side of the barrier. She felt the familiar jolt of dismay as no pictures appeared in her mind, and nothing came to her above the sounds of her Clanmates eating. She shook the feeling away. *Where is Blossomfall going?* There was only one way to find out.

Nodding to the other cats around the squirrel, she stood up. "I'm just going to the dirtplace," she whispered to Bumblestripe to deter him from following her. She used the normal gap through the barrier, noting with relief that it was becoming less prickly. Outside the hollow, the trees clashed in the rising wind, and even though most of the leaves had fallen into heaps on the ground, little daylight seeped down to the forest floor. Dovewing trotted through the shadows, following Blossomfall's scent trail on the leaf mulch. Her heart was pounding and she kept her ears flattened, listening for sounds of danger. The buzzing noise had stopped but her senses still felt dull and heavy, and the half-lit forest seemed far more daunting and secretive than it ever had before.

Suddenly there was a rapid crackle behind her and

Blossomfall pounced on Dovewing's haunches, knocking her over. Dovewing scrambled to her paws and spun around. "What did you do that for?" she cried.

"You were following me, weren't you?" Blossomfall challenged. "Why would you do that? Don't you trust me?" Her fur was fluffed up and her voice was harsh with anger.

Dovewing looked down at her paws, flushed with shame. "I . . . I was just wondering where you were going."

Blossomfall flicked her tail. "You may as well come with me, since you clearly think I'm up to no good." She turned and bounded through the trees.

Dovewing raced to catch up, feeling branches slap her face as they hurtled through the undergrowth. They emerged into a burst of daylight on the old thunderpath. Blossomfall didn't slow as she swerved and headed along the pale stone to the tumbledown Twoleg den. To Dovewing's surprise, she skidded to a halt beside the ivy-covered den and vanished along its side. Dovewing paused. *Is she meeting a Dark Forest cat?* She thrust the thought away. Blossomfall had done nothing to make any cat question her loyalty since the Great Battle! Dovewing trotted after her Clanmate and found her bent over the dark brown soil behind the abandoned den. She was poking at some shriveled plants with one paw.

"I'm looking for catmint," the she-cat hissed through gritted teeth. "Satisfied? I know Jayfeather and Leafpool grew some here, and I wanted to see if there was any left. Our Clanmates are getting sick, and we have to find a way to make them better before we have to dig any more burial holes!" Her voice rose in despair and Dovewing felt a surge of sympathy, and guilt for doubting her.

"I'll help you," she mewed, her voice cracking with emotion. She pressed against Blossomfall's flank in silent apology, then began picking over the loose, damp earth. To her relief, she uncovered a few tiny green stalks still bearing leaves. "Do you think these will help?" she asked Blossomfall.

The warrior nodded. "Bite them off carefully," she instructed. "Leave the roots so they can keep growing."

With a small harvest of stems, they headed back to the camp. "I'm sorry," Dovewing meowed around her mouthful. "I shouldn't have doubted you."

Blossomfall stopped and put down her little burden. "I'd probably have done the same," she admitted. "Joining the Dark Forest was the biggest mistake I could have made. I . . . I'm not sure I can forgive myself."

Dovewing leaned over and pressed her muzzle against Blossomfall's shoulder. "You have to," she murmured. "For all our sakes. We have to move on from what happened, and find new ways to be strong." Her words fell like stones into the cold air. *Does that include me learning to live without my senses?* she wondered. *Just like Blossomfall, I feel as if I can't forgive myself if I am losing them. How will I serve my Clan now?*

CHAPTER 9

❧

Dovewing paused to catch her breath before dragging her prey—a female blackbird, her brown feathers stained with blood after a rather messy catch—through the barrier of thorns. A quarter moon had passed since she and Blossomfall searched for catmint, and more cats had fallen ill. Two sunrises ago, Littlecloud had visited the camp to ask if Jayfeather and Leafpool could spare any catmint for sick ShadowClan cats, so it was clear the sickness had spread beyond ThunderClan's territory. Graystripe appeared behind Dovewing carrying a vole.

"Are you okay, Dovewing?" he asked, laying the vole at his feet.

"Fine," Dovewing meowed. She picked up the blackbird and started to push through the gap in the thorns. She emerged to see Rosepetal placing her catch, a young rabbit, on the fresh-kill pile. Bramblestar padded over to watch the hunting patrol return.

"Well done," he purred. "I know it's hard to keep the fresh-kill pile stocked when there are fewer warriors able to hunt, but we have to do everything we can to feed the Clan. If we're hungry, we're more likely to get sick."

Dovewing looked anxiously at the leader's bony haunches and the hollows above his eyes. She doubted that Bramblestar was taking his fair share from the pile, letting his Clanmates eat the best of the fresh-kill instead. Brightheart was the last to emerge from the thorns, stumbling over a thrush that hung from her jaws. She had left her kits in Daisy's care in order to help with hunting patrols, even though she was exhausted and thin from feeding Sorreltail's kits as well as her own.

She was followed closely by Leafpool, Berrynose, and Poppyfrost, who each carried a bundle of tightly wrapped leaves. Jayfeather came to meet them in the center of the clearing, and Briarlight dragged herself over to help unroll the parcels.

"Did you find any catmint?" Jayfeather asked, his voice taut with worry.

Berrynose shook his head. "We tried all the places you suggested," he meowed. "There was nothing but dead stalks. Sorry."

Jayfeather twitched his ears. "It's not your fault."

"Leafpool said this might help, though," mewed Poppyfrost, nudging her bundle toward Jayfeather so he could sniff it.

"It's fennel," Leafpool explained. "I know we usually use it to treat vomiting, but I've seen it help cats who are having trouble breathing."

Jayfeather nodded. "Good idea. Hawkweed could be helpful too, though I don't know if any grows in our territory."

"I'll take a look tomorrow," Leafpool promised. "I can think of one or two places it might be."

Dovewing felt a rush of pride in her Clan's medicine cats. Was there any plant whose use they didn't know? With their skill, surely ThunderClan would win this battle, too?

Suddenly there was a burst of squeaking from outside the nursery. "Help! Help!" piped Amberkit. "The Dark Forest is coming to get me!"

Dovewing spun around, her fur bristling. She relaxed when she saw Molepaw creeping up on the tiny kit, his front paws extended with claws safely sheathed. Dewkit and Snowkit raced up to join their littermate. "Stay back, traitor!" hissed Snowkit, fluffing up his white pelt. "You say you're a ThunderClan cat now, but we know the truth! You just want to kill us!"

Molepaw arched his back. "Aha! It seems you do not trust me, even though I swore an oath! Well, you're right! I am your most dangerous enemy!" He pounced toward the kits, his tail lashing.

Dovewing bounded over and stood in front of the brown-and-cream apprentice. "What are you doing?" she demanded.

Molepaw blinked up at her. "Playing," he answered innocently.

Dovewing hissed. "You know full well that this is more than a game. Why are you making these kits frightened of the Dark Forest? That battle has been won."

The apprentice's gaze slid sideways to rest on Thornclaw and Birchfall, who were sharing tongues by the tree stump. "Not entirely," he muttered.

"Hey!" Amberkit wailed. "Why did you stop our game,

Dovewing? We were having fun!"

Daisy bustled out of the nursery. "What's going on? Dovewing, is there a problem? I wanted these kits to stretch their legs and get some fresh air."

Dovewing flicked the tip of her tail. "I don't think Molepaw has chosen the best game," she mewed.

The cream-furred queen narrowed her eyes. "All kits play at fighting," she mewed. "No one ever gets hurt. Leave them be, Dovewing. I'm sure you have more than enough to do." She whisked back into the nursery.

Molepaw glared at Dovewing. "You heard her. Stop sticking your muzzle where it's not wanted."

"You know what you're doing, Molepaw," Dovewing growled. "Perhaps you should think about whether it's helping the Clan." She turned away, still bristling. Behind her, she heard the kits leaping on Molepaw, squealing in triumph.

"We killed the traitor!" Dewkit declared. "ThunderClan is safe!"

Dovewing felt her heart sink. *ThunderClan will never be safe if we are divided inside the walls of our own camp.*

The following dawn, Squirrelflight told the cats to organize themselves into hunting patrols while she led a border check. Her voice was quiet and husky, and Dovewing hoped she wasn't getting sick as well. When the deputy and her patrol, which included Bramblestar, had vanished into the thorns, the remaining warriors looked at each other.

"I'll lead one patrol," Poppyfrost offered.

Lionblaze and Cinderheart padded across the clearing to join her.

"I'll come too," mewed Birchfall.

"Actually, I was going to ask Millie," Poppyfrost meowed. "Thanks anyway. Millie, will you join us?"

Looking faintly surprised, the gray tabby she-cat walked over to the group. Dovewing tensed when she saw the hurt in her father's eyes. How obvious could Poppyfrost be? "I'd like to hunt with you, Birchfall," she called. "Thornclaw, Ivypool, Mousewhisker, Blossomfall, will you come with us?" *I will not let my Clanmates shun these cats for the mistake they made!*

The four cats joined her, and Dovewing winced at the gratitude in their eyes. Cherrypaw, Molepaw, and Rosepetal formed another patrol, and the three groups of cats filed out through the thorns. Poppyfrost took her cats toward the old thunderpath, and Rosepetal's patrol headed up the side of the hollow, so Dovewing led her warriors toward the border with WindClan, climbing up the hill to where the trees thinned out and it was easier to spot birds pecking on the ground.

Ivypool caught a thrush almost at once and covered it with leaf mulch at the foot of a holly bush. Dovewing picked up the scent of a rabbit that must have strayed from the moor. She followed it toward the stream, but stopped when it looked as if the creature had hopped across the water and returned to WindClan territory. Disappointed, she turned back and joined her father as he circled around a squirrel that was munching an acorn, so absorbed it hadn't noticed the stalking cats. They drew nearer, placing their paws so lightly they made no sound, and when they were less than a fox-length away, Birchfall pounced. He landed neatly on top of the squirrel, dealt the killing blow, and lifted his head in triumph.

"Nice work!" Dovewing commented. "I'll take it over to the holly bush." She picked up the piece of fresh-kill and carried it through the trees to join Ivypool's catch. She was just sweeping leaves over the fluffy gray body when there was a pounding of paw steps from farther along the ridge. Startled, Dovewing peered up the slope.

Cherrypaw burst out of the undergrowth, her fur standing on end. Molepaw and Rosepetal were close behind, bush-haired and wide-eyed in panic. Dovewing raced to meet them. "What's happened?" she called.

Cherrypaw slid to a stop, almost losing her paws on the loose mulch. "We . . . we . . ." She paused for a moment until her breath steadied. Then she blinked and looked straight at Dovewing. "We found the scent of a fox inside our border. It could be the one that ShadowClan drove out, and it's looking for more cats."

The rest of Dovewing's patrol crowded around.

"That's not good news," Thornclaw growled.

"It's worse than—" Rosepetal began, but Molepaw cut her off.

"We're going to let Bramblestar know," he chirped. "He'll probably want to send a patrol to track it down and chase it out."

"We could go take a look now," Birchfall suggested, and Blossomfall nodded.

"There are five of us," she pointed out. "We should be able to challenge a fox!"

Cherrypaw glanced at her brother with a look that Dovewing couldn't read. "That's a good idea," she mewed. "We'll go tell Bramblestar and then come find you. Come on." She flicked her tail at her patrol and bounded downhill. Molepaw followed, then Rosepetal, who glanced back once over her shoulder before vanishing into the bracken.

Something pricked beneath Dovewing's pelt, as if she should have asked more questions, but Mousewhisker was already running up to the ridge. "Come on!" he yowled. "We can't let this fox get too far into the territory!"

The rest of the patrol raced after him. Dovewing brought up the rear, still fighting the feeling that something was wrong. Ivypool looked back at her. "Are you okay?" she panted.

Dovewing nodded. "When we get to the top of the ridge, we should stop. I might be able to hear the fox."

Ivypool slowed down. "Do you think so?"

"I have to try!" Dovewing hissed.

The warriors tore through the trees and scrambled up the last steep incline to the summit of the ridge. "Wait!" Dovewing yowled, and Mousewhisker skidded to a stop.

"What's wrong?" he called.

"Nothing," Dovewing puffed. "Let's just take a moment to listen out for the fox, or pick up a scent trail." They were close to the border here, and ThunderClan markers hung heavy in the air. Dovewing cast out her senses until her ears hurt. *Nothing!* Just the panting of the other cats and the rush of wind in the trees. *Perhaps the fox is lying still and quiet?*

Suddenly there was a terrible shriek. All the cats jumped, their fur bushing up.

"What was that?" gasped Blossomfall.

"It sounded like a fox," Thornclaw growled. "Let's go!" He took off down the hill, pushing through bracken that whipped back into Dovewing's face as she followed him. The horrific screeching continued, echoing around the woods. Whatever that fox was doing, it wasn't happy.

They burst out into a clear, sandy space on the side of the ridge. At the far side, a she-fox crouched, her lips curled back and her back hunched in pain. Dovewing froze. Had they run straight into an ambush by this dreadful creature?

But the fox didn't move. It pinned back its ears and snarled at them, but stayed exactly where it was.

"Great StarClan!" Thornclaw breathed in Dovewing's ear. "It's caught in a trap!"

Dovewing peered closer. Gleaming silver jaws gripped the fox's foreleg, so tight that white bone could be seen through the torn flesh. Dovewing gulped. She could only imagine the pain this creature was in. The thought flashed into her mind that it could just as easily have been one of her Clanmates caught like this.

"What are we going to do?" hissed Blossomfall. "It can't stay here!"

Ivypool was creeping across the clearing. "Come back!" yowled Dovewing, but her sister didn't stop.

With a howl, the fox exploded to its feet and lunged at

Ivypool, dragging the trap attached to its leg. Dovewing leaped at it, claws out, and landed on its neck as the fox's jaws snapped down toward her sister. Below, Thornclaw and Birchfall launched themselves at the creature's haunches while Blossomfall and Mousewhisker clawed its ears. The fox fought for its life. Half-crazed with pain, it thrashed and bit and lashed with its legs so that the heavy trap crashed into Thornclaw, knocking him to the ground. Ivypool darted right underneath the fox's belly, grabbed hold of Thornclaw's scruff and dragged him clear. Thornclaw shook his head, then leaped side by side with Ivypool at the fox once more, all teeth and claws and yowling.

Dovewing dug into the thick russet fur until she felt skin pop beneath her claw-tips. The fox flicked its head from side to side until Dovewing was dizzy, but she didn't let go. Dimly, she was aware of movement at the edge of the clearing. She glanced up, and her momentary lapse of concentration loosened her grip. The fox flung her off like a bug and Dovewing flew through the air to land with a thud on the earth. She gasped for breath.

A golden tabby face loomed over her. "Keep still. You've been winded." It was Lionblaze. "Watch her, Cinderheart," he ordered. Then he vanished, and Dovewing heard a fresh scream from the fox.

Fuzzily, she made out Cinderheart's features peering down at her. "We heard a commotion and came as fast as we could," the she-cat explained. She glanced up and winced. "I've never seen a fox fight like that before. Oh, Lionblaze, no!"

Dovewing fought to sit up. Cinderheart propped her against her shoulder. Lionblaze was crouched on the fox's back, sinking his teeth into its neck. Blood poured from a rip in his ear but he didn't seem to notice the scarlet liquid pooling into his eyes. Below, Thornclaw and Mousewhisker clawed at the fox's free front leg, while Blossomfall and Ivypool attacked its hindquarters. There was something in the way each pair of warriors moved, matching blow for blow, bite for bite, that reminded Dovewing they had trained together for a long time in skills the ThunderClan cats couldn't dream of.

The fox twisted its head around to snap at Lionblaze. Cinderheart lunged forward. "He's going to be killed!" she hissed.

Dovewing struggled to her feet and put out one paw to stop the she-cat. "He's okay," she mewed. "Let him fight."

Cinderheart turned to face her, her blue eyes ringed with white in fear. "But he doesn't have his powers anymore! He can be hurt now!"

"I know," Dovewing meowed. "My powers have gone too. But he's still the best and bravest warrior that ThunderClan has. Don't take that away from him, Cinderheart."

The gray she-cat held Dovewing's gaze, then slowly breathed out. "You're right," she whispered.

The fox let out another unearthly screech, which was abruptly cut off. With a hideous gurgle, it spat out a mouthful of blood and collapsed onto the ground. Thornclaw and Mousewhisker only just managed to jump clear. Lionblaze leaped down from the fox's back and stood over it, watching its flank heave one last time.

The bracken rustled and Bramblestar burst into the clearing followed by Squirrelflight, Cherrypaw, and Molepaw. The ThunderClan leader stopped dead when he saw the fox and the battered, bleeding warriors around it. "What in the name of StarClan has happened here?" he growled.

Squirrelflight bounded over to Dovewing. "Are you all right?"

"Yes," Dovewing wheezed. She stood up and gingerly tested each paw. Her ribs were bruised on one side from hitting the ground, but there was nothing seriously wrong.

Lionblaze prodded the fox with one paw. Its head lolled away from him and another gush of blood came from its mouth. "She's dead," the warrior announced unnecessarily.

Bramblestar walked over and looked down at the silver teeth still clutching the fox's foreleg. "Cherrypaw and Molepaw said they found traces of a fox inside the border. Did you chase it into the trap?"

Dovewing padded forward. "No," she mewed. "This fox was already trapped when the first patrol found it." She stared at the apprentices. "Wasn't it?"

Cherrypaw nodded miserably.

Bramblestar narrowed his eyes. "That's not what they told me."

"Nor us," Dovewing meowed. "I think they wanted my patrol to find it when it was alive and crazed with pain."

"Why would they do that?" Squirrelflight asked.

Dovewing let her gaze travel over the shamefaced warriors to rest on her brave patrol. "Because my patrol was made up of cats who once trained with the Dark Forest. Cherrypaw and Molepaw feel no loyalty toward them, and were willing to send them into great danger."

Bramblestar's hackles rose. "Is she right?" he demanded.

Molepaw shifted his paws. "We didn't know they'd attack it!" he whined. "We just wanted to scare them!"

There was a blur of movement, and suddenly Lionblaze was looming over the apprentices. "You nearly killed them!" he hissed.

Cherrypaw shrank to the ground. "We didn't mean to!" she bleated.

"Stand down, Lionblaze," Bramblestar ordered. "We'll return to the hollow. All of you who fought this fox, I want Jayfeather to check you over." He turned and stalked out of the clearing. The cats trailed after him, silent now from shame or exhaustion after the frenzy of fighting for their lives. Dovewing's head spun and she leaned gratefully on Cinderheart's shoulder as they pushed through the ferns and descended the slope to the camp.

Inside, Bramblestar was standing on Highledge. "Let all cats old enough to catch their own prey gather here for a meeting!" he roared.

There was a ripple of shock as cats emerged from the dens or put down the fresh-kill they'd been eating. Bumblestripe raced over to Dovewing. "What's happened? Are you all right?"

She breathed in his warm scent and let it comfort her. "I'll be okay," she mewed.

Bramblestar barely gave the cats a chance to settle before

he began speaking. His words were flung into the hollow like stones into a pool. "There are brave warriors among you today," he declared. "Cats who risked their lives to protect their Clan, who rushed into a situation without knowing what they faced but didn't turn back. They fought the most savage of enemies, and won. We are in their debt."

A murmur passed through the crowd and cats turned to one another in confusion. What had they missed? Had there been an attack from another Clan?

Bramblestar continued: "Ivypool, Blossomfall, Mouse-whisker, Thornclaw, and Birchfall, please come to the front."

The five cats limped to the foot of the cliff. Thornclaw's lip was torn, and a scab was already forming above Ivypool's eye. Birchfall and Mousewhisker were missing several clumps of fur.

"Some of you continue to blame these cats for the battle with the Dark Forest," Bramblestar meowed. "You are wrong. Today, these cats saved our lives. They were tricked—yes, tricked—into taking on a wounded fox. I am pleased to report that the creature was defeated and ThunderClan is safe. If you feel anything toward these warriors, it should be grati-tude, respect, and the utmost loyalty. They have proved that they are willing to lay down their lives for you. In future, you will be prepared to do the same."

Dovewing looked around and saw that several of her Clanmates seemed uncomfortable, flattening their ears and shifting their paws. Berrynose and Poppyfrost were among them.

Bramblestar raked the Clan with his amber gaze. "Know this, warriors. The Dark Forest will win if we do not forgive those cats who were once their allies. Forgiveness is far more powerful than hatred and suspicion. United, we are as strong as we ever were. Divided, we will fall. Remember that the Dark Forest is still out there, ready to prey on our dreams. Hostility and distrust among us will give them more force than they deserve. Do you want that?"

"No!" chorused the cats.

Bramblestar tipped his head to one side. "I don't hear you!"

"*No!*" ThunderClan yowled, shivering the leaves on the trees.

Bramblestar lowered his head to pray. "Great StarClan, we thank you for giving courage and strength to these warriors today. May we honor them always."

His words were echoed by the rest of the cats, quietly like a soft breeze. There was a stir of movement near the front, and Dovewing stood on tiptoe to see Cherrypaw and Molepaw approach the cats at the bottom of the cliff.

"We're very sorry," Molepaw mewed. "What we did was wrong, and broke the warrior code."

"It won't happen again," Cherrypaw added.

Birchfall reached out with his tail and stroked the she-cat on her flank. "I believe you," he meowed. He paused. "Will you patrol with me tomorrow, Cherrypaw?"

She nodded vigorously. "It would be an honor to patrol with any of you."

Dovewing let out a sigh of relief.

"I still don't know exactly what's gone on, but whatever you've done, thank you," Bumblestripe murmured. "This means so much to me." He gazed warmly at his sister, who was surrounded by warriors asking if she was okay after the fight with the fox.

"I know it does," Dovewing whispered. She pricked her ears as she spotted Lionblaze padding to his den. "Excuse me," she mewed to Bumblestripe. She trotted after the golden tabby and stopped him at the entrance to the warriors' den. "Lionblaze, we need to talk," she announced. "Now."

The warrior blinked once, then nodded. "I know. Come on, let's find Jayfeather."

The medicine cat was waiting outside the cave. He didn't give them a chance to speak, instead turning his sightless blue gaze to meet them and saying, "It's time. Let's talk outside the camp."

The three cats padded across the clearing and out through the thorns. Jayfeather led them a little way into the trees and jumped onto a fallen tree.

"Our powers have gone," he mewed. "I have not been able to visit other cats' dreams since the Great Battle, nor can I see into their minds when they are awake."

"I can be injured," Lionblaze meowed, sounding as confused as if he had only just noticed.

"And I can't hear or see anything," Dovewing admitted. She raised her head to look at her Clanmates. "Why has this happened?" she wailed. "Are we being punished because the Clan didn't unite again after the battle? Or because too many cats died? Are we still the Three described in the prophecy?"

Jayfeather flicked his tail. "I don't know," he growled. "But I think there is somewhere we can find an answer. Are you two fit enough for a journey?"

"Of course," Lionblaze replied, and Dovewing mewed, "I think so."

Jayfeather jumped down from the tree trunk. "Follow me."

CHAPTER 10

❧

The Moonpool gleamed like a single silver eye, reflecting starlight and the empty night sky. Dovewing caught her breath as she padded down the spiraling path, feeling her paws slot into the impressions left by cats from countless moons before. "It's beautiful!" she breathed.

Lionblaze shivered. "It's creepy."

Jayfeather led them to the edge of the water, as still as polished stone. "Lie down and close your eyes," he meowed.

"What's going to happen?" Lionblaze asked warily.

"StarClan will come to us," Jayfeather answered. "They alone know why we have lost our powers, and what this means for the prophecy." He settled himself on the smooth stone and tucked his paws underneath him.

Dovewing lay down beside him, then Lionblaze on his other side. Dovewing took one last look at the starlit water and closed her eyes. Her pelt prickled with excitement. *StarClan, are you there?*

The sound of rushing wind filled her ears, and she opened her eyes with a start. She was standing on top of a mountain surrounded by dark, starless sky. The wind tugged at her fur and cold seeped into her paws from the hard stone. Lionblaze and Jayfeather were beside her, leaning into the gale to keep their balance.

"Is this StarClan?" Dovewing yowled above the wind. Somehow she had expected it to be more . . . peaceful.

"No!" Jayfeather yowled back. "I don't know where we are!"

Great StarClan! This isn't the Dark Forest, is it? Dovewing thought in alarm.

Lionblaze pointed with his tail to the edge of the rocky plateau. "Look!"

Two figures were walking toward them out of the darkness. Not ancient cats lit with the light of stars, but mismatched, lumpen figures, unsteady in their gait and with fierce glowing eyes. One shape loomed over the other, broad-shouldered and narrow-snouted. The other lurched over the stony ground, its hairless skin gleaming in the half-light.

"Midnight and Rock!" Dovewing whispered. She felt the fur along her spine lie down. Not the Dark Forest, then.

The badger and the blind, bald cat stopped in front of them. Midnight dipped her head. "Welcome you are," she barked. "Come far you have, after difficult time. Something to ask, I think?"

"Why can't I hear anymore?" Dovewing blurted out. "Or see?"

Rock turned his cloudy blue gaze on her. "Oh, I think you can still see," he murmured softly.

Dovewing felt hot with embarrassment. "Yes, of course, but it's not the same. I used to be able to see *everything*! Now I can only see what's right in front of me. And it's the same with my hearing."

"We've lost our powers," Jayfeather put in. "The powers given to the cats in the prophecy. *There will be Three, kin of your kin, who will hold the power of the stars in their paws.*"

"Jayfeather thought StarClan might know why we've changed," Lionblaze meowed.

Midnight turned her striped muzzle toward him. "Not from StarClan came these powers. But from older forces, from earth and water and stone and air. Losing your gifts you are, yes. That I cannot change. But losing them you are because they are not needed now."

Dovewing struggled to untangle the badger's words. "You mean, the Clans are safe now? They don't need us anymore?"

"Your Clan will always need you," rasped Rock in a voice that seemed to come from the wind itself. "And sometimes, so will the other Clans. But you will never face a battle that needs these powers again. The greencough that afflicts you now? That will be hard, but your medicine cats have the knowledge to treat you. You will still fight with your neighbors, but you have the skills to deal with them. Sometimes you'll win, sometimes you won't. That is the way of things."

Midnight lumbered forward and rested her muzzle on Lionblaze's head. "Brave warrior, do not lose faith. To enter battle when injuries are certain, that is true courage." She shuffled along to Jayfeather. "Medicine cat, wise you are, and such you know. Care for your Clanmates you can without walking in their thoughts and dreams. Let those hidden be from your sight." Midnight reached Dovewing, and she felt a blast of stinking breath around her muzzle. "Small warrior, many dangers there are in a world when you are blind and deaf. But eyes and ears you have still. Use them as your Clanmates do. Weaker than them you will never be."

The badger stepped back and heaved a great breath, as if so much talking had tired her. Dovewing wondered just how old she and Rock were. As old as the stars?

"Your powers helped the Clans to win the Great Battle," Rock told them. "That is what the prophecy promised, and that promise has been fulfilled. You will feel lesser warriors without the powers, but you are not. Find strength in the courage and skills shared by your Clanmates. The Great Battle has been fought and won. A new time for the Clans lies ahead."

"Remember also, Great Battle was not won by you alone," Midnight warned them. "All Clans, all warriors, all queens and elders and kits and medicine cats fight together. To protect them all is not for you, powers or not. More has been lost than gift of sight or strength or dreams. But power of warrior code forever lasts."

There was a crackle of lightning overhead, making Dovewing flinch and close her eyes. When she opened them again, Midnight and Rock had vanished and for a moment a ginger cat stood in front of her, his green eyes glowing with love.

"Firestar?" Dovewing breathed, but then the vision was gone and she was standing at the edge of the Moonpool with Jayfeather and Lionblaze. The water was as still as it had ever been.

Lionblaze turned to her. "Are you all right?"

Dovewing nodded. "Better than before," she mewed.

Beside them, Jayfeather flicked his tail impatiently. "I have sick cats waiting for me. Come on, let's see if we can get back before dawn." He trotted up the spiral path, his gray pelt merging with the stone. Lionblaze followed but Dovewing hung back for a moment, staring into the pool. She felt a surge of hope welling up inside her.

The Great Battle has been won. We will survive the greencough. She turned to head after her Clanmates. Suddenly her paws felt lighter. *And the warrior code will last forever!*

ERIN
HUNTER

is inspired by a love of cats and a
fascination with the ferocity of the
natural world. As well as having great
respect for nature in all its forms,
Erin enjoys creating rich, mythical
explanations for animal behavior.
She is also the author of the bestsell-
ing Survivors and Seekers series.

Download the free Warriors app
and chat on Warriors message
boards at www.warriorcats.com.

For exclusive information on your
favorite authors and artists, visit
www.authortracker.com.

Bramblestar pushed his way through the thorn barrier into the camp with the rest of the patrol behind him. The sun shone down into the hollow, casting long shadows across the ground. Above the cliffs, the trees rustled gently and a warm breeze stirred the dust on the ground.

Bramblestar could still see traces of the terrible conflict when the warriors of the Dark Forest had poured into the camp: fresh bramble tendrils entwined with the old in the walls of the nursery, and broken branches on the hazel bush that screened the elders' den. It was too easy to close his eyes and be plunged back into the storm of fighting and blood, with cats both dead and alive attacking from all sides. The Dark Forest cats had flung themselves into battle in a furious quest for power and vengeance, and it had taken all the strength of the living cats—and the strength of StarClan—to beat them back. Bramblestar gave his pelt a shake, trying to recall his earlier optimism. At least the dens were repaired, and the surviving cats had recovered from their wounds.

But the scars we can't see will be harder to heal.

When the battle was over, Jayfeather had propped a bark-stripped branch against the cliff below the Highledge. He had scored claw marks across it, one for each life taken by the Dark Forest.

"It will remind us of the debts that we owe to our former Clanmates," he had explained.

Now Whitewing was standing in front of the branch with her apprentice, Dewpaw, beside her. Seedpaw and Lilypaw stood watching with their mentors, Bumblestripe and Poppy-frost.

"Can you remember all the names?" Whitewing asked her apprentice.

Dewpaw narrowed his eyes in concentration. "I think so. This one is for Mousefur . . ." he began, touching the first claw mark. "She was an elder, but she fought so bravely! And this one is for Hollyleaf. She had been away for a while, but she came back in time to help us when the Dark Forest attacked. And this is for Foxleap, who died of his wounds afterward. . . ."

Bramblestar nodded as Dewpaw went on reciting the names. He had decided that all the apprentices had to learn the list as part of their training, so that their lost Clanmates would be remembered for season after season, as long as ThunderClan survived.

"This one is for Ferncloud," Dewpaw continued. "She was killed by Brokenstar when she was defending the kits in the nursery. And this is Sorreltail. She hid her wounds because she wanted to take care of the kits, but she died just when we thought we had won. She was the bravest of all."

"And the big mark right at the top?" Whitewing prompted. "Do you know who that stands for?"

"That's our leader, Firestar," Dewpaw replied. "He was the best cat in the whole forest, and he gave up his last life to save us!"

Bramblestar felt a familiar stab of grief. *I wonder if he's watching us now? I hope he approves of what I have done.*

"I miss Firestar, too."

Bramblestar turned to see that Jayfeather had appeared at his side, the medicine cat's blue eyes fixed on him so intensely that it was hard to believe he was blind. "I didn't think you could tell what's in my mind anymore," Bramblestar mewed, surprised.

"No, those days are past," Jayfeather admitted, sounding a little wistful. "But it wasn't hard to figure out that you were thinking of Firestar. I heard Dewpaw run his paw over Firestar's mark and say his name, and then you sighed." He pressed himself briefly against Bramblestar's side. "I'm sure Firestar watches over us."

"Has he walked in your dreams yet?" Bramblestar asked.

Jayfeather shook his head. "No, but that's a good omen in itself. I've had enough warnings from StarClan to last me nine lifetimes." With a brisk nod to Bramblestar, he padded away to join Leafpool, who was sorting coltsfoot flowers and fresh-picked catmint outside their den.

"Come on, Snowpaw," Ivypool called to her apprentice. "Time for battle training!"

"Can we go too?" Dewpaw begged, as his sister scampered over to join her mentor.

"Sure we can," Whitewing meowed.

"And me!" Amberpaw raced across the camp and skidded to a halt beside her littermates.

"No, not you!" Spiderleg called from where he stood beside the fresh-kill pile with Cloudtail and Cherryfall. "You did the dawn patrol this morning. You need to rest."

Amberpaw's tail drooped. "But they'll be learning stuff when I'm not there!" she wailed. "I'll get behind, and then I'll never be a warrior!"

Spiderleg padded over to her and gave her ear a friendly flick with his tail. "Of course you'll be a warrior, mouse-brain! Once you've rested, I'll show you the move they're going to learn, I promise."

"Okay." Amberpaw still cast a regretful look after her littermates and their mentors as they left the hollow.

"What about us?" Lilypaw asked, exchanging a disappointed glance with Seedpaw. "Why can't we do battle training?"

"Because we're going hunting," Poppyfrost replied briskly. "Come on! Bumblestripe knows the best place to find mice."

"Great!" Seedpaw exclaimed with an excited little bounce. "Lilypaw, I bet I catch more mice than you."

"*I'm* going to catch enough for the whole Clan!" her sister retorted.

"It's not fair," Amberpaw muttered as she watched them go. "Why don't I get to do anything?"

"I told you," Spiderleg responded. "You did the dawn patrol. Now you rest. But before you do," he went on, "you can fetch some clean moss for Purdy's den."

Amberpaw brightened up. "Sure! And maybe he'll tell me a story!" She darted off and thrust her way into the barrier.

"I wonder if I ever had that much energy?" Bramblestar mewed aloud as he watched the young cat disappear.

Sandstorm popped her head out of the nearby nursery. "You still do!" she told him. She emerged into the open, pushing a ball of moss in front of her. "It's good to see the little ones being so lively. It gives me new hope for our Clan." She paused, her gaze clouding, and Bramblestar wondered if she was thinking about her former mate, Firestar, who wasn't here to watch this group of apprentices grow up. Then she lifted her head again. "Daisy and I are clearing out the nursery," she announced, giving the ball of moss a prod with one paw. "There might not be any kits now, but surely some of our young she-cats will be expecting soon."

"I hope so," Bramblestar replied, remembering his earlier conversation with Berrynose. *I really hope so.* "Surely there are other cats who could help Daisy?" he went on, thinking that Sandstorm didn't need to be struggling with bedding, covered in dust and scraps of moss.

Amusement sparked in Sandstorm's green eyes. "Are you trying to pack me off to the elders' den?" she teased.

"You've served your Clanmates long enough," Bramblestar responded. "Why not let them take care of you now?"

Sandstorm flicked her whiskers dismissively. "I've plenty of life in my paws yet," she insisted, retreating into the nursery to help Daisy wrestle with a huge clump of brittle, musty moss.

Bramblestar watched the she-cats for a moment longer before turning away. His deputy, Squirrelflight, stood near the elders' den, sorting out the hunting patrols with Graystripe; like Sandstorm, the former deputy was one of the oldest cats in the Clan now.

"We need the hunting patrols to go out early," Graystripe was explaining to Squirrelflight. "With the days getting hotter, it's best to avoid sunhigh for chasing around."

Squirrelflight nodded. "And the prey will be holed up by then, too. I've already sent out one patrol," she went on, "but I'll send out another. Brightheart would be a good cat to lead it." She glanced around. "Hey, Brightheart!"

The ginger-and-white she-cat slid out between the branches that sheltered the warriors' den. "Yes?"

"I want you to lead a hunting patrol," Squirrelflight told her. "But stick to one area, and come back before it gets too hot."

Brightheart dipped her head. "Any particular place?" she asked.

"You could try up by the ShadowClan border," Squirrelflight suggested. "Millie spotted a nest of squirrels there yesterday."

"Good idea," Brightheart mewed. "Which cats should I take with me?"

"Millie, obviously, since she knows where the nest is. Apart from her, any cat you like."

"I'm on my way." Brightheart bounded off to call Millie from the warriors' den. Then she rounded up Dovewing and Mousewhisker and headed out through the thorns.

The barrier was still trembling from their departure when Amberpaw reappeared with a huge bundle of moss in her jaws. As she staggered toward the elders' den, Bramblestar noticed that the moss was dripping with water, leaving a line of dark spots on the dusty floor of the clearing.

Squirrelflight stepped out to intercept the apprentice as she drew closer to the den. "You can't take that in there," she told Amberpaw sharply. "That moss is too wet. It'll soak all the other bedding and Purdy will claw your ears off for making his legs ache from the damp."

At the mention of his name Purdy ducked out of the shelter of the hazel bush. "There's nothin' wrong with my legs, or my ears," he snorted.

"How about your pelt?" Amberpaw asked, dropping the moss.

Bramblestar stifled a *mrrow* of amusement: Purdy's tabby pelt looked as if he had crawled backward through the thorns, the fur clumped and sticking up as if he hadn't groomed himself for a moon.

"Eh? Speak up!" Purdy complained. "Why are you mumblin'? Young cats these days always mumble," he added crossly.

"I was explaining to Amberpaw that she can't bring wet moss into your den," Squirrelflight meowed.

"What?" Purdy prodded the bundle of moss. "You're sure you weren't tryin' to bring me a drink instead?" he asked Amberpaw.

The apprentice looked crestfallen. "I was only trying to help."

"Sure you were, young 'un." Purdy stroked Amberpaw's side with his tail. "Come on. You an' I will spread the moss out here, just outside the den, an' it'll soon dry in the sun. An' while it does that, I'll tell you how I once killed a whole nest o' rats."

"Yes!" Amberpaw bounced in delight and began spreading out the wet moss.

On the other side of the clearing, Sandstorm headed out of the camp, pushing a huge bundle of used bedding in front of her. Bramblestar slid into the nursery and began helping Daisy scratch together the next bundle.

"Have you heard anything about new kits?" he asked hopefully.

Daisy shook her head. "No, but I'm sure we'll need the nursery soon, now that newleaf is here." She paused, then added, "Come and look."

She led Bramblestar out of the nursery and pointed with her tail to where Lionblaze and Cinderheart were sharing tongues in a patch of sunlight. "That one will be expecting soon," Daisy mewed, twitching her ears at Cinderheart.

Bramblestar felt a flash of excitement. He remembered play fighting with Lionblaze as a kit outside the nursery, and how he had taught Lionblaze his first pounce. *In spite of all that's happened, I couldn't have loved those three kits more if I'd been their real father.*

Lionblaze looked up and noticed Bramblestar watching him. With a quick word to Cinderheart he got up and limped across the camp to join his leader.

"Did you want me?" he asked.

"No, but since you're here, you can tell me how things are going. It looks as if we might have some new kits soon," Bramblestar meowed with an affectionate nudge.

"Great StarClan!" Lionblaze gave his chest fur a couple of embarrassed licks. "No pressure, then?"

"Are you sure you're okay?" Bramblestar went on more anxiously, spotting a scratch on Lionblaze's shoulder. *He's limping on that forepaw, too.*

Lionblaze sighed. "Yes, I'm fine. Leafpool and Jayfeather checked me out, and gave me a dock leaf for the sore pad. It's just hard to get used to the way I can be hurt now. All I did was trip over a stupid bramble!"

"Too bad," Bramblestar mewed. "You'll have to start watching where you tread!"

"That will make me very fearsome to our enemies. Not," Lionblaze muttered. He limped back to his mate and settled down beside her.

Movement at the entrance caught Bramblestar's eye as the first hunting patrol returned. Dustpelt was leading it; he carried a squirrel in his jaws. Behind him came Brackenfur, Blossomfall, and Poppyfrost, all laden with prey. Bramblestar watched approvingly while they carried their catch over to the fresh-kill pile.

He noticed that Dustpelt looked exhausted as he dropped his squirrel on the pile. The brown tabby tom was still haunted by the death of his mate, Ferncloud, in the Great Battle. Squirrelflight had told him that Dustpelt often woke yowling in the warriors' den, thrashing in his nest. In his dreams he still tried to save Ferncloud from the claws of Brokenstar, and every time he had to watch her die again.

A little more than a moon ago, Bramblestar had suggested that Dustpelt might like to retire and join the elders.

"Anything but that," Dustpelt had growled. "Let me keep busy. I need something to distract me, or the memories hurt too much."

"You'll meet Ferncloud again one day, in StarClan," Bramblestar meowed, trying to comfort the older warrior.

Dustpelt shook his head. "Sometimes I wonder if that's true." His voice shaking, he added, "I kept some of the moss from her nest. But I can't even smell her scent on it anymore."

Bramblestar hadn't known what he could do to help, except to do as Dustpelt asked and make sure he stayed busy.

Bramblestar headed across the camp, intending to praise Dustpelt's patrol for their good hunting, when he heard his name yowled from the other side of the barrier. Startled, he spun around to see Brightheart bursting out of the thorns with the rest of her patrol just behind.

"ShadowClan!" she gasped as she scrambled to a halt.

THE TIME HAS COME
FOR DOGS TO RULE THE WILD

SURVIVORS

BOOK ONE:
THE EMPTY CITY

Lucky is a golden-haired mutt with a nose for survival. Other dogs have Packs, but Lucky stands on his own . . . until the Big Growl strikes. Suddenly the ground splits wide open. The longpaws disappear. And enemies threaten Lucky at every turn. For the first time in his life, Lucky needs to rely on other dogs to survive. But can he ever be a true Pack dog?

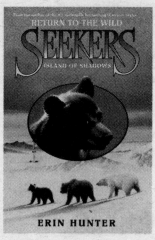

ENTER THE WORLD OF
WARRIORS

Warriors: Dawn of the Clans
Discover how the warrior Clans came to be.

Warriors
Sinister perils threaten the four warrior Clans. Into the midst of this turmoil comes Rusty, an ordinary housecat, who may just be the bravest of them all.

Download the
free Warriors app at
www.warriorcats.com

HARPER
An Imprint of HarperCollinsPublishers

Visit www.warriorcats.com for the free Warriors app, games, Clan lore, and much more!

Warriors Stories

Download the separate ebook novellas or read them in two paperback bind-ups!

Paperback

Paperback

Don't Miss the Stand-Alone Adventures

Delve Deeper into the Clans

HARPER
An Imprint of HarperCollinsPublishers

Warrior Cats Come to Life in Manga!

HARPER

An Imprint of HarperCollinsPublishers